ORIGINS *of* LIBERTY

TIMOTHY AALDERS

Copyright © 2020 Timothy Aalders
All rights reserved
First Edition

PAGE PUBLISHING, INC.
Conneaut Lake, PA

First originally published by Page Publishing 2020

ISBN 978-1-64701-502-2 (pbk)
ISBN 978-1-64701-503-9 (digital)

Printed in the United States of America

Secular humanistic liberalism has done America critical disservice. It has led the United States down a fool's road to a point where the American people, en masse, must either return to the foundation that underlaid the birth of the greatest nation of modern times or continue the false path to an inevitable collision with chaos. And how can the best in genius and skill cope with such a formidable enemy?

Not only has secular humanistic liberalism purposely and willfully obscured the truth of America's origins; it has laid the faulty foundation for her eventual demise, if the people en masse do not return to the foundation spirit, principles, societal and political forms that gave birth to the nation, and build in the right way on that original foundation. Otherwise, there is no hope for the nation's survival.

To see the errors which have created the present critical situation, the American people must go back to the very beginning, which is not 1776, but to the basic fact that America was born of God. In order for you to receive the most benefit from this book, you had to ask yourself a question that is plaguing not only America but humanity in general. Was America created by a group of vigilantes who wanted to create a new rule over mankind and issue rights that were changeable by future generations of America? Or did the founders of our nation, under the guidance of the Lord God, embraced unalienable rights bequeathed to us from him and created the founding documents to protect them from power hungry people?

TIMOTHY AALDERS

One may ask themselves if this even matters, and I would say yes, it has and will continue to determine the course of liberty for every generation to come.

Introduction

The principles that went into the making of America were unique. Their origins were the light of the Holy Spirit, acting in the lives of people, and they bear the mark of their creator—the light of Christ. One of the great ideas gave birth to liberty was the idea of individual conscience. When this inner illumination of the light of Christ struck the individual in his heart and soul when he read the Bible and began to receive the flow of the Spirit as an inner light, the enlivened word produced that which is called the *auto pistos*, which is a Latin term. "A-u-t-o" is auto, which you can put in front of the word mobile, and what do you have? Automobile—a machine that that can move without being pulled by horses. And the word *pistos*, as a Latin word, can denote a piston. Now what do you have? Something that moves. The popular idea then was that the words *auto pistos* had power in itself and that it enlightened conscience. As one German historian put it, conscience became the basis for unalienable rights. And conscience became the basis of the age of reason.

Yet it was not reason as understood by the classic world. The Fathers of Liberty called it "right reason." It was right because it was illuminated by the Holy Spirit. That Spirit was the Spirit of Truth. This was its scriptural name. It was the Spirit of Truth—the Spirit of Light that enlightened the mind. As a result, an age of reason began that lasted until about 1825, near the end of the Axial period. It was not mere humanistic reason; its character was the Spirit of Christ.

The same thinking was true of "unalienable rights." I prefer the term "unalienable" over the more popular "inalienable," which is a softening of the term. Unalienable means absolute, unqualified, you can't get rid of them, and no one can take them away from you. They were yours. They came from God—that is, Christ. For example, George A. Sabine stated, "The interest and distinctive features of the Leveler philosophy," as a group in the Axial Hub, "is the new form which it gave to the ancient concepts of natural rights and consent." They looked different, they breathed different, and their character was different. America, then, was born of unique principles, not just the gathering of ideas from the Greeks and the Romans. America was born of a new type of ideas, which were new in character. Sabine states, "They interpret the law of nature as in valuing human individuals with innate and inalienable rights which legal and political institutions exist only to protect and the construed consent as to an individual act which every man is entitled to perform for himself." Those are the principles that truly gave birth to the United States of America.

They were the living enlivening principles of individual conscience and unalienable rights that centered in Christ as a divine glorified Being, who infused His divine nature into those who exercised the requisite faith On this basis, they were all related to that inner illumination that people of true faith received, which brought forth the principle of unalienable rights and the idea of a covenant society. That inner spirit began to transform the person of faith, and he or she began to live outside themselves in service toward others; and this because they began to feel the love of Christ in their souls. The only social instrument that can satisfy that kind of impulse from within is the principle of covenant wherein they freely join together on the basis of stipulated requirements that guaranteed their freedom, justice, equity, or a true sense of brotherhood for each other.

These ideas came into America and made America a unique nation different from the Greeks and the Romans. In the colonization of America, this same spirit moved the colonists to come here. They came because they responded to the powerful transforming inner spiritual power. They, therefore, said, "We go to practice the positive part of church reformation and to propagate the gospel in America." That "positive part" was the inner spiritual prompting. The Puritans migrated first to Holland then to New England. This migration was carried on, and I quote, "In the interest of their mission to found a purely democratic church." They went on to explain "that the church is governed not by man but by the spirit of Christ." This is only another illustration of the effect of preeminently spirit on the whole.

Now a little about the idea of a New Jerusalem, which was not merely an ethereal thing. The New Jerusalem was conceived to be a practical Christian society based on free individuals bound together my mutual covenant. And they understood that it was going to be built before the second coming. They had read the Psalms 102, which states, "When the Lord shall build Zion then He shall appear in His glory." When the Puritans came to America, they came with the idea of establishing that ideal. The historian Christopher Dobson explains, "The modern western beliefs in progress in the rights of man and in the beauty of conforming political action to moral ideals whatever they may owe to other influences derive ultimately for the moral ideals of Puritanism, especially separatism, and its faith in the possibility of realizing a holy community on earth by the efforts of the elect." That's what they were attempting to establish here in America.

Edward Johnson, a first-generation layman, declared that God would erect Mt. Zion in the wilderness. Governor John Winthrop said as he came to Massachusetts, "We shall be as a city on a hill. The eyes of all the people are upon us so that if we shall we deal falsely with our God in this work we have undertaken and so cause Him to withdraw his presence and help form us we shall be made a story and a by word through the world." Did they have a fully correct understanding? No. But they had its overall idea.

Men like Roger Williams were talking about Zion, and there were others as well. I will not spend time discussing their comments but move on to the conclusions I would like to present, and that is to talk about the Founding Fathers in their day and what they hoped for. When they got the Constitution established, that was not the end of their vision for this country. They had the idea that there was to be still two revolutions. First was the spread of civil political liberty justice and equity from the new nation to other areas of the world. Second, the further spiritual renewal of the individual, the family, the upgrading of society, by the further unfolding of the spiritual truth leading to Bible Christianity, and eventually, they hoped for a restoration of Bible Christianity. David Austin put it this way, "It seems that no unnatural conclusion from prophecy and from present appearances that in order to usher in the universal dominion of our glorious Emanuel, as predicted to take place and usually called the latter-day glory, two great revolutions are to take place. The first outward and political, the second inward and spiritual. This first is now taking place it is having the effects that we in this country already enjoy and all that the Lord would graciously put into the hearts of his ministers and churches are now all under the dominion of civil and religious liberty to begin the second revolution that which is inward and spiritual." He went on to say, "Behold the revolution through the agency of the hero of America," whom he calls Christ, "why it not now then begin the second."

Now one final idea: They did not think the great Second Coming of Christ was going to take place in their day. They put it two hundred years in the future. They had read the book of Revelation where John saw the book sealed with seven seals. They interpreted each seal as a thousand-year period of their temporal existence. They understood from the book of Revelation that Christ would only come after the opening of the seventh seal or during the seventh-seal period. They viewed the future then on that basis.

Writing in 1793 Samuel Hopkins says, based about two hundred years from the end of the eighteenth century, "God has given us the victory and ratified the peace and independence of America but we are not to conceive this the ultimate object in the divine plan he has done it in subservience to the glorious scheme of the gospel of redemption and brought by the empires and learning and religion have in past ages been traveling east to west and this content is their last Western heritage. The great Pacific Ocean which abounds the western part of the country will bind their further progress in this direction." He continues by referring to the West, saying, "Here then is God erecting a stage on which to exhibit the great things of his kingdom. The stage is spacious the territory extensive such as no other part of the globe can equal. We may expect God's greatest works out here in the West. In no doubt this Christian revolution of America and independence," that is what has just been completed, "is a leading step. The world is far advanced in age from prophecy it is apparent that the latter-day glory is at no great distance and when we consider about three thousand miles of western territory the most fertile part of America, yet uninhabited can we suppose this vast region was designed merely for beasts of pray or may we not rather suppose this is the wilderness and a solitary place that shall be glad and the desert that shall blossom like a rose."

Secular humanistic liberalism has done America critical disservice. It has led the United States down a fool's road to a point where the American people, en masse, must either return to the foundation that underlaid the birth of the greatest nation of modern times or continue the false path to an inevitable collision with chaos. And how can the best in genius and skill cope with such a formidable enemy?

Not only has secular humanistic liberalism purposely and willfully obscured the truth of America's origins, but it has laid the faulty foundation for her eventual demise if the people en masse do not return to the foundation spirit, principles, societal, and political forms that gave birth to the nation and build in the right way on that original foundation. Otherwise, there is no hope for the nation's survival.

To see the errors that have created the present critical situation, the American people must go back to the very beginning, which is not 1776, but to the basic fact that America was born of God. In order for you to receive the most benefit from this book, you had to ask yourself a question that is plaguing not only America but humanity in general. Was America created by a group of vigilantes who wanted to create a new rule over mankind and issue rights that were changeable by future generations of America? Or did the founders of our nation under the guidance of the Lord God embraced unalienable rights bequeathed to us from him and created the founding documents to protect them from power hungry people?

One may ask themselves if this even matters, and I would say, yes, it has and will continue to determine the course of liberty for every generation to come.

CHAPTER 1

The Search for American Origins

In a letter to John Adams, in 1805, Dr. Benjamin Rush, a signer of the Declaration of Independence, mentioned an effort he once made to show how the United States of America came into being. "I once intended to have published a work to be entitled *Memories of the American Revolution*," he wrote, "and for that purpose collected many documents and pamphlets. But perceiving how widely I should differ from the historians of that event, and how much I should offend by telling the truth, I threw my documents into the fire and gave my pamphlets to my son Richard." Said he, "From the immense difference between what I saw and heard of men and things during our revolution and the histories that have been given of them, I am disposed to believe with Sir Robert Walpole that all history [that which is contained in the Bible accepted] is a romance, and romance the only true history."

To Dr. Rush's confession, John Adams replied, "I am half inclined to be very angry with you for destroying the anecdotes and documents you had collected for private memoirs of the American Revolution. From the memoirs of individuals the true springs of events and the real motives of actions are to be made known to posterity."

Adams's response to Dr. Rush's admission raises two compelling questions: What were the 'true springs' and 'real motives' of the American Founders who brought forth the United States of America?' And, Can they still be determined?

The Revolutionary Base of the United State of America

The United States of America was the product of an extraordinary revolution, unique in its driving spirit, principles, and character, which began centuries before 1776. Alexis de Tocqueville, the noted French student of American life, society, and government, based his Democracy in America (1835–1840) on the fact that a remarkable revolution in the West was the foundation of the new nation's way of free life, society, and political government. "There is one country in the world," he stated at the beginning of his classic work, "where the great social revolution that I am speaking of seems to have nearly reached its natural limits… [It is] a fact already accomplished, or on the eve of its accomplishment; and I have selected the nation, from among those which have undergone it, in which its development has been the most peaceful and the most complete."

Tocqueville continued, "The Anglo-Americans are the first nation who has escape[d] the dominion of absolute power. They have been allowed by their circumstances, their origin, their intelligence, and especially by their morals to establish and maintain the sovereignty of the people."

By this revolution, promoted by the earlier labors of inspired courageous reformers and those in their time, the vital principles, concepts, and forms of human value, dignity, and liberty arose and were institutionalized in the founding documents of the United States of America, including such vital factors as freedom of speech, freedom of the press, freedom of assembly, freedom of religion, freedom to petition for redress of grievances, an enlivened sense of unalienable rights, the concept of society by covenant and/or contract, society and government based on the consent of the people, the separation of church and state (not the separation of God and the state), and the vertical and horizontal separation of powers.

Though generations of scholars have studied and written scores of treatises on the origins of American society and America's constitutional republic, after more than two hundred years the understanding of the American people's renewing life and dynamic spirit and character that gave birth to the new nation on the western hemisphere is still critically lacking and is being greatly distorted.

The Question of American Origins

Many have tried to determine the true nature and sources of the Revolution Tocqueville described and to acquire a correct understanding of the order of free society and government that it produced. The revolution glowed "with heat," Jacob P. Mayer notes, and it displayed a "strong spirit of independence." John Stuart Mill saw it as "that go-ahead spirit; that restless, impatient eagerness for improvement in circumstances; that mobility; that shifting and fluctuation—now up, now down, now here, now there; that absence of classes and class-spirit; that jealousy of superior attainments; that want of deference for authority and leadership; that habit of bringing things to the rule and square of each man's own understanding."

Frederick Jackson Turner, who emphasized the role of the frontier in American history, described the revolution as "that coarseness and strength combined with acuteness and inquisitiveness; that practical inventive turn of mind, quick to find expedients; that masterful grasp of material things, lacking in the artistic but powerful to effect great ends; that restless, nervous energy; that dominant individualism working for good and evil, and withal that buoyancy and exuberance which comes from freedom."

Since the spirit and thrust of the revolution brought the individual to the fore with his sense of personal dignity and individual rights, Tocqueville suggested that the urge for equality gave rise to dynamic life in America and to the vigorous democratic order; to him, the "ultimate ascendancy of the democratic principle" assumed the "character of a law of nature." Mill challenged Tocqueville's opinion, asserting that, while the revolution brought the individual to the fore, an equality of conditions was not "the exclusive, or even the principal cause" of the revolution. The French Catholics in lower Canada enjoyed an opportunity for a similar equality, yet no energetic spirit prevailed among them, which suggests that the mere opportunity for equality is not the key to an understanding of American democracy.

Turner concluded that the "striking characteristics" of American life, democracy and progress were "traits of the frontier." True, the frontier did release people from the limitations of aristocratic society and opened the way for the elements that moved the prevailing revolution to operate more freely and effectively. But to assign America's enormous contributions to the modern world merely to the frontier disregards her religious-spiritual, as well as ideological, heritage and makes secondary factors primary causes.

Changing Views of the American Founding

The great majority of colonists on the eastern seaboard of North America believed that the liberty they came to enjoy was a gift from God. Advance Reformers among them saw themselves in the vanguard of a prolonged revolution, with God at the helm, inspiring men to build an ideal life, society, and government. They viewed the new order as a "City upon a Hill" that would show the world that a genuine society and government, "along the lines set forth in the New Testament" could be built on God's law. While reform convictions varied and the vision of a free society and government in some was more restricted and less liberal than in others, ministers, political leaders, and writers emphasized God's special concern for his "Chosen People in their effort to build a New Canaan." The New England experience, therefore, revealed "God's mercy" toward mankind. The unfolding saga was "one long record of the revelation of God's providence toward his people." And their Christian view of history affirmed the actuality of "supernatural causes" in the origins of the United States of America.

God's place at the foundation of the new nation, with the conviction that liberty came from Him, is obvious in two national documents. The Declaration of Independence states, "We hold these truths to be self-evident, that all men are created equal, that they are endowed by their Creator with certain unalienable Rights that among these are Life, Liberty and the pursuit of Happiness." Reaffirming the American tradition in his Gettysburg Address, Abraham Lincoln declared that the American Founders "brought forth on this continent a new nation, conceived in Liberty, and dedicated to the proposition that all men are created equal." Amid the tragedy of Civil War, Lincoln concluded his address with an expression of hope "that this nation, under God, shall have a new birth of freedom; and that government of the people, by the people, for the people, shall not perish from the earth."

But since the creation of the United States of America, each generation of citizens has rewritten national history "to suit its own image." Reasons for the continuous reinterpretations of American history vary, but the dominant one is "the changing climate of opinion" among the people.

Toward the end of the eighteenth century, emphasis on the religio-spiritual foundations of American life, society, and government (with the "supernatural causes" of the rise of America as understood by the colonists and founders) began to give way to a more secular view that stressed "human progress, reason, and material well-being." The move was away from God to emphasize on the practical fruits of the revolution—a shift away from the Giver to the gifts. Emphasis on the Holy Spirit was set aside, and attention was placed on liberty, justice, equality, and progress.

The Enlightenment of eighteenth-century Europe, which was characterized by rationalism, learning, skepticism, and empiricism in social and political views, helped foster this shift. Promoters of the Enlightenment took principles of liberty, equality, and fraternity from seventeenth-century England where liberty and Christian democratic constitutionalism were born, then severed them from their living religio-spiritual roots. In like manner, the liberal principles and concepts that John Locke (1632–1704) advocated and the scientific views and vision set forth by Sir Isaac Newton (1642–1727) were separated from their religio-spiritual foundations in the European Enlightenment. Both Locke and Newton were deeply religious men who penned more words on religious topics than on social and political principles, and their writings reveal their full acceptance of God's Word and law as the true foundation of human life, society, and government. By the skewed emphasis that leaders of the Enlightenment gave to the thought of these leading men, they promoted the view that by man's "use of reason" alone he could "control his destiny and determine his…material and intellectual progress." This narrow secular approach was so widely received that most historians "abandoned the Christian theory of history" for a view of the universe in which, for a time, natural law became a major motivating power in life.

Some historians still continued to give God credit for the founding of America. In his twelve-volume *History of the United States from the Discovery of the American Continent* (1834–82), George Bancroft affirmed that mankind's march toward freedom was according to "a preordained plan conceived by God." America was "the fruition of God's plan," and Americans had a "unique mission" to promote democracy in the world. But with a few exceptions, American historical writing in the first three quarters of the nineteenth century did not give credit to God for the origin of the nation. History became "essentially the story of liberty," which evolved from "a progressive advance toward greater human rights."

By the 1870s, two major developments began to influence the writing of American history: (1) the rise of professionally educated historians with broad ranges of social interests and (2) the impact of Darwinism and related schools of thought. Historians from about 1910 to 1945 rejected the view that "natural laws governed human society." Unlike early Fathers of Liberty who affirmed the reality of the renewing power of Bible Christianity and, on that basis, gave credit to divine and natural law, the new breed of historians were moved by a "climate of opinion and methodology" that viewed history as "an ideological weapon." This conceived weapon was used to explain the present, and to "control the future," while ignoring the elements of the past that gave birth to liberty and progress. To them, society was merely "open-ended and dynamic" with little, if any, emphasis on primary causes. Social development was not determined by God and his blessings, or even by divine or natural laws, but, as Karl Marx argued, by "economic and social forces" that arose out of the interaction of individuals with their environment.

The assumption that the events of society result from an "evolutionary developmental process" encouraged attempts to explain social realities by "emphasizing the interplay of economic, technological, social, psychological, and political forces." Historical scenes in America were portrayed as a "conflict…between the polarities of life"—aristocracy versus democracy, the "haves" versus the "have-nots," the overprivileged versus the underprivileged, people of one sectional interest in the country versus those of another.

Applying this "overt class conflict hypothesis," Charles A. Beard proposed that, instead of representing "a judicious combination of wisdom and idealism," the Constitution of the United States was the product of a group of propertied men intent on establishing a strong central government to protect their interests from encroachment by the masses. While the commitment of Beard and Vernon Louis Parrington lay with democracy, their works rested on the Marxian thesis that American ideology was "determined by the materialistic forces in history."

The humanistic approach to American origins virtually ignores the vital religio-spiritual foundations that gave birth to the spirit of liberty, private and public virtue, and the democratic principles, concepts and forms of society that provided the base of the American founding. "A long and rich tradition of American political thought has been ignored" while the names and writings of important advocates of the Christian Democratic-Republican tradition have either been omitted or obscured. Consequently, rising generations of Americans have never known the roots and foundations of American liberty. Some concerned scholars lament that Americans have "well-nigh forgotten" the sources of their domestic harmony and accord, their rights, freedom, and prosperity, and they act as if emphasis on the "paraphernalia" of their free system is enough to "make it operate—as if there are no hidden sources" of liberty, democratic society, and free constitutional government.

TIMOTHY AALDERS

The Rediscovery of America's Ideological Heritage

In the 1950s, Professor Clinton Rossiter began the work of rediscovering the "intellectual dimensions of the American Revolution." He was followed by the contributions of Caroline Robbins, Bernard Bailyn, and Gordon S. Wood, who established the basis of a more comprehensive study of the origins of the United States of America. By their combined efforts, these scholars demonstrated that ideals and ideology—not economic considerations—played leading roles in the formation of American society and republicanism.

Robbins's work on the English Commonwealth men—a school of "prolific opposition theorists, 'country' politicians, and publicists" in the latter seventeenth and the eighteenth centuries—who continued to advance the free ideological principles that emerged in the English Revolution of the mid-seventeenth century became a "turning point" in the understanding of the foundation sources of American republicanism. She precisely delineates the "English libertarian heritage" from which Americans drew heavily in the years that led to the American Revolution.

The Commonwealth men were men of principle, not expediency. They were the "Real Whigs" of England. Representing no political party, they spoke and wrote freely on the liberal Bible principles, concepts, and societal forms that emerged in the English Renaissance of the mid-seventeenth century. And while their writings had little effect on England, they profoundly influenced the American mind. The Constitution of the United States of America came to embody "many of the devices" that they had in vain counseled their fellow Englishmen to adopt. Yet few, if any, historians, prior to the second half of the twentieth century, had made use of their works in discussing the "origins of the American Revolution."

The views voiced by the two most influential Commonwealth men, John Trenchard (1662–1723) and Thomas Gordon (d. 1750) on contemporary issues in the British Empire, had a distinctly New Testament base and character, and they were "very close" to colonial beliefs in the 1760s. Their "fine, clear, concise" declarations had an immense influence on Americans in clarifying and consolidating a Bible Christian "philosophical basis for the whole American argument." With their primary emphasis on Bible Christianity, they condemned the narrow, distorted views and practices of organized Christianity—of man-made churches. And on the positive side, they championed the new order of Christian life, society, and republicanism that arose in the 1640s and gave birth to modern liberty and democracy, with emphasis on the need for just and equitable laws to guarantee the unalienable rights of the people.

Until Robbins illustrated the powerful impact of the English Commonwealth men on American thinking, historians paid little attention to their writings. Trenchard and Gordon had published the classical works, *The Independent Whig* and *Cato's Letters: Essays on Liberty, Civil and Religious*. But except for "rare and fugitive references" to these important publications, they were unread during most of the twentieth century, even by specialists in the history of American political and constitutional theory and intellectual history.

The "central occurrence" in establishing a new more accurate approach to the origins of America was Bernard Bailyn's *The Ideological Origins of the American Revolution*. His study of more than four hundred pamphlets published in America between 1750 and 1776 (and over 1500 by 1783), bearing on the British-American controversy, is of particular significance. In them, the role of ideology in the American Revolution is made clear. Bailyn found that the American Revolution was primarily "an ideological, constitutional, political struggle" out of which existing political principles and objectives were consolidated to mature and establish a new idea of government. The Constitution of the United States did not arise, as Beard had argued, by controversy between groups seeking to change the "organization of the society or the economy." And it is clear that the vital ideological ideas came from the liberal thought that emerged in mid-seventeenth-century England.

In 1969, Wood followed Bailyn's work with *The Creation of the American Republic, 1776–1787* in which he described how the synthesis of ideas that Bailyn discovered had influenced the writing of state and federal constitutions between 1776 and 1789. He demonstrated that in the era of the American Revolution, the people of the emerging nation "insistently fought their battles in terms of theory" and that there can be no doubt that the use of this "habit of thinking" was the major cause of their break with England. The ideology of a free faith and spirit had emerged with sufficient force and power in the minds and souls of Americans to bring on the American Revolution.

The rediscovery of the intellectual dimensions of the American Revolution also makes clear the extent to which the American consciousness was "shaped by a Dissenter"—by the Advance Reformer. And it shows that the writings of the English Commonwealth men perpetuated the liberal spirit and principles that had blossomed in the English Revolution of the mid-seventeenth century, with enormous influence on many American Colonists.

The publications of Rossiter, Robbins, Bailyn, and Wood launched an important "reinterpretation of Anglo-American eighteenth-century social and political thought." They produced a "major upheaval in American historiography" and revealed the critical need for a reassessment of America's constitutional heritage. But there is little evidence to indicate that historians have accepted that challenge, and more than twenty five years after the publication of Bailyn's work, Barry Alan Shain could write, "During the past half century, liberty's meaning has greatly changed and the history of the concept has come to be manipulated in multiple ways."

The Line of Liberty

Because Luther, Calvin, and other mainline Protestants did not follow and build upon the line of liberty that began to rise among such groups as the Friends of God, the Franscicans, and the Lollards and Hussites, they cannot be classed among the Fathers of Liberty. The line of liberty, instead, extended forward in England among the Lollards, into the separatist movement that was initiated by Robert Harrison and Robert Browne. It was then broadened out into the Congregationalists, Baptists, and Independents; and it finally exploded in the Age of Christ and of the Holy Spirit, by the spirit of enlightened faith, freedom, individualism, and desire for open covenant union, in the 1640s and early 1650s. There, it arose in mighty expressions, in the upsurge of Seekerism; the many Free Churches that emerged, where freedom was born and practiced; the Fifth Monarchists, who misinterpreted the prophecies of Daniel and thereby brought the whole prophetic tradition into disrepute; and the theodemocratic Quakers who exploded on the English scene in the early 1650s. Nor should the many free individuals be neglected, who did not affiliate with any church group, with William Walwyn and John Milton as superb examples. The lunatic fringe must also be noted, not because it contributed to the rise of freedom and progress in any substantial way, or ways, but because, in perverted expressions, it revealed the fact that there truly was an underlying spirit of the age.

On the continent of Europe, after the departure of Luther and Calvin from the early path of the line of liberty, the free tradition continued among the more sober Anabaptists and, in its most insightful and effective expressions, among the Continental Spiritual Reformers. Meanwhile, the New Learning, which arose in Italy and was carried to England by John Colet, then broadcast over all Europe by Erasmus and others, worked its way effectively into the lives of reformers in Germany and Northern Europe to lay the groundwork on which Descartes formulated the objective principles of the modern scientific method.

From the Continental Reformers, who greatly contributed to the rise of objective analysis and thought, the line of liberty expanded into the Dutch Collegians, where the Seeker movement emerged in power and produced many Fathers of Liberty and proto Quakers. And from the Continental Spiritual Reformers, the free Spirit/spirit, with the free principles and concepts to which it gave birth, then helped create the views of Jacobus Arminius, whose free principles had a mighty influence in the Arminian movement that not only effected many people itself but were taken into the Anglican Church at a time when Englishmen were colonizing Virginian and the Carolinas from which many freedom loving Episcopalians emerged to become signers of the Declaration of Independence.

The writings of the Continental Spiritual Reformers and the Dutch Collegians also found their way into liberal English reforms thought to build the idea of the Spiritual Church, with its free views, to great heights among several liberal minds who raised ideas of individual liberty to their highest conceptual levels in the mid-seventeenth century.

Also, the thought and emphasis of the familists should not be neglected. Works like William Walwyin's *The Power of Love* (1643), from wherever he got his initial ideas and proposals, played powerful roles in the rise and birth of the new Christian civilization that was born in the 1640s and '50s.

The Religio-Spiritual Foundations of the United States

In discussing "Freedom and the Historian," in his treatise of *Liberty Before (Modern) Liberalism*, Quentin Skinner stresses that historians should study the issue of freedom in the context in which it arose, not merely by focusing on "a canon of so-called classic texts" related to it but in the context of the "broader traditions and frameworks of thought." And Dr. James Hastings Nichols of Chicago University wrote his insightful volume, *Democracy and the Churches*, on the premise that "religious and moral attitude and dynamic... alone gives a political system real vitality."

The religio-spiritual basis of American life, society, and constitutional republicanism was well stated by Patrick Henry, who said, "It cannot be emphasized too strongly or too often that this great nation was founded, not by religionists, but by Christians; not on religions, but on the Gospel of Jesus Christ." To see the Gospel foundation of the American nation, one must go back at least 150 years before 1776, to liberal revolutionary thought and experience in England and the Low Countries of Northern Europe, with roots in earlier times, and consider the possibility that God—by the use of transforming truth and the enlivening power of the Holy Spirit—was working in the minds and souls of many people. Serious studies thought in this period clearly indicates that modern liberty was first a Spirit/spirit of renewing life in the souls of Advance Reformers and Reformists, which gave them the required enlightenment to bring forth free principles, concepts, and societal forms with a desire to progress. Here, the word "Spirit" is an abbreviation of the "Holy Spirit," and the word "spirit," in lower case, has reference to the quickening life of the Western Awakening. The renewing life of the Holy Spirit combined with the quickening power of the Western Awakening to produce the determining power of the reform initiative that gave birth to liberty.

To Henry and other prominent early Americans, Christ's Gospel had deeper and more significant substance than mere theological or ideological principles or the letter of written law. The Reverend Jonas Clark, an early supporter of the American Revolution, affirmed that "the gospel of Jesus Christ is the source of liberty, and the soul of government and the life of a people." Stating his "observations relative to the true principles and Spirit of the Christian religion," as underlying factors of American social and political life, Zephaniah Swift explained, "Moral virtue is substantially and essentially enforced by the precepts of Christianity, and may be considered to be the basis of it. But in addition to moral principles, the [new life and enlivening power connected with] Christian doctrines inculcate a purity of heart and holiness of life which constitutes its chief glory." Swift emphasized, "When we contemplate it in this light, we have a most striking evidence of its superiority over all the systems of pagan philosophy, which were promulgated by the wisest men of ancient times."

In a sermon before the governor, Senate, and House of Representatives of Massachusetts, in October 1780, Samuel Cooper emphasized the vital role of divine enlightenment in "the principles and arguments upon which," said he, "the right of our present establishment is grounded." Americans were "illuminated," and they were "nurtured by their ancestors in the love of freedom"—"a people to whom divine providence was pleased to present so fair an opportunity of asserting their natural right as an independent nation." They were, therefore, morally responsible to accept "the heavenly call" that enabled them to acquire "the glorious wreaths and peculiar blessings" that could only be bestowed by divine means.

The question must be asked, Did John Adams and Thomas Jefferson—the two leading minds in the American Revolution—have a similar insight and understanding? Historical evidence indicates that they did. A study of Adams and Jefferson in the context of the extended revolution that gave birth to liberty makes it clear that they perceived that living transforming elements that went beyond ideological principles, concepts, and societal forms produced American independence.

Writing to Jefferson in 1813, Adams voiced his strong conviction that the causative factors that gave birth to American independence were "the general principles of Christianity." These, he emphasized, were not "the general principles, institutions, or systems of education of [any Church or]...of the Philosophers." Instead, "the general principles on which the [American] Fathers achieved independence were...the general principles of [Bible] Christianity," which indicates that Adams was speaking of the deep transforming Spirit and power of Bible Christianity. In solemn testimony of the divine nature of the factor of which he spoke, he stated, "I will avow that I then believed, and now believe, that those general principles of [Bible] Christianity are as eternal and immutable as the existence and attributes of God." Of those divine "principles," he added, "I could therefore safely say, consistently with all my then and present information, that I believe they would never make [further] discoveries [toward liberty, justice, and human well-being] in contradiction to these general principles." To make genuine progress toward greater liberty, Americans would have to build on the foundation of divine and eternal elements that gave birth to the nation.

Jefferson, who denounced man-made systems of religion and looked hopefully for the return of Bible Christianity, stressed that "the precepts of philosophy and of the [earlier] Hebrew code laid hold of actions only." Then, alluding to the enlivening power of Bible Christianity, he emphasized that Jesus "pushed his scrutiny's into the heart of man; erected his tribunal in the region of his thoughts, and purified the waters at the foundation head." Both Adams and Jefferson recognized that the roots of American independence were the eternal—not merely the outward theological or ideological properties of Bible Christianity.

Jefferson saw a vital free spirit working in the lives of the American people that was the substance, or essence, of their free democratic life and society and made them possible. By this dynamic spirit, Americans could enjoy "voluntary associations" that produced a much different type of free life than that which existed in ancient classical times. Said Jefferson of the Greeks, "So different was the style of society then, and with those people, from what it is now and with us, that I think little edification can be obtained from their writings on the subject of government." He added, "They had just ideas of the value of personal liberty, but none at all of the structure of government best calculated to preserve it." The problem was that "they knew no medium between a democracy [the only pure republic, but (to them) impracticable beyond the limits of a town] and an abandonment of themselves to an aristocracy, or a tyranny independent of the people." The Greeks lacked the Spirit/spirit or vital substance of liberty—the inner living elements of free open life and union—that were foundations of early American liberty and democratic republicanism.

The power of a Bible Christian Spirit, with the free and open principles, concepts, and forms that it generated, brought many insightful Americans to sense how and why they had "the right to choose" and support "a Republican, or popular, government" capable of being expanded "over any extent of country." Said Jefferson, "The introduction of this new principle of representative democracy has rendered useless almost everything written before on the structure of government; and, in a great measure, relieves our regret, if the political writings of Aristotle, or of any other ancient, have been lost, or are unfaithfully rendered or explained to us."

Americans had little need to consult Greeks, Romans, or philosophers on matters of political government. Jefferson urged, "My most earnest wish is to see the republican element of popular control [which had developed in the tradition of liberty that came into being in America] pushed to the maximum of its practicable exercise." His ideal order of republicanism would instill the fundamental elements of private and public virtue, the spirit of liberty, free and open union, right reason, etc. into the people. If this were done, Jefferson added, "I shall then believe that our government may be pure and perpetual."

Tocqueville perceived that early Americans had a special source of power that gave foundation for all facets of free life and society.

"Religion in America takes no direct part in the government of society," he explained, "but it must be regarded as the first of their political institutions; for if it does not impart a taste for freedom, it facilitates the use of it... Americans combine the notions of Christianity and of liberty so intimately in their minds that it is impossible to make them conceive the one without the other; and with them this conviction does not spring from that barren, traditionary faith which seems to vegetate rather than to live in the soul."

Along with the changing views that have occurred of America's constitutional order of government, secular-minded scholars have made what they hold to be objective studies of the renewing spiritual life of Bible Christianity as it was experienced, in part, by insightful reformers who tried to return to the New Testament order of life. Yet this requires them to rationalized primary factors. With their narrow view of man as a mere physical creature, the transforming life that combined with the enlivening power of the Western Awakening and gave direction to insightful reformers who became Fathers of Liberty can only be their "imagination." This, to them, is the foundation of the Single Tradition of Liberty. Thus, Sacvan Bercovitch edited a book entitled *The American Puritan Imagination*, published at Cambridge in 1974. And John R. Knott Jr., in his *The Sword of the Spirit: Puritan Responses to the Bible*, which he introduces with the chapter entitled "The Living Word" states, "It is reasonable to talk about a Puritan imagination, as Sacvan Bercovitch and others have done in connection with American Puritanism, and to pay more attention than we have given to works that best embody this imagination."

This rationalization, based on blind unwillingness to insightfully objectively weigh clear historical evidence, is a major fallacy of the greatest importance for these are the roots of modern freedom and constitutional republicanism, and evidence suggests that a nation cannot permanently survive on the mere ideological and outward forms of liberty. When first things are set aside, secondary things open the door for the disintegration of the freedom that people possess.

Nowhere in the New Testament is there a hint that Jesus and his apostles conducted their lives on the basis of mere imagination.

Nor did insightful reformers who struggled for the light of the Spirit and found it in various shades and degrees. Nor did the hundreds of martyrs who made the ultimate sacrifice to sustain the light and renewing life that they found. Fair consideration must, therefore, be given to the foundation on which they worked, which was that on which modern freedom and constitutional republicanism were born. Their personal experiences and teachings reveal that renewing life and regenerating truth and light—which these Fathers asserted they received by faith in God, through the Holy Spirit and the living Word of Scripture, with added inner enlightenment and strength from the quickening power of the Western Awakening—were dominant powers underlying the Single Tradition that finally gave birth to the United States of America. And the American Founders saw in these free elements, with their power to give birth to the spirit of freedom and promote liberal principles, ideology, and procedures, the vital sources of their independence.

The Need for Further Study

While studies of the ideological origins of the United States contribute much to knowledge of the American founding, they fail to deal with the roots and ultimate sources of liberty and democracy, which were religious and spiritual in character. A basic factor that moved the Fathers of Liberty was a desire to return to Bible Christianity and the New Testament Church. This fact is key to an understanding of the wellsprings of America and the transforming power of the scriptural Word among reformers. And it justifies the need to state the principles and program of Bible Christianity and the New Testament Church, compared to the program of subsequent "Christianity." And it is suggested that all this will show that Bible Christianity and the New Testament Church were vital foundations of modern liberty and the urge to progress.

To get to the roots of the United States of America, the liberal spirit and elements within Bible Christianity must properly be noted and four major divisions of reform within the overall revolution that gave birth to freedom and democracy investigated, with a focus on the vital elements that were central to the Single Tradition of Liberty: (1) reform efforts from the end of the New Testament era to 1517 when the eruption which Martin Luther initiated severed Teutonic Europe from the Roman Catholic Church; (2) reform movements from 1517—with emphasis on a group called the Continental Spiritual Reformers—to the beginning of the last quarter of the sixteenth century; (3) reform efforts beginning with the last quarter of the sixteenth century to the Glorious Revolution in England, in 1688, which was the birthing period of modern freedom; and (4) liberal reform efforts and writings that elaborated on the free spirit and principles that had emerged to the time when freedom and democratic republicanism were institutionalized in America's state and federal governments in the last quarter of the eighteenth century.

There is need to study each of these areas to show the rising elements of liberty and progress and their connection with earlier and later ages. Since all leading reformers in the liberal tradition had an eye single to the glory of God and relied on Christ and the Holy Spirit for renewing life and truth, certain central points must be kept in mind in each division of reform thought and activity, such as the following: Who were the major reformers? What influence did the Bible, especially the New Testament, have on them? What was the nature of the religious, social, and political setting of their day? What contributions did they make toward liberty and democratic society? What evidence, and testimony, is there that the principles and concepts that they brought forth came from Christ through the Holy Spirit? And which of their ideas later found place in the free societies and constitutional republicanism of the United States of America?

Evidence presented in this study shows clearly, without valid reason to question, that the primary causative elements that moved reform minds in the liberal tradition were religious and, especially, spiritual in nature. The plain facts of history show that, strengthened by the quickening power of the Western Awakening, a living renewing Spirit acquired by Bible-type faith brought forth free principles, concepts, and societal forms from New Testament Christianity, and that these combined factors gave birth to American life, liberty, and democratic constitutional republicanism.

CHAPTER 2

Wellsprings of America

Note: It is one thing to focus attention on the general growth of freedom and democracy and discuss the merits of those who promoted their growth, as many historians do. It is quite another thing to find the original line of freedom and progress, with those who brought them forth and promoted them, and, especially, to determine the vital elements that gave life and moving power to the spirit of freedom and progress. But until this last work is done, there can be no true foundation on which free people can meet the challenges of maintaining freedom and progress and promoting them in the world.

Opinions vary on the question of why civilizations develop in given ways. Some credit the influence of great men who stand at pivotal points in time while others hold that natural conditions and ideas play decisive roles. Still, others give preeminence to economic causes. But while men, ideas, and economics were important factors in the rise of free progressive Western and Anglo-American life and society, historical evidence presented in this study shows clearly that a Bible Revolution, which soon became a New Testament Revolution, with added strength given by the quickening life of the Western Awakening (with no natural earthly antecedents equivalent to effects produced), promoted the rise of the West and eventually gave birth to the United States of America. Yet after more than a half millennium since the mighty transformations began to occur, a popular history text reflects the dilemma that has prevailed. "Precisely why all this took place when and where it did," it confesses, "is still a puzzle."

The dynamic powers that nurtured the prevailing revolution that lay at the foundation of America contributed in three determinative ways to the birth of the United States of America and the Modern Age of the world: (1) the discovery of the New World by Christopher Columbus; (2) the early colonization of British America; and (3) the creation of free religio-spiritual-based social, economic, and political principles, concepts, and forms that finally produced a free Christian civilization and fashioned the progressive practices and character of American life, liberty, and constitutional republicanism.

The Living Spiritual Base of Western Liberal Reform
Getting to the Source of Western Reform

1. The testimony of historians—the New Testament Revolution
2. The Western Awakening, a basis of life and strength for the New Testament Revolution.

Christ: The Anointed One

1. Christ came to earth with glory in Himself.
2. Christ's testimonies of Himself as the life and light of the world—Living Water, Bread of Life (after feeding the multitude).

The Testimony of John the Baptist
The Testimony of the apostle John

Note: Stress 1 John 1–2, etc.

The Testimony of the Apostle Paul
The Testimony of Advance Reformers

Note: They may be called Advance Reformers because they focused on living truth and power derived from their faith in Jesus Christ and the renewing life and power that they found in the scriptural word, instead of merely promoting a reform position based on given views and principles.

The Discovery of America

With few exceptions, early Americans accepted Samuel Miller's declaration, in 1795, that God provided enlightenment and strength in the major events that led to the establishment of the Constitution of the United States. Oliver Hart spoke of the "great, unexpected, and marvelous things" which the Supreme Being "wrought for America," declaring, "God raised up CHRISTOPHER COLUMBUS to make the discovery… By means of COLUMBUS, God discovered to the enlightened nations this vast continent,…intended in Providence, no doubt, for a theater of great and marvelous events." And Bishop James Madison of Virginia called attention to the "displays of divine providence which the history of America exhibits," beginning with the guidance and support given to Columbus to open these "distant regions of the earth."

Yet later, historians began to portray Columbus's voyage in a humanistic light. This depiction, which rested on a "slender repertoire of texts," was not depicted as a spiritually motivated and directed venture but one made by a "bold and innovative explorer" armed with a "'rational' geography," who battled the ignorance of powerful ecclesiastics.

Not until the mid-1980s—five hundred years later—did scholars seriously consider that Columbus's "personal spirituality, or the spirituality of his age" could have been the inspiration for his voyage. A book written by Columbus that lay virtually unread for nearly half a millennium in the *Biblioteca Colombina* of the Cathedral of Seville, Spain, shows the fallacy of the restricted view. Columbus's

Libro de las Profecias (*Book of Prophecies*), written in 1502, had been but rarely and superficially regarded by historians, and not until 1991 was it published in an English translation. Historians had long ignored it because they were "reluctant to admit" that the great mariner "was influenced by prophetic ideas," which were recorded in his study notes as early as 1481. The volume refutes the idea that Columbus merely "applied [human] reason in conceiving his bold venture." For centuries, the "secular mind-set of the Western World" produced extensive literature on Columbus, but with rare references to the "essence of what motivated him, to wit, his deep and enduring faith in Jesus Christ." But due to this "most reliable documentary evidence," the motivation behind the admiral's voyage of discovery can be seen with greater insight and understanding.

Columbus's intended preface to his *Book of Prophecies* is an unfinished letter written between September 13, 1501, and March 23, 1502, and addressed to King Ferdinand and Queen Isabella of Spain. The body of the volume is a compilation of scriptural statements, prophecies, and authoritative commentaries collected and arranged by Columbus. The book opens a "window onto the motives and consuming passion" of the great mariner. As a "most important and revelatory" work—one of "incalculable value"—it reveals the "faith and the vision" and exhibits the "heart, of one of history's greatest heroes."

Conclusive evidence of the admiral's "principal motive" in planning his voyage shows clearly that his faith in Christ was the "most powerful incentive in his life," and that the Bible, with insights and personal witnesses given by the Holy Spirit, was the "principal source of inspiration" for the Columbian Enterprise. Reminding the Spanish monarchs of the "many promises which our Savior made to us," Columbus declared, "All that is requested by anyone who has faith will be granted. Knock and it will be opened to you." The admiral asserted, "No one should be afraid to take on any enterprise in the name of our Savior, if it is right and if the purpose is purely for his holy service."

Columbus made it amply clear that promptings by the Holy Spirit were the motivating factors behind his voyage. "Neither reason, nor mathematics, nor world maps," he stated in his letter intended for the Spanish monarchs, "were profitable to me." Instead, he was "convinced to the bottom of his heart" that he was "speaking the truth" when he stated that he was "inspired by the Holy Ghost." This was no "rhetorical flourish, no hypocrisy, no attempt to ingratiate himself" with church dignitaries; it was "bitter [due to the reluctance of many to credit his spiritual motivation] deep, earnest."

Never doubting the Spirit's enlightenment, Columbus ardently believed that if he did his part he would not fail. "Our Lord with provident hand unlocked my mind," he declared, "sent me upon the sea, and gave me fire for the deed. Those who heard of my Emprise called it foolish, mocked me, and laughed, but who can doubt but that the Holy Ghost inspired me?" To Ferdinand and Isabella, he affirmed, "I attest that he [the Holy Spirit] with marvelous rays of light, consoled me through the holy and sacred Scriptures, a strong and clear testimony,...encouraging me to proceed, and continually, without ceasing for a moment, they inflame me with a sense of great urgency." Like Advance Reformers who gave birth to liberty, Columbus's view of the Spirit was neither restrictive nor elitist. "I say," the admiral declared, "that the Holy Spirit works in Christians, Jews, Moors and in all others of every sect, and not just in the learned, but also in the ignorant."

Columbus read a "wide range of books" in his search of scientific and geographic data to give to the Spanish monarchs and their board of examiners as "proofs" to verify the soundness of his view. He looked into "all the Scriptures, cosmography, histories, chronicles and philosophy and other arts." These, said Columbus in his intended letter to Ferdinand and Isabella, "our Lord opened to my understanding [I could sense his hand upon me],...and he [God] unlocked within me the determination to execute the idea."

Neither worldly "sciences...nor the authoritative citations from them, were of any avail," the admiral emphasized. He reminded the Spanish monarchs, "I spent seven years in your royal Court arguing the case with so many persons of such authority and learned in all the arts, and in the end they concluded that all was idle nonsense, and with this they gave up [the project]."

There can be no doubt that the admiral's faith and communion with the Holy Spirit were "integral parts of his personality, central to the development of his global plans." His book may be read as "compelling evidence" that the Spirit was the living "force motivating his vision and sustaining him through years of ridicule, hardship, and achievement." Without the Holy Spirit's enlightening influence, he probably would not have been able to "sustain the single-minded persistence it took to win support for the Enterprise."

The New Christian Civilization

Belief in divine causation and guidance had profound effects on the American founding in various ways. In response to inward enlightenment like Columbus and the early American colonists received, English and American Fathers of Liberty affirmed that the free spirit, principles, concepts, and democratic forms of the new Christian civilization they brought forth in mid-seventeenth-century England and America were derived from Bible Christianity and the influence of enlivening power received from the Holy Spirit. Bible Christianity and the Holy Spirit were the vital wellsprings of the American Republic. Noting that as early as the thirteenth century, "the Pentecost Spirit" began to rise on a wide scale, Jones writes, "The most characteristic religious note of the popular movement was the call to follow Christ. It occurred to multitudes, as it did to St. Francis (of Assisi), that traditional Christianity had lost the way the Master made for it and was on a bypath. Throughout all, Christendom prophetic spirits were striving to restore apostolic and evangelical piety and to discover how to bring religion vitally into the lives of the people. It was a time of vast upheaval and ferment, like that which four centuries later appeared in the English commonwealth...swarms of sectaries...fill the period... Cathari and Waldenses are already numerous. The Franciscan and Dominican movements are the most powerful expressions of the profound desire for a return to the religion of the Galilean."

The vital elements that underlaid the above movements were derived from Bible Christianity, and from them came the faith and

Spirit-based components on which Advance Reformers brought forth liberty and democracy. Many reformers who were "moved by the Spirit of God and according to Holy Writ," the American congregationalist John Wise wrote, "led the way [toward reform] in the face of all danger." And in this scenario, many Advance Reformers not only made the arduous voyage to America in the interest of their faith, but there they unfolded its free spirit, principles, concepts, and societal forms with good effect on their brethren who remained in the mother country while they, in turn, benefitted from the achievements of Advance Reform in England.

A new age had dawned, which William Dell, a leading Reformer in the English Renaissance—the birth period of the Modern Age—held to be the product of practical experience with the Holy Spirit. Those who opposed the rise of reform early in the West, he explained, reproachfully called the "breaking forth" of renewing truth and power the "New Light," which consisted of "the truth and light and life and Spirit of the Gospel." And he affirmed that in and of the Holy Spirit, the power of the latter was made manifest with even greater transforming affects to produce a new order of free life and society.

John Saltmarsh also indicated that religio-spiritual "experience" led to the birth of liberty and democracy. The "Spirit" was the moving power that operated in "the first pure Gospel-day or [New Testament] time." And the same Spirit, in "some faint and small discoveries," said he, enlightened "Hus, Luther, Wyclif, Calvin, Peter Martyr and…the…many martyrs in the kingdom, who were glorious lights respectively to the darkness of that generation." Thus, John Owen (1616–1683), dean of Christ Church, Oxford, vice-chancellor of the university, and one of Oliver Cromwell's chaplains in the English Revolution, stated that "God revealed to Zwingli a strong confirmation" of certain points of doctrine. And John Foxe (1516–1587), whose acts and monuments had a powerful effect on the growth of the rising free Christian civilization in England, saw the invention of printing as "a miracle performed by the Lord for the express purpose of bringing the reformation of his Church to its final consummation." Said Foxe, "The Lord began the work of his

Church, not with sword and target to subdue his exalted adversary, but with printing, writing and reading."

Owen reminded the Commons that in earlier years, God "stirred up" the spirits of certain men "to reform his Church," adding, "the most whereof died in giving their witness." Following this line of experience, the Quaker historian Rufus M. Jones found abundant evidence of "spiritual struggles" that finally culminated in the blossoming of the free spirit and its liberal principles and concepts in the English Commonwealth, where liberty and democracy were born. They "were the normal fruit of the Reformation Spirit, when once it had penetrated the life of the English people and kindled the fire of personal conviction in their hearts."

The Levelers, who diligently labored to give England a democratic republic, affirmed in the strongest possible terms that the life and power of the Holy Spirit lay at the base of the order of political government that they proposed. They saw God's blessings in their efforts to recover their "liberties" that were lost in the Norman Conquest of AD 1066, and they positively declared their faith that God desired England to be a free nation.

John Milton (1608–1674), the leading intellect among other English reformers whose views Milton often reflected, was fully convinced that through the Holy Spirit, Christ was the central moving power in Western Reform, and that in mid-seventeenth-century England, God was "decreeing to begin some new and great period." The Lord had "ever had this Island under the special indulgent eye of his providence," said Milton; he "began the reformation of his church by sending 'that glimmering light which Wyclif and his followers dispersed.'" Milton made reference to "an extraordinary effusion of God's Spirit upon every age and sex, attributing to all men, and requiring from them, the ability [in the spirit of the New Learning] of searching, trying, examining all things, and, by the Spirit, discerning that which is good." In this way, many were brought to a state of "musing, searching, revolving new notions,...reading, trying all things, assenting to the force of reason and convincement." To Milton, this was the true base of the English Renaissance.

Milton affirmed that many reformers experienced a "sudden assault" of God's "reforming Spirit," which was "warring against human principles and carnal sense, the pride of flesh, that still cried up Antiquity, Custom, Canons, Councils and Laws, and cried down the truth for novelty, schism, profaneness and sacrilege." "If God had left undone this whole work so contrary to flesh and blood till these times," he reasoned in referring to the Spirit's work in earlier ages, "how should we have yielded to his heavenly call, had we been taken as it were in the starkness of our ignorance?"

Then contemplating the rise of a new more peaceful society in the Anglo-American world, Milton voiced the hope that as God had dignified their "father's days with many revelations above all the foregoing ages" since Christ's ministry on earth, he would also "vouchsafe to [people in his day]...as large a portion" of the Holy Spirit as he pleased. Addressing the living Christ as "the Ever-Begotten Light and perfect Image of the Father," Milton exclaimed, "Thou hast opened our difficult and sad times and given us an unexpected breathing after our long oppressions; thou hast done justice upon those that tyrannized over us; ... thou hast taught us to admire only that which is good, and to count that only praiseworthy which is grounded upon the divine precepts."

Asserting the obvious, Milton confidently exclaimed, "Who is there that cannot trace thee now in thy beamy walk through the midst of thy sanctuary, amidst those golden candlesticks [i.e., churches] which have long suffered a dimness amongst us through the violence of those that had seized them and were more taken with the mention of their gold than of their starry light. Everyone can say that now certainly thou hast visited this land, and hast not forgotten the utmost corners of the earth, in a time when men had thought that thou wast gone up from us to the farther Est end of the heavens."

The spirit of liberty and the free ideas that emerged in this way then spread to British America through various channels. The Pilgrim migration, first to Holland, then to New England, says Troeltsch, was carried out "in the interest of their mission to found a 'purely democratic church.'" Their early covenant associations promoted "the line of development which led to the so-called Congregational

Church principle." Says Troeltsch, "The statement that the Church is governed not by man but by the Spirit of Christ is only another illustration of the influence of a preeminently 'spiritual' type of thought upon the whole."

The unyielding belief of many reform people that the Holy Spirit was the indispensable foundation of society based on mutual covenant clearly reveals the spiritual character of their venture in America. Their purpose, or "interest," in going to New England, said Jonathan Mitchell, who sat at the feet of the first American ministers, was the "erecting of Christ's Kingdom in whole societies,… tho' with respect to the Inward and Invisible Kingdom, as the scope thereof,"—the inner life and truth created by the Holy Spirit, which was the determining factor. Perry Miller uses Mitchell's statement to support the view that the Puritan colonization of America was undertaken as a "positive crusade" for their covenant ideal. The early American clergy, he found, were united by their former associations in England and their allegiance to the views of particular theologians. And, above all, they were "consciously united, almost to the man, in the conviction that the form of church order decreed explicitly by revelation from heaven was Congregational." The heart of the "church theory was the covenant" in which people enlightened and renewed by the Holy Spirit "covenanted together, and out of their compact created a Church." Miller emphasizes that the desire to develop covenant societies, as a major causative factor in American colonization, resulted from "the piety, from the tremendous [religio-spiritual] thrust of the Reformation and the living force of the theology."

Within the Advance Reform Tradition of Anglo-America, John Locke (1632–1704), whose writings helped mature and refine the principles, concepts, and forms of society that emerged earlier that century, made it clear that the great Messiah—a designation of Christ that he often used—and the Holy Spirit were fundamental to his life and thought. While one could employ reason to acquire knowledge of truth, said Locke, there are some truths that "lie too deep for our natural powers easily to reach and make plain and visible to mankind without some light from above to direct them." Yet, Locke observed, it often happens that once a truth is revealed it is taken for granted. "A great many things which we have been bred up in the belief of," he stressed, "we take for unquestionable obvious truths and easily demonstrable, without considering how long we might have been in doubt or ignorant of them had revelation been silent. And many are beholden to revelation who does not acknowledge it." He concluded, "It is no diminishing to revelation that reason gives it suffrage too, to the truths revelation has discovered. But it is our mistake to think that, because reason confirms them to us, we had the first certain knowledge of them from thence, and in that clear evidence we now possess them."

Although Locke referred more specifically to revelation given in Christ's ministry on earth, he included immediate personal revelation through the Holy Spirit as a source of truth to true believers. Jesus, "who is faithful and just," he declared, promised the Holy Spirit to his disciples; and the prominent Englishman stated emphatically, "We cannot doubt of the performance."

Personal enlightenment by the Holy Spirit, Locke made clear, was the basis of his own written works, and he assumed that others would judge his views by the light of that same Spirit. "As far as they carry light and conviction to any other man's understanding," he said, "so far, I hope my labor may be of some use to him; beyond the evidence it carries with it, I advise him not to follow mine nor any man's interpretation." Each person was to rely on his own acquired light. While this was not the fuller view and use of the inner light that the Quakers made the base of free life and theodemocracy, Locke was suggesting that one rely on the same principle of illumination. Confessing that he and others did not have this light to the same degree Christ's Apostles did, Locke stressed the need to rely on it for truth and enlightening power. Faith in the living Christ and enlightenment by the Holy Spirit, with the added power of the Word/Spirit, were the wellsprings of the new order of life, society, and government that had emerged and had been planted in British America where it was growing to greater maturity.

TIMOTHY AALDERS

The Humanist Fabrication

By the use of devised techniques, without consulting historical evidence, secular humanists have created a picture of the rise of the Modern Age and of the United State of America that is quite different from that which is found in the experiences, teachings, and testimonies of the Fathers of Liberty; and in their efforts, they pay considerable attention to classical history and literature while implying that they are factors of primary importance in the rise of the Modern Age.

After the Western Awakening had been underway more than a century, an ecumenical council was held at Florence, Italy, in 1438–39, which brought many Greek scholars to the city, and their presence helped stimulate a rising interest in classical literature. Then, with the fall of Constantinople to the Turks in 1453—which caused many Byzantine refugees to seek a livelihood in Italy by teaching, copying, and translating Greek manuscripts—the Revival of Antiquity gained momentum in the West. But even though the Western Awakening had been underway for some time, there is no evidence that classical writings produced a rise of liberty and progress among the people of Constantinople comparable to that which was then beginning to occur in the West.

When the power of the Western Awakening began to be felt, many authentic humanists emerged in Italy, with an exclusive focus on the natural man: his intellect and his ability to direct his life and the affairs of society. Yet the contributions of these humanists to liberty and progress were "rare and dubious." As self-made men, they tended to worship their creator, and in championing the natural man without a firm foundation of moral and ethical values, many nurtured erotic interests that led to debauchery and the disintegration of society. The powerful reformer, Girolamo Savonarola (1452–1498), who organized a free republic in Florence, Italy, in the late fifteenth century, got to the root of their deficiencies when he said, "How… will the desire of our hearts be gratified if we have not a clear view of God? Nothing finite can fill the capacity of our soul—our spirit always goes beyond the finite."

There are different meanings of the word "humanist" and "humanism." At the height of the Renaissance, the term *humanista*—the origin of the modern word "humanist"—was given to those who were interested in the humanities. The term had been used by the Romans to designate a liberal or literary education by studying authors like Cicero, and that usage of the term was resumed by Italian scholars in the late fourteenth century. "The studia humanitatis [then] came to stand for a clearly defined cycle of scholarly disciplines, namely grammar, rhetoric, history, poetry, and moral philosophy; and the study of each of these subjects was understood to include the reading and interpretation of its standard ancient writers in Latin and, to a lesser extent, in Greek." The term *humanist*, used in student slang at Italian universities, was apparently derived from the older term *studia humanitatis* or the "humanities." But instead of denoting "a philosophical tendency or system," this term referred to "a limited cultural and educational programme, and as such should not be used to characterize Renaissance thought in general."

The term "classical humanism" arose from the word "humanista" and "from this designation...nineteenth-century historians derive the present term 'Humanism,'" which, as a philosophical system, has two points of emphasis: (1) man, the sole focus of life—the center and highest form of life in a conceived godless evolutionary scale and (2) the limiting of man's interest and abilities in acquiring truth to the natural order of life found on earth. This connotation (which is more ardently voiced today) has been extended back to the Renaissance, implying that early humanists gave roots to the modern concept.

Humanists now justify the view that the special "cultivation of the classics or 'the Humanities' is...[valid] because it serves to educate and to develop a desirable type of human being. For [they wrongly contend that] the Classics represent the highest level of human achievement and should hence be of primary concern for every man." And they tend to mold historic facts to their opinions, instead of deriving conclusions from the facts of history, to create a narrow incomplete secularized view of the origins and growth of the vital sense of human dignity and value, which shows their failure to apply objective analysis to the get to the origins of liberty and democratic associations.

Kristeller recognizes the central fact that "practically all Renaissance humanists, before and after the Reformation, were [what he and others erroneously call] Christian humanists." To combine the two irreconcilable words, "Christian" and "humanist," is to create a contradictory name—a nonsense term. These Reformers are more accurately "Christian Reconstructionist." The cardinal hope of early Reformers, whom humanists now call "Christian humanists," was to return to Bible Christianity. They held to the fundamental scriptural view that a Christian is one who, by faith, centers his life in Jesus Christ, the Son of God, and receives regenerating life, truth, and power from the Holy Spirit to put off the natural person and to achieve a newness of free open life and dignity in and through Christ. And having entered the path of salvation, they desired to grow up in the truth and Spirit of Christ. Such a person is not a "Christian humanist." A humanist holds that the natural man is the sole focus of life, and that by his natural powers, he can achieve a life of freedom, success, and happiness. This view cannot be reconciled with the principle goal of a Christian, which is to be perfected in Christ.

Although there is well-documented evidence that the leading early figures in the revolution that finally gave birth to liberty, whom Kristeller calls "Christian humanists," centered their lives in Christ, he rationalizes, "Regardless of the particular philosophical or theological opinions held by individual humanists, and of the theological, philosophical, scientific, or juristic training which individual scholars may have combined with their humanist education, we might choose to call Christian humanists all those scholars who accepted the teachings of Christianity and were members of one of the churches, without necessarily discussing religious or theological topics in their literary or scholarly writings."

Humanists who believe that the dignity and value of man arose from within himself have developed and propounded a restricted view of the origins, growth, and achievements of the modern age. But historical evidence makes it clear that humanism did not produce the widespread Western Awakening, nor did it promote the regenerating life, truth, and transforming power that Advance Reformers derived from Christ and the Word/Spirit. When these and related elements came to a crest in the mid-seventeenth century, humanists did not give birth to liberty and the concept of constitutional democracy. They are not found among the prominent minds of the Age of Christ and of the Holy Spirit.

Historians like A. G. Dickens take sharp issue with secularists who credit humanism with producing the renewing life, the enlarged intellect of people in general, the new inquisitiveness, the objective posture of analysis and right reason, and the democratic elements that created a new Christian civilization and continued to unfold and bring forth liberal fruits for generations after the synergistic developments that occurred in the mid-seventeenth-century Anglo-American world had produced the nucleus of the new Christian civilization. Dickens challenges, "The label 'humanism' with its Classical, Italian and Erasmian connotations seems quite inadequate to express the whole of this tidal movement, the direction and depth of which can best be ascertained by examining the intellectual interests, not of great or even eminent minds, but of ordinary readers and writers in Tudor England."

By contrast, historical evidence clearly attests, says Troeltsch, that the "real supporters" of the new age were Christians who had "been born again through the Word." Reformers who applied a program of spiritual renewal moved the Renaissance spirit and objective outlook forward on a progressive foundation, with the Word/Spirit playing a major role in giving direction to reform initiatives that finally gave birth to liberty and democracy. The renewing life that Reformers acquired had practical effects in all realms of thought and human endeavor. It helped them to fight their way up and out of totalitarian darkness, superstition, and vain sophistry into the light of liberty, democracy, and progress, and eventually to give birth to British America and the modern world. The source of this renewing life was Jesus, the Christ, the Anointed One. And the ability of Advance Reformers to perceive vital elements of Bible Christianity from the patriarchs, prophets, and apostles of Scripture, and to apply them in practical ways represents "the highest level of achievement" among true liberal Western minds.

The Colonization of America

Many early American colonists were convinced that, like Columbus, they were directed by promptings of the Holy Spirit to set sail to the New World. As early as 1584, the Separatists under Robert Browne considered leaving England in order to practice their faith more freely in another land. Yet their ultimate consideration was "whether God did call them to...depart out of England," and they concluded that a proposed move to Scotland was not consistent with their "duty" to God. They first had to accomplish "that good in England which...they might do before their departure." They were not to "remove before they had...further testified [of] the truth, and the Lord had with strong hand delivered them from these responsibilities" to fellow Englishmen. Redemption had to come from God, not by a "cowardly fleeing of their own devising." Browne's followers also considered moving to the channel islands of Jersey or Guernsey, but here again, they received no compelling promptings. "At last, when divers of them were again imprisoned, and the rest in great trouble and bondage out of prison, they all agreed and were fully persuaded that the Lord did call them out of England."

Temporal, as well as spiritual considerations, figured in the Pilgrim decision to leave their native land. "At no time," in the "long course of English history were the claims of the monarchy more exorbitant than...from 1603 to 1642, just when the tide of immigration began to flow towards America, and when the governments of the colonies were being established." Yet the presence of one motive did not "prove the absence of any other." To Tocqueville, the faith of the early colonists was not "merely a religious doctrine," it "corresponded in many points with the most absolute democratic and republican theories." Said he, "It was this tendency that had aroused its most dangerous adversaries. Persecuted by the government...and disgusted by the habits of a society which...their own principles condemned," they went to America to seek a place "where they could live according to their own opinions and worship God in freedom." "We go," said the early colonists, "to practice the positive [religio-spiritual] part of church reformation, and propagate the Gospel in America." "Never doubting that he was setting down the cause' of the great migration,'" an early American historian wrote, "God sifted a whole [English] nation that he might send choice Grain over into this Wilderness."

In accepting the view that God directed the early colonists to go to America, Tocqueville quoted the New England historian Nathaniel Morton, who wrote, "I have for some lengths of time looked upon it as a duty incumbent especially on the immediate successors of those that have had so large experience of those many memorable and signal demonstrations of God's goodness, viz. the first beginners of this Plantation in New England, to commit to writing his gracious dispensation on that behalf; having so many inducements thereunto, not only otherwise, but so plentifully in the Sacred Scriptures: that so, what we have seen, and what our fathers have told us [Psalms lxxviii. 3, 4], we may not hide from our children, showing to the generations to come the praises of the Lord; that especially the seed of Abraham his servant, and the children of Jacob his chosen [Psalms cv. 5,6], may remember his marvelous works in the beginning and progress of the planting of New England, his wonders and the judgments of his mouth; how that God brought a vine into this wilderness… He has guided his people by his strength to his holy habitation and planted them in the mountain of his inheritance in respect to precious gospel enjoyments."

Said Tocqueville, "It is impossible to read this opening paragraph without an involuntary feeling of religious awe; it breathes the very savor of Gospel antiquity. The sincerity of the author heightens his power of language. In our eyes, as well as in his own, it was not merely a party of adventurers gone forth to seek their fortune beyond seas, but the germ of a great nation wafted by Providence to a predestined shore."

The colonization of New England was representative of "the new Age of the Holy Spirit in the New World." Many of these early colonists testified that they were enlightened by the Spirit of God in the work of colonization. Charles M. Andrews calls attention to the "curious mingling of the religious with the pecuniary spirit." The settling of New England was primarily an "enterprise of the Puritan spirit," and the Independents, or Pilgrims, who landed at Plymouth in 1620, had the "same spiritual preparation" as many searching Puritans who came later. The journey of the *Mayflower* was "inspired by the ideals common, not only to Separatists but to [more liberal] Puritans in general," with their "faith and character, and the dream of a godly Utopia." John Robinson and William Brewster wrote in 1617, "We verily believe and trust that the Lord is with us,…and that he will graciously prosper our endeavors according to the simplicity of our hearts therein."

Tocqueville quoted the American clergyman, Cotton Mather, on "what motives led the Puritans to seek a refuge beyond the seas." Said Mather, "Briefly, the God of heaven served as it were, a summons upon the spirits of his people in the English nation; stirring up the spirits of thousands that never saw the faces of each other, with a most unanimous inclination to leave all the pleasant accommodations of their native country, and go over a terrible ocean, into a more terrible desert, for the pure enjoyment of all his Ordinances."

In his preface to Mather's *Magnalia Christi Americana* (1702), John Higginson spoke of the early colonists. "It has been deservedly esteemed one of the great and wonderful works of God in this last age," said he, "that the Lord stirred up the spirits of so many thousands of his servants…to transplant themselves…into a desert land in America…in the way of seeking first the kingdom of God." The colonizing venture, to those who undertook it, was indeed a "redemptive journey" toward a "new heaven and a new earth" in America.

CHAPTER 3

The Life and Revolutionary Power of the Word

The Scriptures teach that the Holy Spirit is a spirit of freedom and liberty. Paul said of the inner life and power of "the New Testament"—not the mere letter but the living power that can accompany it when studied with faith in Christ, "Where the Spirit of the Lord is, there is liberty" (2 Cor. 3:2–6, 17; Heb. 8:8–11). And it is said in the Book of Mormon, "The Spirit of God...is...Spirit of freedom" (Alma 61:15). Paul, thus, admonished, "Stand fast...in the liberty wherewith Christ hath made us free, for...ye have been called unto liberty" (Gal. 5:1, 13). For the Scriptures indicate that the Holy Spirit not only dictated scripture (see 2 Pet. 1:21), but it is connected with scripture when God's Word is properly read or spoken. Thus, Jesus declared, "The words that I speak unto you, they are Spirit, and they are Life" (John 6:63).

Reformers who promoted the rise and birth of freedom and progress by their personal experience left many testimonies in their writings that the "life" that they acquired from the Word to promote the Revolution of Life and Liberty. They understood that the Spirit as a living power, a transforming force connected with the Word of Scripture, led them to formulate the ideas and concepts that historical evidence shows led to the rise of freedom and democratic republicanism and, eventually, to the birth the United States of America.

Through thoughtful prayerful study of the Bible reformers found that as they applied the Word with faith in God a power, which they held to be the Holy Spirit, gave them renewing life and truth, and this discovery became a "common Reformation assumption" with far-reaching benefits. Believing that God gave life and truth "in Scripture, through the action of the Spirit," which enlightened, strengthened, and guided reformers. The reformers motto was "Word and Spirit." The two "go together," said the prominent English reformer Richard Sibbes. "If we will have the comforts of the Spirit we must attend upon the Word…then wait on the Spirit to quicken the Word, that both Word and Spirit may guide us to life everlasting."

Due to the union of the Word and Spirit, the term *Word/Spirit* is often used in this book. The combined power was a major driving force in the Revolution of Life and Liberty. Historical evidence shows clearly that, among other things, it promoted a general resistance to some programs of the Roman Church; gave further impetus—beyond the enlivening power of the Western Awakening—to the highly significant awakenings that occurred in the West; further enlightened the conscience of man, to foster the rise of individualism and the freedom of the masses; and helped elevate the concept of "reason" to that of "right reason"—reason enlightened by the enlivening power of the Spirit—that reached its height of popular expression in the West in the mid-seventeenth century.

Reform groups throughout the revolutionary ages gave the Word/Spirit different shades of acceptance and degrees of emphasis. And while reformers in earlier years were more concerned with freedom from arbitrary power in the church, their ideas were later extended to other realms of society and government. The point is, there is a living principle connected with the scriptural Word and to better see its place in the revolution that gave birth to freedom and progress one must also understand such aspects of the Word/Spirit as are discussed in this chapter.

William Dell (d. 1664), who was prominent among liberal English reformers in the birthing period of modern liberty, stressed the practical application of the power of the Word/Spirit in a sermon before the House of Commons, in 1646. The fact that the eternal Word, as a living Word, could be planted in the heart of man was the basis of "true gospel reformation." There could be no true reformation under the Law of Moses, Dell reasoned, until Christ, "who was God in the flesh, came with the ministration of the Spirit." "Then indeed," said he, "was the Time of Reformation." He stressed, "The time of the Gospel is the Time of Reformation. Whenever the Gospel is preached in the Spirit and power of it which is the Time of Reformation." The specific means by which "Christ brings this reformation about," Dell declared, is "by these two, and them only: to wit, the Word, and the Spirit."

Advance Reformers found in the Bible that the Spirit of God connected to the Word was a spirit of liberty, and in their personal experience, the Spirit of renewing life and of liberty became the very heart of their liberal reform initiatives. Claiming to receive support and guidance from the Spirit, John Lilburne (1614?–1657), the Leveler leader who fought for liberty against arbitrary power in every sphere of society and government in the birthing period of liberty, could not be checked by the lash, the pillory, or prison bars. And when faced with the scaffold, Sir Henry Vane the Younger (1612–1662)—next to Oliver Cromwell, the most influential man in the English Revolution—walked by faith, without flinching, to his death, as did Algernon Sidney (1622–1682), whose *Discourses on Government* in later years became a Bible of Christian Revolution in the cause of liberty.

The Living Word

The written word in Scripture, when made alive by the Spirit of God, became the living Word. Reformers equated it with life, with truth, with power, with light; and the ultimate goal of some reformers was to have the Spirit so completely within them that they would experience their own inner scriptures—a manifestation of Christ to themselves. The English reformer Edward Dering attested that the Spirit engraved on Scripture "an express image of eternal truth" that gave it life and made it a living power. John Calvin reasoned, "Read Demosthenes or Cicero, read Plato, Aristotle, or any other of that class: You will, I admit, feel wonderfully allured, pleased, moved, and enchanted. But turn from them to the reading of the Sacred Volume, and whether you will or not, it will so affect you, so pierce your heart, so work its way into your marrow, that, in comparison to the impression so produced, that of orators and philosophers will almost disappear; making it manifest that in the Sacred Volume there is a truth divine, a something which makes it immeasurably superior to all the gifts and graces attainable by man... Whether you read David, Isaiah, and others of the same class, whose discourse flows sweet and pleasant; or Amos the herdsman, Jeremiah, and Zechariah, whose rougher idiom savors of rusticity; that majesty of the Spirit to which I adverted appears conspicuous in all."

All reformers held that, by faith, the Word embodies "a divine power or energy," and its renewing life and truth can affect the "manner in which the Word acts" on faithful individuals. The Word, "confirmed and authenticated by the witness of the Spirit," Coolidge states, means that "the new life in Christ which Paul preached as the end of Scripture is...itself conveyed by Scripture." In Scripture, believers found "life itself in untrammeled variety." Through the Word, a "life-giving Spirit" was infused into them, and by practical experience, they learned that "the Spirit of the new law [of the Gospel] quickens" people of faith. "To hear the Word of God 'means life,'" declared the early Continental Spiritual Reformer Hans Denck, "to hear it not means death." And later, John Saltmarsh, a leading English reformer, emphasized that, comparatively speaking, "nothing is pure, spiritual, divine, Gospel, but that which is light, life, glory, Spirit, or God-revealed."

Troeltsch explains that "the saving energy of God joins forces with the movement of transient emotion; and faith is certain that it is able to distinguish the motion of the Divine Spirit from all merely human opinion and desire." He added, "The Spirit of God can only recognize his own Presence in the Scriptures and in the Church, and only thus can strength and nourishment be drawn from them; left to themselves, both the Bible and the Church are merely a dead letter or an empty ceremonial." This was neither fantasy nor emotion but evidence of the power associated with the Word.

To English reconstructionists who placed great reliance on the Word/Spirit, Scripture was much more than a written symbol. Nuttall explains that "'the letter' is not only dead but kills, is death-bearing, whereas the Spirit gives life." Early in the Elizabethan age, John Jewel stressed that church "sacraments were but seals of the faith that sprang from the experience of the Word." And in the 1570s, Thomas Cartwright declared that the Word carries "its own miraculous evidence along with it." "No pen of man," he reasoned, "is able to lodge so much matter in so small room, and with such facility of speech." And the Spirit's living power in the Word, he emphasized, has "such an effect and working in men...as will easily sort it and single it from all men's words."

"Scripture generates its own light for believers," William stressed in 1588; the Word has "inherent power" to "convince one of its truth, make itself plain, and act upon the heart." He, thus, concluded, "The sum of our conviction is that the Scripture is autopistos. It has all its authority and credit from itself; is to be acknowledged, is to be received, not only because the Church has so determined and commanded, but because it comes from God. And we certainly know that it comes from God, not by the Church, but by the Holy Spirit."

The idea that the scriptural Word or God was enlightened by the Spirit of God to the person who read with faith rose to prominence in the Age of Christ and of the Holy Spirit, when even the more conservative Westminster Confession stated, "Our full persuasion and assurance of the infallible truth and divine authority [of the Bible] is from the inward work of the Holy Spirit, bearing witness by and with the Word in our hearts." So entwined were the Word and the Spirit that Peter Sterry, a fellow of Emmanuel College at Cambridge, a London preacher on Cromwell's Council of State and a prominent ally of Sir Henry Vane the Younger in the cause of liberal reform, insisted that "the Word of God is the Spirit of God."

To Sibbes, the Spirit was "the life and soul of the Word." Said he, "The Word is nothing without the Spirit; it is animated and quickened by the Spirit." He stressed, "The Spirit of God goes along with the Word, and makes it work." "When the Word is most revealed" in the heart, said he, "there is [the] most Spirit; but where Christ is not opened in the Gospel, there the Spirit is not at all visible." He concluded that those who care not for the Word "are strangers from the Spirit," and those who "care not for the Spirit never make right use of the Word." In full accord with this view, the leading Quaker Robert Barclay stated, "The Word of God is, like [God] himself, spiritual, yea, Spirit and Life."

Enlightenment by the Spirit was so vital that insightful students of the Word gave writers who centered on it a special place in scriptural study. Erasmus, thus, counseled, "Above all...make Paul your intimate friend. Him you should always cling to, 'meditating upon him day and night' until you commit to memory every word." In the preface of his *Exposition of 1 Peter* (1523), Luther stated that those apostles—John, Paul, and Peter—who most often treat how faith in Christ justifies "are the best Evangelists." Paul's Epistles, he asserted, are "more a Gospel than are Matthew, Mark, and Luke, for these do not set down much more than the story of the works and miracles of Christ." The need for the renewing light and power of the Spirit is stressed "especially in his [Paul's] letter to the Romans." Said Luther, in the preface of his *New Testament* (1524), "John's Gospel, St. Paul's Epistles, especially that to the Romans, and St. Peter's First Epistle are the right kernel and marrow of all books,...for in them one finds,... in a quite masterly way expounded, how faith in Christ overcomes sin and death and hell, and gives life, righteousness, and peace."

The Bible translator William Tyndale (1492?–1536) was among those who stressed the need to use the living Word as "a light and a way." Everything in Romans 8, in particular, Coolidge adds, "means what it does by virtue of its function in the developing experience of participation in the death and new life of Christ." "If one began one's study of Scripture" with Romans 8, the influential Puritan William Perkins explained, "and then went to the Gospel of John, one had the key to the whole." Paul's Epistle to the Roman saints, Thomas

Draxe exclaimed, "is like...paradise itself, enclosing 'the quintessence and perfection of saving doctrine,' and the Eighth Chapter...is like a conduit conveying the waters of life; rather it is the Tree of Life in the midst of the Garden."

The importance of the study of Paul's writings to the rise of the Modern Age, and the United States of America, is implied in Gerald Parshall's article, "History's Hidden Turning Points," which identifies the apostle's "Momentous Mission" in proclaiming renewing life in Christ as the first major "turning point" in the rise of the modern world.

Learning by the Light of the Spirit

The "new life in Christ" that Advance Reformers received by spiritual renewal became the foundation of their reform initiatives. With it, the student of Scripture received spiritual sight that gave him a special approach to understand all Scripture. Since the Word is "Spirit and Life," Barclay stressed, it "cannot be heard and read with the natural external senses."

Advance Reformers, especially, "insisted on a continuity of the Spirit's action" that to other Christians "was often unwelcome." "The same Spirit who worked in those who wrote the Bible and in the first Christians" had to work in readers of the Word. A person understood the Word only if he was "in the Spirit." Yet one began by studying the written word. Said the early Italian reformer, Girolamo Savonarola, "It is necessary that we should attain to the knowledge of invisible things by means of visible, for all our knowledge commences with the senses, and the senses only apprehend external accidents; but the intellect by its subtlety penetrates to the very substance of things, whence it elevates itself to the knowledge of that which is...invisible: for while man seeks the substance and propriety, order, causes, and movements of visible things, he is led by induction to the knowledge of invisible things, and even raises himself to God; so that by the accidents, the movements, and the exterior operations of man we arrive at a knowledge of our own soul."

There was the same need to have the light of the Spirit to preach the Word. To light the candle of the Lord in people, Roger Williams emphasized, requires the work of a "spiritual minister of the Gospel." Said he, "No man ever did, nor ever shall, truly go forth to convert the nations but by the gracious Inspiration and Instigation of the Holy Spirit of God." The written word was "at best only the…testimony which assists the soul to find the life-giving Word." Not only did the Holy Spirit witness the truth of the Word, but its vital life and light was the "highest witness," certifying the "truth of its own testimony."

The basic "work of the Spirit," said John Owen, was twofold. First, it communicated "spiritual light." The Spirit enlightened "the mind to discern the saving truth, majesty, and authority of the Word." Second, it gave each person "a spiritual sense." "The Spirit," said Owen, "does…persuade the mind concerning the truth and authority of the Scripture, and therein leaves an impression of an effectual testimony within us."

True gospel teaching, Dell, thus, affirmed, was "clear and evident"; there was "certainty in what [was]…taught." He emphasized, "It is an inward teaching by the outward Word; reaching to the inward soul and spirit, to the hidden man of the heart." The Holy Spirit gave "sweet, inexpressible, heart enamoring…manifestations of itself, and of divine love," Petto declared. And conviction of God's truth was conveyed by a "secret" touch of the Spirit, said he, that "irresistibly strikes the soul into such clear, firm and strong apprehensions and persuasions…that…[one] cannot but say, as Job 19:25, 'I know'—or as Romans 8:38, 'I am persuaded.'"

In studying Scripture by the "contemporaneous work" of the Holy Spirit, a living power impressed the "hearts" of the readers as well "as their heads," which required them to read the Bible in "a different way" than other books. The Spirit illuminated that which was written, or the mind and soul was enlightened "to understand it." Erasmus gave instructions on the correct way to read Scripture: "Let him approach the New Testament not with an unholy curiosity, but with reverence; bearing in mind that his first and only aim and object should be that he may catch and be changed into the Spirit of what he then learns." "It is the food of the soul," said Erasmus of the living Word, "and to be of use, must not rest only in the memory or lodge in the stomach, but must permeate the very depths of the heart and mind."

The living Word gave life, through revelation from God, to the person of faith. The living Word, Dell stressed, "is a spirit of power in us by being in us a spirit of truth." "This inner Scripture," said the Continental Spiritual Reformer Caspar Schwenckfeld, "has an active creative power of holiness…[in] those in whose hearts it is written." The Holy Spirit, he asserted, "is, in fact, God himself operating as Life and Spirit and Light upon the spiritual substance of the human soul." This "Inner Word," said he, "is in reality nothing else than the continued manifestation of Christ." And, in reality, the Spirit "leads the obedient soul on into all the Truth, and perfects it into the likeness and stature of Christ."

In citing Paul's statement in Romans 10:17, that "faith comes by hearing, and hearing by the word of God," Dell said, "The word of the Gospel…works faith and…is called the word of faith… As the Word works faith, so faith apprehends the word, even that Word that was with God and was God. This living and eternal Word dwells in our hearts by faith, as the Apostle says, 'that Christ may dwell in your hearts by faith.' And this Word dwelling in us by faith, changes us into its own likeness, as fire changes the iron into its own likeness, and takes us up into all its own virtues. And so the Word dwelling in the flesh, reforms the flesh."

Dell explained, "'The natural man,' says Paul, 'knows not the things of the Spirit, neither can he, for they are spiritually discerned [1 Cor. 2:14].' Now a man that is not born of God and his Spirit [to "see the kingdom of God" (John 3:3)], with all his parts, abilities, reason, wisdom, prudence, learning, is but a natural man still, and so has no right knowledge of the things of God and his Spirit." Urging the fact that enlightenment by the Holy Spirit is required to understand Scripture, Roger Williams likewise asserted that a natural person in an unregenerate state cannot be "nourished and edified" by the Word/Spirit any more than a dead child can "suck the breast, or a dead man feast." Said he, "So also is it as impossible for a dead man yet lodged in the grave of nature to contribute spiritually [I mean, according to Scripture's rule] as for a dead man to pay a reckoning."

For a partially enlightened individual to learn gospel truth may, in some cases, also be difficult. Though there is in the Word "an evidence of truth commending itself to the consciences of men," yet, said Owen, "many men who are not stark blind may have yet so abused their eyes [of faith] that when a light is brought into a dark place they may not be able to discern it." They may be "so prepossessed with innumerable prejudices—principles received by strong tradition—corrupt affections making them hate the light—that they may not behold the glory of the Word when it is brought to them."

Varying Emphases on the Word/Spirit

In the ongoing Revolution of Life and Liberty, the Word was "more alive for some than for others." Some read Scripture and practiced outward requirements but showed "no spiritual profit" because, it was said, "truth runs into no one by a pipe!" By greater faith, some were more "dramatically changed" than others, and more persuaded by experience of the Spirit's blessings.

The several branches of Christendom, therefore, differed in emphases on the Word/Spirit. The order of compulsion and the notion of infallibility that emerged in the Roman Catholic Church replaced the free Spirit-enlivened order of the New Testament Church. And while Roman authorities cited Augustine that one could not see scriptural truth "clearly unless the organized church held the candle for him and pointed in the right direction," the reformers who brought on the cleavage of Teutonic Europe from Rome in 1517 stressed that every person had to receive personal guidance by the Holy Spirit. And to them, the Bible was "the center of the Church, the absolutely inspired authority, and the operative power of salvation through the converting power which dwells within it." Advance Reformers, in particular, put more emphasis on the Spirit than on the written word alone. The Bible, they held, "proves and manifests its own infallibility by the Holy Spirit who dwells within it." Likewise, the early English reformer, John Colet, wrote, "Observance of the law comes by means of a life-giving principle; and it is by this that men are justified."

On the principle role of the Bible and the Spirit, Luther launched the outburst of 1517. Justification before God, he held, came by an exercise of Bible-type faith, which, aided by the quickening power of the Word, gave renewing life and enlightenment to the believer. Said he of his own experience, "Night and day I pondered until I saw the connection between the justice of God and the statement that 'the just shall live by his faith.' Then I grasped that the justice of God is that righteousness by which, through grace and sheer mercy, God justifies us through faith. Therefore I felt myself to be reborn and to have gone through open doors into paradise. The whole of Scripture took on a new meaning."

Luther's clarion call stressed the reality of "faith in the miraculous power of the 'pure Word,' which alone contains converting power." And he believed that the Word "would finally triumph." Tyndale, his English disciple, declared, "The Scripture is the cause why men believe the Scripture." The Holy Spirit would "demonstrate the 'internal clarity' of Scripture," and it would "banish darkness" from the mind.

But Luther failed to maintain primary emphasis on the Word/Spirit with its liberal effects. When other reformers continued to build on the liberal doctrines of the Word/Spirit, and to move forward along a path of free and open union, he and other Mainliners not only opposed their rising individualism but began "to close the door" to inquiry and to regulate the teaching of the Word by "fixed standards." "Thus," Troeltsch observes, "with Luther himself, the rudimentary beginnings of a free historical human interpretation of the Bible disappeared, and the process was completed in the subsequent period of orthodoxy." The result among Mainline Protestants—Lutherans, Calvinists, etc., which came to include Anglicans and Puritans—was "a kind of literary Incarnation of the Divine" that corresponded to the Catholic "Incarnation in the Priesthood." Theological determinism, administrative regulations, and concessions to arbitrary power in the State subordinated the individual to man-made theology and coercive systems of church and state.

The Protestant Reformation is often equated with Mainline Reformers, and the Anabaptists, Continental Spiritual Reformers, English Separatists, and Dutch Remonstrates and Collegians, who rejected the arbitrary dogmas of Luther, Calvin, and others are considered as side currents to the Reformation. These reformers, whom Luther, Calvin, and other Mainliners, sought by ruthless means to suppress, never ceased quoting Luther's early teachings on the living power of the Word but echoed them "again and again,...down to the time of the English Independents and the German Pietists." And unlike Mainline Protestants, the Advance Reformers based their views and their lives on the affirmation that the Holy Spirit was "a real Presence in the deeps of men's consciousness," who was "ceaselessly voicing himself there as a living Word," which it was "life to obey [individually and socially] and death to disregard and slight."

The contrasting views of the Puritans and the Baptists on the Word/Spirit reveal the more arbitrary verses liberal beliefs in the English Renaissance. Puritans centered more emphasis on the letter than on the Spirit. Puritans like Perkins held that while Scripture was dictated by the Holy Spirit, "human hands [merely] held the pens;... mortals were only amanuenses." Speaking of the Old and New Testaments, he stated "that 'not only the matter of them but the whole disposition thereof, with the style and the phrase, was set down by the immediate inspiration of the Holy Ghost.'" These views tended to lessen the dignity, not only of the prophets who wrote by the Spirit but the people who read their words.

By contrast, John Smyth, who combined Separatist and Anabaptist views to create the English Baptists, saw the written word as but "a preparation for worship." He did not rely wholly on the letter of Scripture. Instead, the heart of true worship was "the fire of the Spirit working with the Word." Smyth "objected to any book...being used in the actual worship service," with translations sharing "in the same general ban." "Worship technically began after the books were laid aside."

The Quakers went beyond the Puritans and Baptists in their emphasis on the role of the Holy Spirit. When George Fox was charged with saying that the Scriptures were carnal, he replied, "The letter is carnal and kills: but that which gave it forth is spiritual, eternal, and gives life." And when James Nayler, his fellow Quaker leader, was asked, "Is there not a written Word?" he responded, "Where read you in the Scriptures of a written word? The Word is spiritual, not seen with carnal eyes: but as for the Scriptures they are true." "There is," William Penn, thus, affirmed, "something nearer to us than Scriptures, to wit, the Word in the heart from which all Scripture came." The question Advance Reformists asked "was not, or not only, 'Has he Scripture for it?' but 'Has he the Spirit?'"

The Word/Spirit and Light in Advance Reform

Advance Reformers in the Age of Christ and of the Holy Spirit differed from other reformers in that they placed greater emphasis on the role of the Holy Spirit in Christian life and society. Dr. John Everard, who popularized vital teachings by the Continental Spiritual Reformers, stressed that "the Bible [alone], as it consists of words, syllables and letters, is not the Word of God." Except for the Holy Spirit, he added, "the Word is a spring shut up, a fountain sealed." The Leveler, author of *The Ancient Bounds or Liberty of Conscience* (1645), also stated, "The Scriptures themselves are but a sealed book except Christ by his Spirit speak in them, and by them, to our understandings and hearts."

As Advance Reformers gained strength, such views in the Age of Christ, they built increasingly on the conviction that the Spirit made the Word more than an external authority. Since "the Spirit accompanies the Word," Dell declared, "the Gospel is called the ministration of the Spirit that is, the Word and Spirit in union and operation."

The idea of light was also connected to the living Word. Reformers In the seventeenth century were "no less interested in the idea" of light than were reformers in earlier times. From early times, "the Christian tradition used the metaphor of light to stand for Christ and the inspiration of the Holy Spirit in humanity." This "standard metaphor," which portrayed the in-workings of the Holy Spirit," had continued in the Middle Ages and throughout the Renaissance and Reformation in religious and philosophical thought. Interest accelerated by Advance Reform movements then led to the rise of a Seeker groundswell in the 1640s and an explosion of Quakers, with their emphasis on the Inner Light, in the early 1650s.

Two leading chaplains at the headquarters of the New Model Army, Saltmarsh, and Dell emphasized Advance Reform thought on light and the Spirit in the sermons they published with great influence in the lives of the soldiers who played a leading role in the birth of liberty. Sibbes asked, "How do we know divine truth out of the Book of God to be divine?" Then stated, "By the light in itself, by the majesty of the Scriptures, by…the miraculous preservation of it,… but especially by the powerful work of it on the heart, by the experience of this blessed truth." Scripture, he stressed, has "a supreme authority from itself." The "supreme Judge is the Word, the Spirit of God in the Scriptures," and the "motions of the Spirit…carry their own evidence with them, as light does." This testimony Sibbes freely shared with others, stating, "I know this to be an undoubted truth."

Similarly, Milton wrote, "The Scriptures themselves pronounce their own plainness." Inviting others to base life on "the plain field of Scripture," he spoke of "the transparent streams of divine truth" that flow through the Word. Although Milton may have differed with the Quakers on some points, like them, he insisted "on the illumination of the soul by a Light within; 'a celestial light,' he calls it in Paradise Lost, which shines inward and irradiates the mind through her powers, and supplies an inward sight of things invisible to sense—a Light which steadily increases as it is used by the obedient soul."

To Milton and other Advance Reformers, "the origin of this inward Light" was Christ, "the eternal Word of God, who [in the cosmic order] is before all worlds, and who is the source of all revelation, whether inward or outward." The Life and the Light of the World, the Eternal Word, was the Giver of the Word and, said Milton, "the Great Teacher of man is the Holy Spirit." Like the Quakers, Milton called the Holy Spirit "a more certain guide than the Scripture." Coolidge, thus, observes that when an English Reformer of this class "says that 'the Word of God directs a man in all his actions,' he is insisting that the transformation of life which he finds in the Bible as he reads it should extend throughout the whole range of experience."

The Inner Versus the Outer Word

Some reformers differentiated between the Word and the Spirit and their many ramifications by using the term "the Inner and the Outer Word." Peter's statement infers the two features when he states that Scripture came "not…by the will of man but holy men of God spake as they were moved by the Holy Ghost." While the Outer Word is the written letter of divine communications, the Inner Word is the revelatory Spirit of truth connected with it in a fundamental primary way. Jesus, thus, said on the latter point, "The words that I speak unto you, they are Spirit, and they are life." Said Erasmus in affirming the truth of this statement: "The flesh accomplishes nothing; it is the Spirit that gives life."

The early reformer, Johannes Tauler (1300?–1361) said, in speaking of the "sweet voice" of Scripture in believers, "We know that the eternal Word is still so unutterably nigh to us inwardly, in the very principle of our being, that not even man himself, his own nature, his own thoughts, nor aught that can be named, or said, or understood, is so nigh or planted so deep within him, as the eternal Word is in man."

Dell stated further, "In the Gospel, the Word and the Spirit are always joined: and therefore, says Christ, 'The words that I speak are Spirit and life'; that is, they come from the Spirit and carry Spirit with them." Nuttall, therefore, writes, "The work of the Holy Spirit in connection with Scripture is…twofold: the Spirit…[1] inspired its writers, and [2] enlightens its hearers or readers," suggesting "a double revelation of God" to man: (1) the living revelation given by the Holy Spirit, which can be heard by the person of faith, and (2) the verbal or written word, with the living Word and Law being "eternal, spiritual, [and] inward." Thus, God's revelation is "primarily…a living Word [written] in the soul of man, and secondarily… an historical word."

Only "when the inward word, or…Spirit, and the outward word, or ministry" act together can Christ "more effectually knock and stir up the heart." The outer letter, when reflected upon with faith, became a living Word and as an important "key to the mysteries" of the Word. This introduced believers to the renewing life and light that the ancient prophets and saints enjoyed.

Though Savonarola stressed the need for the Spirit's action, he explained, "Because our Savior knew that by reason of sin, the Spirit would be driven from the hearts of men, and that iniquity would increase therein, therefore, to the end that the holy doctrine written upon the hearts of the apostles might never fail, but be dispersed abroad to them that were afar off, and preserved for them that were to come after, being kept sound from the corruptions of wicked men, it was his will that the Gospel should also be committed to writing." One could then come to the "life-giving Word," through the written word that was designed "to awaken the mind and...direct it to the inward Word."

Besides perpetuating these teachings, the Continental Spiritual Reformers, beginning with fundamental principles, extended them to the idea of the Spiritual Church. Schwenckfeld taught, "The Word, when spiritual messengers preach or teach, is of two kinds with a decided difference in their manner of working." The Outer Word was "written and read in letters" and was heard by "the external man with his ears of sense." The Inner Word was "of God, even is God, and lives and works in the heart of the messenger... Christ... is inwardly revealed and heard with the inward ears of the heart." One who merely read or heard the letter of the word had "not heard the Gospel of Christ, the Gospel of Grace," nor had he "received or understood it." The "living Word," said D. V. Coornhert, one of the most important Continental Spiritual Reformers, is "vastly different from the written word." And being eternal, it is "the source of all spiritual light and truth that have come to the race in all ages." And another Continental Spiritual Reformer, Johann Bunderlin, concluded, "The true spiritual goal of life is the formation of a rightly fashioned will, the creation of a controlling personal love, the experience of a guiding inward Spirit, which keep the awakened soul steadily approximating the perfect Life which Christ has revealed."

The views of the early English Separatists, Robert Browne Henry Barrow, extended into the seventeenth century. Browne taught that God the Father sent Jesus Christ into the world "to work out our salvation by taking our manhood unto his Godhead—by assimilating believers spiritually into himself, so that he might be in them and they in him." To this end, the Father filled Christ "with his Spirit... and the fullness of all graces." Barrow, thus, distinguished between the Outer and the Inner Word, identifying the Spirit in believers as "the fruit of the Word." When teachings of the Continental Spiritual Reformers were combined with views like those of Browne and Barrow the liberal compound blossomed in the mid-seventeenth century to produce the English Renaissance—the Age of Christ and of the Holy Spirit.

Among the Englishmen who voiced the mounting views was Milton, who explained, "We have, particularly under the Gospel, a double Scripture...the external Scripture of the written word and the internal Scripture of the Holy Spirit, which he...has engraved upon the hearts of believers." Milton explained, "Nowadays, the external authority...is of very considerable importance and, generally speaking, it is the authority of which we first have experience... [But] the preeminent and supreme authority...is the authority of the Spirit, which is internal, and the individual possession of each man." Individuality, self-determination in Christ, freedom of expression, the right of choice, etc., were inherent within the rising assurance that each person had equal and practical access to the Spirit of God, and that he was not dependent on pope or priest to receive it.

Similarly, Saltmarsh held that the Gospel was "distinguished into the spiritual nature of it and into the administration with which it is clothed." Said he, "Whatsoever is of mere letter, form, [or] ordinance is of the administration or Gospel-clothing and appearance, as to men and as in the flesh; things that are seen are temporal, things that are not seen are eternal."

Sibbes, thus, emphasized, "There must be a Spirit in me, as there is a Spirit in the Scripture before I can see anything." Beyond the "bare naked reading" of Scripture, he stressed, "there must be a spiritual knowledge...like the truth itself... We must see and know spiritual things in their own light...[which is] to know them by the Spirit." Only then is "the breath of the Spirit in us...suitable to the Spirit's breathing in the Scriptures." The Leveler, John Wildman, therefore, emphasized, "It must be the spirit of faith [in a person] that must make him believe whatsoever may be spoken in spiritual matters." "Real knowledge," Sterry affirmed, "comes when the Day Star rises in the heart." The Spirit then carries believers beyond the bounds of human reason and of natural capabilities. Still, it was only by "long processes of tutorship and discipline" that one could truly live by "the Seed of Life and Light of Truth within."

The Reform Power of the Word/Spirit

"The essence of the Word," Troeltsch explains, "consists in its power of forming personal conviction and of producing the New Birth" and of creating a vigorous Christian society. Historical evidence, thus, affirms that the "real supporters" of the rising age of liberty and progress in the West were Christians who were "born again through the Word."

The living Word was the major fundamental power of liberal reform in the Revolution of Life and Liberty. Luther held that the Word was a living force, "an invincible warrior," that open-minded people of faith could not resist, and by the "automatic working of the Spirit" in Holy Writ, the elect would "be reformed." The Word was the "medium by which the Spirit of God worked a radical transformation of individuals and whole societies." Based on the conviction that the Spirit accompanied the Word, Luther and others felt that a "right-minded man had only to look at the Bible to recognize its perfection." "Let an unprejudiced man study it for himself, with the assistance of the Holy Spirit," they affirmed, "and he will be convinced." "So alive and strong and powerful" was the Word that the Swiss reformer Ulrich Zwingli (1484–1531) declared that "all things" had to obey it. Likewise, the American minister Thomas Hooker (1586–1647) wrote, "When the truth of God is delivered with a holy violence and hearty affection by God's servants, it makes way, it bears down, and breaks all before it."

The transforming power of the Word/Spirit was particularly evident in the Age of Christ and of the Holy Spirit. The Inner Word "is the only Word that works reformation," Dell could argue in *Right*

Reformation: Or, the Reformation of the Church of New Testament, Represented in Gospel Light (1646). Said he, "This Spirit that is present in the Word of the Gospel, and works in it, and is given by it, reforms mightily." He explained, "[Jesus sent forth his Apostles] to reform the world" with "the Lord working with them (Mark 16:20)." They were "poor, illiterate, mechanic men," unarmed with "swords or guns…or with any power of states, or armies." Yet they possessed "the power of the Word." Dell, thus, observed, "Behold what wonders they wrought by that power alone! They turned the world upside down; they changed the manners, customs, religion, worship, lives, and natures of men." All Christian reconstructionists took this approach to bringing forth modern liberty and democracy.

Citing Scripture for authority, the Leveler, writer of *The Ancient Bounds*, stated, "Christ has a sword for the vindicating of truth, for the propulsing of errors, for the conquering of enemies." To the question, "What is that?", he replied, "Why, the sword of the Spirit, the Word of God." Paul had spoken not merely of "the sufficiency, but [of] the mightiness of this means (2 Cor. 10.4): 'The weapons of our warfare are not carnal, but spiritual, and mighty through God.'"

In the preface to the *Bloudy Tenent*, Roger Williams also equated the "Word of God" in the reform movement with the "Sword of God's Spirit." The Word's "powerful persuasions…[was] that two-edged sword coming out of the mouth of Christ Jesus in his true ministers." Their trust was in the "heavenly and spiritual, even the sword of the Spirit with which Christ fights, which," Williams affirmed, "is exceeding sharp, entering in between the soul and spirit, and bringing every thought into captivity to the obedience of Christ Jesus." "He that submits not at the shaking of this sword," he declared, "is cut off by it; and he that despises this sword, all the power in the world cannot make him a true worshiper."

It was not the work "of the civil sword," Milton declared, "but of the spiritual [sword], which is the Word of God," to destroy "popery and [English] prelacy, then…heresy, schism, and profaneness." The Word was a sharp sword for repudiating error and for the progressive reconstruction of reform doctrines and practices.

Like other Fathers of Liberty, Milton held that when the power of the Spirit was connected with the Word, it cut through darkness and error and gave enlightened understanding to believers. By means of the "divine light" that "it expresses," the Word acts as a "scourge of error." In *The Reason Of Church-Government* (1642), Milton, in attacking the Anghlican Church, denounced the "mass of slime and mud, the slothful, the covetous and ambitious hopes of church-promotions and fat bishoprics" that prelacy fostered until the "pestiferous contagion to the whole kingdom" was, like "a great python,... shot to death with the...pure and powerful beams of God's Word." In contrast, he praised the "inherent power" of Scripture "to make its truth felt." "This is certain," said he, "that the Gospel, being the hidden might of Christ,...has ever a victorious power joined with it, like him in the revelation [of John on Patmos] that went forth on the white horse with his bow and his crown conquering, and to conquer." The Word was "proving a sharper divider than any two-edged sword," says Nuttall, "and was revealing who were serious in their Christian profession and who were not."

It is said at the beginning of this chapter that the living power of the Word/Spirit was the underlying power that give birth to many liberal elements within the new Christian civilization that emerged in the mid-seventeenth century Anglo-American world. This fact has not yet been demonstrated, but it has been shown that a mighty transforming power pervaded the lives of many people in the English Renaissance where freedom and progress finally emerged on a permanent foundation. The role that this pervading power played in the rise of specific elements in the new order of freedom and progress will be demonstrated hereafter.

CHAPTER 4

The Revolution of Life and of Liberty

Changes occur in every age, and every generation remodels the world in some way. But Preserved Smith observes that on rare occasions, there comes a transformation so "startling and so profound" that it signals the "beginning of a new season in the world's great year." Dr. Smith compares that "startling" transformation of the Western world in the sixteenth century to the sudden bursting out of spring, when the casual observer, who perceives no change, suddenly beholds that "almost within a few days, the leaves and blossoms put forth their verdure." In a very tangible way, the new season has arrived.

The Foundations of the Revolution

The Revolution of Life and Liberty was an awakening within Western man toward free and open union and progress that finally gave birth to the Modern Age and, in particular, to the United States of America. In this chapter, the revolution includes all movements and all individuals who contributed to the rise of the new age. The central reform initiative within the revolution is called the "Single Tradition of Liberty" (abbreviated, "Single Tradition"). From the beginning, reformers within it unitedly affirmed that their reform initiatives arose from a desire to "return to primitive Christianity."

Moving from an initial general emphasis on the Bible to the New Testament, they made it their ideal and sought for the gifts and blessings of the Holy Spirit that were given to the saints in New Testament times. Not mere scriptural truth and doctrine but transformation of life in Christ was their ultimate goal. And they used experience with the renewing life and power of the Spirit, supported by the practices they saw in the New Testament Church, to create free principles, concepts, and outward forms of free associations.

Since the Revolution of Life and Liberty centered in the New Testament, the Scriptures are used in this study to describe the key reform assumptions of these Reformers, which were the following: First, there is a God in heaven, the Father of all, and Jesus Christ is his Son, conceived and born as a divine being on earth of the Virgin Mary.

Second, Jesus had "life in himself," as his Father "has life in himself," and the Son of God extends this renewing life, through the Spirit of God—sometimes called the Light of Christ—to give life to all men on earth. John, therefore, wrote that Christ is "the true Light which lights every man that comes into the world."

Third, by faith and repentance toward God, believers can receive the manifestations of this quickening "light of life" in its higher degrees—the divine rheostat can be turned up within them—by which they may be raised to higher levels of quickened life than the natural order that prevails on earth. In the Sermon on the Mount, Jesus stated, with promise, "The light of the body is the eye: if therefore thine eye be single [to God], thy whole body shall be full of light." More specifically, he declared, with promise, "I am the light of the world: he that follows me shall not walk in darkness, but shall have the light of life."

Predicated on faith and obedience, God declared to the ancient patriarch Jacob, whose name was changed to Israel, "I will pour out my Spirit upon thy seed, and…they shall spring up…as willows by the water courses." And after Christ's crucifixion, the promise of the Spirit (through the Gospel) was given to believers in Western society, scripturally called "Gentiles."

The renewing life and light within the Single Tradition of Liberty—as a historical fact of the greatest importance—"exhibited...freedom, variety, [and] personality"; and abundant historical evidence shows these things to be the root sources of modern liberty, democracy, and progress. The Single Tradition is represented historically by unbroken lines of Advance Reformers who strove to transform society by applying the renewing life and truth that they saw in Bible Christianity and the New Testament Church. With an eye single to Christ and his glory, they affirmed that they received renewing life from him. Their faith and the new life they found in Scripture were sources of this transforming truth and life that gave them the urge to improve their conditions and bring the free principles, concepts, and outward forms of society and constitutional republicanism, with power centered in the people under God. By these means, they emerged out of medieval darkness, and the renewing life they found in Christ and the Holy Spirit, with its free spirit—not merely the free principles and concepts to which these fundamental factors gave birth—were vital features in the birth of the new American nation.

The Nature of the Revolution

In the civilizations of the world, an essential sameness existed during the Middle Ages until the dawn of the Western Awakening that quickened the lives of the people and gave support to the Bible Revolution that could then move forward with added strength and power. The stupor of centuries was "suddenly" interrupted, and the West, which was inferior in some ways to the more progressive Ottoman Empire, then took an "unprecedented step" forward.

The transformations that then began attest to the reality of the inner powers that began to operate in the lives of Western people. Signs of the awakening started to appear in the fourteenth century, and the new spirit began to blossom in the fifteenth and sixteenth centuries. The individual man was beginning "to discover himself and to assert himself," and "the spirit of democracy" was apparent in almost all the new movements. "The people are no longer dumb and obedient," Jones observes; "they are restless, and on occasion clamorous for rights and privileges."

Emphasizing the effects of the New Testament on the rising reform movement, Jones continues, "There is at work, at first silently and then vocally, a spirit of revolt from authority and a growing consciousness that the personal soul ought to work out its own salvation." There was a "hidden leaven…fermenting beneath the surface," which prompted an outbreak of reform activities—movements that were "strangely alike"—"almost simultaneously in widely sundered places." The "Pentecost Spirit" was abroad, and "the Rhine dweller, the Italian peasant, the French weaver" all spoke the "same spiritual tongue."

The breadth and power of the awakening are evident in the new signs of life that began to appear all over Europe, and "nearly every [Western] nation" made contributions to the new age. The individual awakened and began to break the ties that were giving him "security and narrowing him at…the same time." The dreamy "half awake…veil" of passive belief, superstition, and fantasy began to dissolve, and feudalism and serfdom were soon dealt death blows in several Western countries. People started to move forward "armed for untried experience and ready to watch with hopefulness a prospect of incalculable change." Many who had been content to eke out a bare subsistence and prepare through ceremonial religion for life beyond the grave were filled with intense energy and burning curiosity. The changes that followed were among the most significant in human history—such as the world "has rarely seen"—and they occurred in all areas of life. During the fifteenth and sixteenth centuries men discovered, "not in metaphor but in sober fact, a new heaven and a new earth."

The Closed Society of Traditional Christianity, which largely determined the "intellectual construction" of life, socially, economically, politically, etc., in the Middle Ages, was "a completed world," nonindividualistic in character, where each person could "feel secure and at home." But powerful inner forces fundamentally different in character from those of the closed system then began to wreck the old order "on the ethical and political side" by liberal elements that

Advance Reformers brought forth, and "on the intellectual side, by the rise of the applied sciences." And to the degree, the new impulses inspired a tendency to assert "the moral supremacy of the individual conscience, the old basis of political and social order disappeared."

With the ascendancy of the single person "pure individualism," Troeltsch notes, produced "an actual change in the whole general situation" in Europe, destroying medieval culture and giving rise to the Modern Age. The new life and truth in the Bible-type Christianity that began to emerge produced a lay sect-type form of Christianity that was a "new type" faith that "had no desire for an [outwardly] organized fellowship" but an extreme "religious individualism." The "isolated individual...and [objective] analysis became everything." All that was left of the former Lex Christi was "the example of Christ," and this individualistic Christian faith, life, and objective thought finally "attained its universal historical significance" among Dissenters in the mid-seventeenth-century Anglo-American world, who gave birth to modern liberty and democracy.

All these new theories of free life and progress, Troeltsch emphasizes, "were not merely the logical outcome of thought; they were the result of conditions which had awakened the impulse to transform and recreate social life. Their basis was an actual change in the whole general situation, which alone really destroyed the whole fabric of the medieval world." The aspirations of men soared beyond the values of society, even of leading reformers. Many became "absorbed in theological restatement, in scientific investigations, in exploration and mercantile development" while "political and economic interests freed themselves from the international control of the Church, and from its cramping economic ethic."

The introduction of paper from the East and the invention of printing greatly aided the growing Revolution of Life and Liberty and helped produce an age "of fermentation" and "free discussion." With the upsurge of new life, the knowledge of reading rapidly increased and printing facilitated a vast circulation of written materials—in particular, vernacular Scripture and commentary literature—that promoted a Bible Revolution that, while retaining its rising power, moved on to become a New Testament Revolution that created a "high tradition" of life and many free associations.

Responding to the living power of the Holy Spirit associated with the scriptural Word and strengthened by the quickening life of the Western Awakening, many began to realize a new "ethical value" of life on earth—"of marriage, of children, of daily labor, and of success and prosperity." The novel age stirred many people with "a new warmth," which was coupled, consistently, with "a general yearning to bring men nearer to God." Many affirmed that this inward illumination came from the power of the Holy Spirit coupled with the Word, which brought them "into direct communion with their God, without the intervention of the priest."

This new faith in God "finally rescued mankind from the abyss of skepticism and corruption in which all at that time were more or less engulfed." Theologians, philosophers, and potential martyrs were fired with "fresh enthusiasm." Enlivened by the combined Spirit and quickening power of the new age that nurtured their "new aspirations," hope arose by "the force of ideas and principles," which gave "new youth to society," initiated "modern culture," and "reawakened science."

The rising approach to discovery, called "the New Learning," spread over Europe and found receptive minds in many places. Its emphasis on the objective analysis of Scripture promoted the early Seeker Tradition that later helped produce the Continental Spiritual Reformers and many leading reformers in mid-seventeenth-century England who gave birth to liberty. The "universal spirit" of the rising age was revelatory in character, as may be seen in the flashes of insight that many spiritual and political reformers, as well as scientific innovators, experienced. This, for example, was later manifested in the conviction of Rene Descartes (1596–1650), who affirmed that intuition played a principal role in the scientific processes of the day. Influenced by men who promoted the liberal movement toward objective analysis, Descartes stated the rules of empirical analysis that greatly helped strengthen the emerging Scientific Revolution. By objective methods of analysis, the French philosopher and mathematician proved to his own satisfaction that there is a God. It is not a "far step from the inner enlightening witness of the Holy Spirit to the Cogito, ergo sum [I think; therefore, I exist] of Descartes."

These advancements produced "a Creative Tradition," in testimony of the inner powers that brought it into being, and the "forward movement" increasingly divided the new "from the older world." The persisting "universal spirit of investigation and discovery" withstood recurring reactionary efforts. Successive deliverances, with a gradual passing "from subordination to independence," was a "phenomenon of primary import," and historical science was one of its effects and instruments. In the middle decades of the seventeenth century, the kindling movement began to move triumphantly forward, and when it became "massive, and…one investigator began to cooperate with another," Western Europe "broke out into a galaxy of names that outshone the utmost scientific reputations of the best age of Greece."

Revolutionary Awakenings

The motivating and transforming influence of the Revolution of Life and Liberty gave rise to a number of specific awakenings. These awakenings, corresponding directly to particular facets of Western society, were manifest in different ways and to varying degrees. The foundation of the Revolution of Life and Liberty was a literal life awakening—an actual increase of life in the inner man that came from God and produced enlivened conscience, enlightened reason, the spirit of liberty, feelings of personal dignity, a posture of objective analysis, and an inner urge to progress. Strengthened by the quickening power of the Western Awakening, it was literally a new birth in the fundamentals of life, which did not "owe its existence, primarily, to the Revival of Antiquity."

The roots of the revolution "were fixed firmly in the Middle Ages" before the Revival of Antiquity began. Lord Acton, therefore, affirms that the modern age did not rise "by normal succession, with outward tokens of legitimate descent." There was, instead, "an awakening of new life" that caused the Western world to revolve in "a different orbit, determined by influences unknown before." Men were governed in earlier ages by "usage and the will of masters who were in their graves," and many were "persuaded of the headlong decline and impending dissolution of society."

Powerful spiritual forces then created a shift from "outer to… inner"—from "external to…internal"—life. In the late Middle Ages, the "personality of man," not merely the "structure of society… changed." And by the power of enlivening forces, "intimations of a new and profounder social justice" spread throughout "the general body of…Western civilization."

There was a soul awakening—a religio-spiritual enlightenment—that turned men from arbitrary ecclesiastical systems toward personal spiritual renewal. There was a "deep yearning among serious people for a religion of inward experience…based…on the native capacity of the soul to seek, to find, and to enjoy the living God." The new rising age was unlike, in religio-spiritual foundations, any prior age. In response to rising religio-spiritual elements in the lives of many people, the Latin Vulgate Bible was issued in about a dozen printed editions before a classic of ancient Rome was published. (The Literary Revival also predated "the Revival of Classical Learning," and "the Artistic Reawakening was in full progress before attention was drawn to Classical Representative Art.") It is, therefore, a serious error to say that classical literature or thought was a primary, or determinative, factor in the rise of the West.

Men were, at first, satisfied to read the Bible "historically and to treat it as a wondrous story," but new life made manifest in Scripture soon began "to speak inwardly to the hearts of the most sensitive and conscientious" reformists. From personal experience in spiritual renewal came inner strength and determination to meet arbitrary power head on, as hundreds of martyrs did. Advance Reformers, in particular, were "interpreters of an inward light in the human soul," which brought a reorientation in religious belief and ethos, with the conviction that each person had a right to his own reading and understanding of Scripture. The soul awakening was the foundation of private and public virtue, right reason, individual value and dignity, unalienable rights, consent, and society by covenant and/or contract.

There was an intellectual awakening—a mental awakening—that enlivened the thinking processes of man and opened new vistas of thought to perceptive inquirers who began to shake "themselves free from the bondage of ecclesiastical authority and corporate society." Whether due to a "natural selection of circumstances or to the inward urge of vital force," there can be "no doubt that the average intellect…of the European races as a whole" grew steadily greater in the late fifteenth and sixteenth century. The "direction and depth" of this new life awakening, Dickens explains, can best be seen by examining the "intellectual interest, not of great or even eminent minds but of ordinary readers and writers." Surveys conducted by Dickens disclose a "striking mental development" among the masses around the mid-sixteenth century.

America's John Adams also commented, "By what causes it was brought to pass, that the people in the Middle Ages became more intelligent in general, would not, perhaps, be possible in these days to discover. But the fact is certain; and [said he of its effects] wherever a general knowledge and sensibility have prevailed among the people, arbitrary government and every kind of oppression have lessened and disappeared in proportion."

Aided by the new art of printing, many began to read and think with independence and objectivity. "In the last thirty years of the fifteenth century, ten thousand editions of books and pamphlets are said to have been published throughout Europe." The important objective "process of light and thought" that was later epitomized in Descartes and Seeker-type Christians helped strengthen "newly awakened intellectual energies" and kindled a desire to reconstruct personal life, church organizations, and society. With nearly every European nation making contributions, great social, as well as intellectual, developments were in progress." Many began to appreciate the splendor of the natural world, and throughout Europe, natural philosophers rejected old dogmas and objectively applied new light to probe nature's mysteries. The Florentine Leonardo da Vinci (1452–1519), for instance, was "a naturalist, an anatomist, an engineer, as well as a very great artist." Scientific minds of the seventeenth century came to the conclusion that mathematics was "the skeleton of God's plan of the universe"; and men like Christian Huygens (1629–95), the Dutch physicist, astronomer, and mathematician, contributed significantly to this view.

While scientific experiments were being made on plants and animals, and innovative studies were being conducted in the fields of physics, botany, and medicine, Copernicus, Galileo, Kepler, Newton, and others made discoveries that revealed a new more meaningful universe. And the Flemish physician Andreas Vesalius (1514–64), one of the world's foremost anatomists, explored the inner structure and functions of the physical body. The universal result was the Scientific Revolution, symbolized by its first eminent work, Copernicus's *De Orbium Coelestium Revolutionibus* (*Concerning the Revolutions of the Celestial Sphere*), published in 1543. And fittingly, the same year Vesalius issued *De Corporis Humani Fabrica* (*Concerning the Fabric of the Human Body*), which has been called the discovery of a new world.

The momentous age of science reached a new height in 1665 when Newton concluded his first investigations on gravity and motion; and within a few months, he made important discoveries in optics, formulated the binomial theorem and invented differential and integral calculus. The significance of the intellectual awakening nature of these times is evident in the similar findings of the French mathematician Pierre de Fermat (1601–65), who developed the idea of calculus before Newton but whose collected works were not published until after his death. Also, Baron Gottfried Wilhelm von Leibnitz (1646–1716), held by some to be the most universal scientific genius of modern times, developed components of calculus independently, contemporaneously with Newton; and there was a dispute as to who deserved the glory. It is said that the combined achievements of Descartes, Galileo, Huygens, and Newton have some right to be seen as the "greatest single intellectual success which mankind has achieved."

There was an economic awakening—an inner-motivated incentive toward material gain—that produced its greatest results, first, in Italy, then the Iberian Peninsula, the Netherlands, and, finally, in England. And later, the United States of America emerged as the dominant economic power. While combined awakening forces produced "deep-lying tendencies away from the bondage and traditions of the past," they also fostered "aspiration for economic and social reforms to liberate the common people and give them some real chance to be persons." These interests were "deeply felt and shared" by many reformers on the continent and in England, and this phase of the Revolution of Life and Liberty accelerated the shift from the medieval guild to production by capital and wages and the expansion and greater free flow of trade. People in general came to enjoy the benefits of productive labor, which produced an emerging commercial or middle class. As wealth and industrialization increased, enterprising men and nations gained new strength, and Asia and Africa lost the contest for world power with Europe. As the lines of seaborne commerce were rerouted, Venice and Genoa declined while, in succession, Antwerp, Amsterdam, and London rose to economic supremacy, followed in later centuries by the United States of America.

There was a geographic awakening—an inward impulse toward movement—that, beginning in the twelfth century, stimulated an increase in trade, and "a great revival of town life" began in Europe that produced population movements and the rise of urban centers. The vitality of the geographic awakening was also evident in the many explorations that were undertaken. Early on, Portugal became "the most progressive and Western-minded of the European kingdoms." Portuguese sailors developed new trade lines on the Atlantic coast of Europe and Africa. As early as 1460, they passed the site of Dakar, on the northwestern coast of Africa. Fifteen years later, they completed the exploration of the Gulf of Guinea and opened up a channel of trade "that made Lisbon the envy of Europe." And in 1488, the Portuguese navigator Bartolomeu Dias rounded the Cape of Good Hope. The Portuguese also developed a sailing vessel, the *Caravel*, that was fast, sea-worthy, and weatherly, the type used by Columbus to make his voyage "far less difficult and dangerous."

Building on achievements by Portuguese and Spanish sailors, Columbus, Vespucci, Dias, Vasco da Gama, Cortez, Pizarro, Magellan, and others made their respective discoveries, which affected all Europe and bore "witness to the intrepidity and greatheartedness that characterized these…nations." In 1492, Columbus sailed to America. In 1497, John Cabot discovered the coast of North America. From 1497 to 1503, Amerigo Vespucci sailed to the West Indies and to South America. In 1498, da Gama navigated around the southern tip of Africa to India. In 1519, taking a southern route, Ferdinand Magellan began a voyage around the world, and though he was killed by natives in the Philippine Islands, his crew completed the journey in 1522. And in 1534, while searching for a northern passageway to the Pacific, the French navigator Jacques Cartier discovered the Gulf of St. Lawrence.

By these explorations and other factors, ideas of the size and structure of the earth were changed, and former theories of organization and power among nations became obsolete. Awakening forces in Europe brought about more extensive changes than those that were witnessed by Alexander the Great or Augustus Caesar. And they gave foundation for the prophetic vision later popularized by the English philosopher and bishop George Berkeley, who said in a commentary on the prophetic vision portrayed by the prophet Daniel, in chapter 2 of his writings, "Westward the course of empire takes its way."

There was a literary awakening—an illumined interest in things and ways of expression—that began in the fourteenth century. An immense outbreak of "creative literature" resulted from the awakening of "Western European intelligence," and the books and treatises that were written enormously affected "the popular mind." Eminent among the writers of the new age were Dante Alighieri (1265–1321), Francesco Petrarch (1304–1374), Geoffrey Chaucer (1340?–1400), Luiz Vazde Camoes (1524–1580), Miguel de Cervantes (1547–1616), William Shakespeare (1564–1616), and John Milton (1608–1674). As Roger Bacon and other scientific men broke through "the bookish science of the [scholastic] scholars" and as painters and sculptors "broke through the decorative restraints and [narrow] religious decorum of medieval art," these and other men broke through "the dignity and heroics of formal literature to let in freedom and laughter." It is said that Cervantes's *Don Quixote* is unsurpassed for its masterful, withering, witty, yet courteous, taunts at the evils of the day.

Throughout Europe, there was "a rapid replacement of local dialects" by Standard Italian, Standard English, Standard French, Standard Spanish, and Standard German. All these became "literary languages" in their respective countries; they were "tried over, polished by use, and made exact and vigorous." Lorenzo Valla's *Elegantiae Latini Sermonis* (*The Elegance of the Latin Language*), a treatise on correct Latin usage to replace the faulty grammars in the Middle Ages, was first published in 1471, then issued in about sixty editions during the period of the Renaissance alone.

There was a cultural awakening—a new deep-centered interest in the aesthetic features of life—with "multifarious revivals of domestic and decorative art," and other forms of ornate expression; and many great painters, sculptors, etc. emerged. In the thirteenth century, at Florence, Italy, "a strictly scientific research into the artifices of realistic representation" was begun, and toward the end of the fourteenth century, Florence became the center of "the rediscovery, restoration, and imitation of antique art." Later, classical influences that flowed "strongly in literature spread into the already active world of artistic creation," and Florence enjoyed "a second 'Periclean age.'"

Painters acted with a new assurance "to represent depth" in their pictures and a "veracious rendering of details." The effort to portray reality "was at best bold and splendid and often harsh and brutal." The exhibition of creative insight by artists and composers "shot the world through with a matchless radiance of color and meaning." From the eleventh century on, sculpture developed slowly and naturally in Germany, France, and North Italy." Then bridging the fifteenth and sixteenth centuries, the brilliant Michelangelo (1475–1564), painter, sculptor, architect, and poet, produced works of a towering force and dignity and unparalleled anatomical vigor that stunned his successors into imitation.

Advancements in architecture occurred, and between the eleventh and fifteenth centuries, "a multitude of very distinctive and beautiful buildings, cathedrals, abbeys, and the like" sprang up in Western Europe, Italy, and Spain. The fifteenth century is renowned for the "birth of beauty," which was expressed "in every field of human activity." It set a new ideal for man that in time "touched every aspect of life." As the masses awoke, "elegance became the object of riches." The nobility moved out of their castles into houses that "began to express the grace, proportion, and light of the Renaissance." The forbidding towers and narrow streets that dominated many towns "gave way to spaciousness and order." The new Christian idea that "the glory of man should be reflected in all his activities" produced a move toward general refinement in all spheres of life that lasted for centuries and affected "the taste and manners of the entire population of Europe." Under a newly formed Christian code of life, "consideration for others" was made "a custom of society."

The cumulative power of all these awakenings gave strength to a political awakening—an ideological governmental revolution—with immense practical effects. The progress of the Revolution of Life and Liberty was evinced not merely by the development of science, exploration, and the dissemination of knowledge but by a new inner "craving for freedom and equality." Kings and magistrates did not respond immediately to this aspect of the awakening, but the ultimate "political consequences of this vast release and expansion of European ideas" was most significant. The old mental and moral framework "was breaking up." As internal political weakness ceased, national states—Spain, Portugal, France, England, etc.—began to achieve maturity. Especially in England, subtle working tendencies led "towards a new method in government—the [Saxon] method of parliament—that was to spread later on over nearly all of the world."

Revolution in one sphere promoted related developments in others. Changes in religious faith and thought altered the way people felt and conducted their lives in social, economic, and political matters, and the growth of modern science was "connected with all the major social and cultural developments of Western Europe." The combined factors—the rising Bible-type faith and individualism, the new Copernican universe, the knowledge of civilizations in distant lands, the emerging middle class with the "substitution of the family man for the chivalric and monastic orders," etc.—were "swiftly reshaping the mental contours" of the people. Migrant Englishmen in the rising age then transplanted elements of the Revolution of Life and Liberty to other areas of the world, especially to the Atlantic seaboard of North America.

Enlightened Breaks with Arbitrary Systems

The ongoing revolution with its enlivening powers produced multiple breaks with the past, in all areas of life and human experience. As the new age dawned, men broke with ignorance, superstition, and the fears of the day, and with false ideas and narrow views about life, nature, and the sidereal heavens. In these breaks, they repudiated current doctrines, systems, and schools of thought. Perceptive minds like Roger Bacon (1214?–1294), William of Ockham (1300?–1349), Johannes Tauler (1300?–61), Francesco Petrarch (1303–74), John Wyclif (1320?–84), John Hus (1369?–1415), Jerome of Prague (1365–1416), Lorenzo Valla (1407–57), Marsilio Ficino (1433–99), Girolamo Savonarola (1452–1498), Giovanni Pico (1463–94), John Colet (1467–1519), and Desiderius Erasmus (1466?–1536) moved toward breaks with the scholastic order that prevailed in the West. And in the realm of social idealism, though not fully founded on a free spirit, Sir Thomas More (1478–1535) broke with supporters of the status quo.

Though Luther later produced an arbitrary reform system of his own, he used the impetus of the Revolution of Life and Liberty, with the life, spirit, and principles of the Single Tradition, to break with the ecclesiastical and political powers of Rome. In the same period Anabaptists on the continent, moved by renewing life and vitality acquired in personal religious experience, broke with both Traditional and Reform Christianity to create independent congregations too liberal for the time and, in some cases, too erratic to be condoned by Mainstream Protestants. Building on the liberal Christian views of men like Erasmus, in further efforts to recover Bible Christianity, the Continental Spiritual Reformers, promoted the principles of spiritual renewal with more clarity than most others and, thus, broke with Luther, Calvin, and other Mainline Reformers to bring forth early

Seekers and proto Quakers. The familists, Arminians, Mennonites, remonstrants, and collegiants also arose after breaking with others.

In England, Henry VIII broke with the pope to establish himself as head of the English Church, which opened the way for tactful reformers to publish the first official English Bible. With the support of Queen Elizabeth in the final days of their revolt, the Scots broke with their Catholic Queen Mary and her French and Spanish supporters to establish the first National Reformed Church in their land. And encouraged by England, the Dutch broke with Philip II of Spain to assert their national freedom.

Though the Puritans remained within the national church, they broke with the Anglicanism's closer union with Traditional Christianity to give birth to a strident and in some ways repressive type of Christian life and society. The Separatists, as an important liberal group, then broke with both Anglicans and Puritans to repudiate the idea of the national church and to promote a theodemocratic order of congregationalism, free society, and democratic republicanism. And led initially by the Puritans, all English dissidents broke with Charles I and the Anglican bishops to bring on the English Revolution of the 1640s and '50s.

Liberal Independents then broke with the Presbyterians who sought to establish their religion as the new national faith of England, with the power of the state to enforce its program. The numerous Free Churches that arose in the mid-seventeenth century broke with all other systems, including, in some instances, each other, to finally create the foundations of the Open Society. And during the same period, Advance Reformers in England and America broke with the narrow restrictive dogmas of Grace and Elite Election that Puritans and Mainline Protestants held to create broad basic and liberal views of universal grace and justification as foundations for a new order of free Christian life, society, and constitutional republicanism.

In the vanguard of the Advance Reform Movement, the Seekers broke with all existing churches to promote the idea of the spiritual church that many Advance Reformists in mid-seventeenth-century England and America embraced and made the foundation of the most liberal theoretic political views of that ingenious age. And in the wake of the Seeker groundswell in England, the Quakers emerged and broke with the Anglicans, Puritans, and Separatists to establish their lives and society on the Inner Light, or Holy Spirit, within their pure theodemocratic movement.

Liberal Reformists who learned the lessons of freedom and democracy within the many Free Churches that arose in the Age of Christ and of the Holy Spirit broke with current views of royal authority and aristocratic society to propose the idea of a government of the people, by the people, and for the people. To them, political government was to be separate from all churches, with the responsibility to administer justice and equity for all, and to maintain the freedom and unalienable rights of the people in an Open Society. Prominent among these liberal religio-political minds, the Levelers, led by Seeker-type reformers, broke not only with royal and aristocratic society and with Presbyterian regimentation in the English Parliament, but with Oliver Cromwell, a majority of the officers of the New Model Army and the influential Baptists, in a noble effort to establish a constitutional democracy based on An Agreement of the Free People of England.

Early in the seventeenth century, the Pilgrims broke with more conservative Puritans to found the Plymouth colony in America, and the migration of many Puritans to Massachusetts constituted a silent break with the English Church. Moved by growing Seeker convictions, Roger Williams broke with the Massachusetts hierarchy, then with the American Baptists (who had broken with the established Church of England and with Puritanism) to set up the free colony of Rhode Island, to which Anne Hutchinson and Samuel Gorton gathered dissenting groups. Thomas Hooker also broke with the arbitrary power of Massachusetts. In Connecticut, in 1639, Hooker and others framed the first formal political Constitution of modern times. Similarly, when the self-governing Quakers who broke with all other Christians settled in America, William Penn made his "Frame of Government" (1682), the basis of religious liberty in the colony of Pennsylvania.

In the Glorious Revolution of 1688, English Whigs and Tories, supported by Newton and other liberal minds, broke with James II to validate the right of revolution and, bolstered by the writings of Locke, to confirm lastingly the supremacy of parliament in the government of England. In various ways and degrees, Reformers like John Wesley and his friend George Whitefield broke with established churches and gave mighty impetus to the basic elements of free Christian life, society, and constitutional government in England and in America.

Finally, in the grand tradition of renewing life, scriptural truth and practice, Christian dissent, and cleavage the English colonies in North America, bound together by a spirit of free and open union that leading minds like George Washington credited to God, broke with England to establish "a new nation, conceived in liberty, and dedicated to the proposition that all men are created equal," and "that they are endowed by their Creator with certain unalienable Rights," among which "are life, liberty, and the pursuit of happiness." In these proceedings, the renewing Christian spirit, principles, concepts, and free societal forms that arose, as effects and causes of prior cleavages back to the beginning of the Revolution of Life and Liberty, became the substance and foundation of a free system of republican government.

And in the ongoing march of renewing life, the enlightened dissent and cleavages that the light of life from Christ produced helped create a unique order of Christian society and constitutional republic government in the United States of America.

CHAPTER 5

The Nature of American Life and Society

Henry David Thoreau

The Political Fruits That Arose in America from the Concept of the Spiritual Church That Goes Back to the Continental Spiritual Reformers and That Blossomed in the Mid-Seventeenth Century

Thoreau called himself a transcendentalist, and he implies in his writings that the spiritual-type individualism that he espoused gave rise to America, and that it had to be built upon if men were to reach higher realms of free life and society. When he was asked by the Association for the Advancement of Science to specify which branch of science he was especially interested in, he said, "Though I could state to a select few that department of human inquiry which engages me,…I felt that it would…make myself the laughing-stock of the scientific community to…describe…that branch of science which specially interests me, inasmuch as they do not believe in a science which deals with the higher law. So I was obliged to speak to their condition and describe…that poor part of me which alone they can understand."

He championed practical political views that first emerged from the idea of the spiritual church that Continental Spiritual Reformers devised and that later gave birth to the highest ideal of liberty to emerge the English Renaissance of the mid-seventeenth century. He is, therefore, called a true "Renaissance man," who created for himself "a life above mere money-grubbing." And while he was familiar with other historical sources, he had great enthusiasm for poets in the Elizabethan Age, "and still more for the leading [English] verse writers of the seventeenth century," while preferring John Milton over Shakespeare. His centered his primary emphasis "on free will and the spiritual independence and responsibility of the individual" which, to great liberal minds of the English Renaissance, was "both good poetry and good doctrine." No verse was more often quoted by Thoreau than the lines from Samuel Daniel's "Epistle to the Lady Margaret, Countess of Cumberland" (1610)—"Unless above himself he can erect himself, how poor a thing is man!"

Thoreau spoke of the ideal of the totally free individual within the existing order of political government in his day. This ideal set forth the primacy of individual conscience over the rule of expediency and popular opinion.

Thoreau began his essay on "Resistance to Civil Government" with the statement "I heartily accept the motto—'That government is best which governs least;' and I should like to see it acted up to more rapidly and systematically. Carried out, it finally amounts to this, which also I believe—'That government is best which governs not at all;' and when men are prepared for it, that will be the kind of government which they will have."

Thoreau explained, "When I converse with the freest of my neighbors, I perceive that, whatever they may say about the magnitude and seriousness of the question, and their regard for the public tranquility, the long and the short of the matter is, that they cannot spare the protection of the existing government, and they dread the consequences of disobedience to it to their property and families."

This was the dilemmas that totally free men, when they viewed their lives within the political state. "For my part," said Thoreau, "I should not like to think that I ever rely on the protection of the State.

But, if I deny the authority of the State when it presents its tax-bill, it will soon take and waste all my property, and so harass me and my children without end."

He explained, "I have never declined paying the highway tax, because I am as desirous of being a good neighbor as I am a bad subject; and, as for supporting schools, I am doing my part to educate my fellow-countrymen now."

Thoreau's views were not based, primarily, on the spirit of rebellion but on the idealism he saw in the essence of America and the principles and concepts that emerged from it. Said he, "I ask for, not at once no government, but at once a better government." Thoreau understood that there was a higher law of liberty, based on greater purity of conscience, and he stated, "They only can force me who obey a higher law than I." Because he looked primarily to the essence of life and liberty of America, he said of those who merely sustained the outward order of her constitutional government, "They who know of no purer sources of truth, who have traced up its stream no higher, stand, and wisely stand, by the Bible and the Constitution, and drink at it there with reverence and humility; but they who behold where it comes trickling into this lake or that pool, gird up their loins once more, and continue their pilgrimage toward its fountain-head." He asked, "Is a democracy, such as we know it, the last improvement possible in government? Is it not possible to take a step further towards recognizing and organizing the rights of man?" And he concluded, "There will never be a really free and enlightened State, until the State comes to recognize the individual as a higher and independent power, from which all its own power and authority are derived, and treats him accordingly."

Thoreau concluded his essay with the statement "I please myself with imagining a State at last which can afford to be just to all men, and to treat the individual with respect as a neighbor; which even would not think it inconsistent with its own repose, if a few were to live aloof from it, not meddling with it, nor embraced by it, who fulfilled all the duties of neighbors and fellow men. A state which bore this kind of fruit, and suffered it to drop off as fast as it ripened, would prepare the way for a still more perfect and glorious state, which also I have imagined, but not yet anywhere seen."

The following are some statements by Thoreau within the body of his essay:

> Can there not be a government in which majorities do not virtually decide right and wrong, but conscience?—in which majorities decide only those questions to which the rule of expediency is applicable? Must the citizen ever for a moment, or in the least degree, resign his conscience to the legislator? Why has ever man a conscience, then? I think that we should be men first, and subjects afterward. It is not desirable to cultivate a respect for the law, so much as for the right. The only obligation which I have a right to assume is to do at any time what I think right. It is truly enough said, that a corporation has no conscience, but a corporation of conscientious man is a corporation with a conscience.

> A wise man will only be useful as a man, and will not submit to be "clay."
> I am too high-born to be propertied,
> To be a secondary at control,
> Or useful serving-man and instrument
> To any sovereign state throughout the world.

> How does it become a man to behave toward this American government to-day? I answer that he cannot without disgrace be associated with it. I cannot for an instant recognize that political organization as my government which is the slave's government also.

A wise man will not leave the right to the mercy of chance, nor wish it to prevail through the power of the majority.

Oh for a man who is a man, and, as my neighbor says, has a bone in his back which you cannot pass your hand through!

The American has dwindled into an Odd Fellow—one who may be known by the development of his organ of gregariousness, and a lack of intellect and cheerful self-reliance; whose first and chief concern, on coming into the world, is to see that the alms-houses are in good repair; and,…who, in short, ventures to live only by the aid of the mutual insurance company, which has promised to bury him decently.

I was not born to be forced. I will breathe after my own fashion.

For eighteen hundred years…the New Testament has been written; yet where is the legislator who has wisdom and practical talent enough to avail himself of the light which it sheds on the science of legislation?

Having stated his views on government, Thoreau makes some clarifications. First, he states, "I do not wish to quarrel with any man or nation. I do not wish to split hairs, to make fine distinctions, or set myself up as better than my neighbors. I seek rather, I may say, even an excuse for conforming to the laws of the land. I am but too ready to conform to them. Indeed I have reason to suspect myself on this head; and each year, as the tax-gatherer comes round, I find myself disposed to review the acts and position of the general and state governments, and the spirit of the people, to discover a pretext for conformity."

He then explained, "Seen from a lower point of view [than that which he held], the Constitution, with all its faults, is very good; the law and the courts are very respectable; even this state and this

American government are, in many respects, very admirable and rare things, to be thankful for, such as a great many have described them; but seen from a point of view a little higher, they are what I have described them; seen from a higher still, and the highest, who shall say what they are, or that they are worth looking at or thinking of at all?"

Daniel Webster was a superb example of those who relied primarily on the practical features of America's constitutional system. "Webster never goes behind government," Thoreau explained, "and so cannot speak with authority about it." To understand, one must get back of the Constitution and see and understand the essence of new life and liberty by which it was brought into being as a practical system. Thoreau continued, "His words are wisdom to those legislators who contemplate no essential reform in the existing government; but for thinkers, and those who legislate for all time, he never once glances at the subject." Thoreau did not see himself as standing alone in these views. Said he, "I know of those whose serene and wise speculations on this theme would soon reveal the limits of his [Webster's] mind's range and hospitality."

"Yet," Thoreau explained, "compared with the cheap professions of most reformers, and the still cheaper wisdom and eloquence of politicians in general, his are almost the only sensible and valuable words, and we thank heaven for him. Comparatively, he is always strong, original, and, above all, practical. Still, his quality is not wisdom but prudence. The lawyer's truth is not truth but consistency or a consistent expediency. Truth is always in harmony with herself and is not concerned chiefly to reveal the justice that may consist with wrongdoing. He well deserves to be called, as he has been called, the Defender of the Constitution. There are really no blows to be given by him but defensive ones."

Viewed from the vantage point of America's true original spirit and essence, Thoreau said of Webster, "He is not a leader, but a follower. His leaders are the men of 1887. 'I have never made an effort,' he says, 'and never propose to make an effort; I have never countenanced an effort, and never mean to countenance an effort, to disturb the arrangement as originally made, by which the various States came into the Union.'"

Thoreau got to Webster's deficiency when he stated, "Notwithstanding his special acuteness and ability, he is unable to take a fact out of its merely political relations, and behold it as it lies absolutely to be disposed of by the intellect."

America's liberal Puritan heritage embodied such basic elements as higher law, which, to liberal Puritans, was a clearer revelation of the elements in natural law and, therefore, superior—natural rights and the rights derived from spiritual renewal and life in Christ; private and public virtue; the principle of Christian liberty, with the spirit of liberty that came from Christ; and the ideal of free and open union, with the Holy Spirit making that ideal real and meaningful among regenerated individuals. But the fact that God and his law were central to all these elements, and the basis of them, meant that the American heritage of higher law was much broader than its mere legal principles and features. To liberal Puritans, higher law was in a very real sense a living law, written by the Holy Spirit on the tablets of the human heart; and the life-giving principle extended far beyond the legal concepts to provide a unique context of activated forces and quickened elements in which higher law was received and applied. It was by the expression of faith in Christ that liberal Puritans received and applied the law of God; and their acceptance and application of that law, in faith, yielded the blessings of the Holy Spirit, which they identified as being germane to the spirit of liberty, the inner substance of private and public virtue, and the spirit of free and open union. These and other by-products of the Word or law of God made the liberal Puritan heritage much broader, inclusive, and significant in a living, dynamic way than its mere legal principles.

This combined body of activated principles and living power undergirded and gave life to the republican order that the American Founders establish. The above elements of Biblical Christianity, therefore, had a direct—indeed, a central and dominant—bearing on the American governmental system, which in the minds of several leading Founders was based indispensably on the realities of the spirit of liberty, private and public virtue, and the spirit of free and open union among the citizens of the nation. These were the fundamental ingredients that undergirded their republican concept and made it all possible, as a higher order of life, society, and government than many since their day have grasped or sought to implement. While the need for virtuous leadership had been set forth by such men as Bolingbroke (Henry St. John) in the *Idea of a Patriot King*, which John Adams, Jefferson, and other Founders studied and sought to apply, clear evidence not fully heretofore considered suggests that they recognized that they could do so only by the existence of this undergirding foundation.

Because many students of America's origins do not give full consideration in early American life and thought to the ideal of free and open union and the significance of its undergirding religio-spiritual elements, they generally approach the Founders from the premise that in their nobility, they were above party, then follow with the qualification: Yet in the practical affairs of political life, based on later political realities, the Founders reveal a degree of naivety in their thinking and actions. But contrary to this conclusion, when the Founders are studied within the context of the liberal Puritan tradition, spiritually, ideologically, and historically, there is need for a more insightful premise, namely, the American Founders were nobly above party, and in this, they were not naive. They were, instead, operating within a vital and dynamic contextual framework that was largely lost to America after their day.

The American Founders thought and acted within the framework of the liberal Puritan tradition that was planted in America by the Pilgrim fathers and such leading men as Thomas Hooker and Roger Williams, and that was matured and refined by the influence of liberal minds in that tradition, like John Milton, John Locke, Algernon Sidney, and the English Commonwealth men. When viewed in relation to the elemental ingredients that comprised the liberal Puritan tradition, the Founders were operating in the context of the spirit of liberty that liberal Puritans saw as being one of the sacred fruits of the Holy Spirit and the spirit of free and open union, another even more sacred fruit of the Spirit. Ketcham, therefore, repeatedly equates the views of Washington, Adams, Jefferson,

ORIGINS OF LIBERTY

Madison, Monroe, and John Quincy Adams on nonparty leadership with that of John Winthrop, who, as discussed later, set forth the view of government under the dominant principle of Christian liberty. These vital, fundamental elements largely set the mold of the vision of their minds.

To be more specific, the vision of the American Founders embodied the needs that were incident to two planes of human experience—the spiritually unregenerated and the regenerated plane of human life. There was the need, first, to establish adequate means to govern unregenerated individuals and groups, where self-interest, personal and class conflict, and a lust for power often (if not largely) prevailed. To this end, the Founders devised the auxiliary precautions that they built into the American republic—the vertical and horizontal separation of power, the doctrine of limited government, the republican principle and form of government based on a democratic spirit, the guarantee of individual rights, etc. But these were merely precautionary devises. In addition to their role and benefits, it took the elements that pertained to the second plane of human experience to more fully move America forward on the pathway of higher purpose and progress. Here, the liberty that America's constitutional system provided enabled the people to freely acquire and express such deep, positive and noble elements of Biblical Christianity as those which motivated the discovery of America by Columbus and the colonization of the New World by the Pilgrim and Puritan fathers and by which an order of liberty, progress, open union, and good will was brought forth and established through the instrumentality of sensitive, intelligent people working within the liberal Puritan tradition. On this foundation, the initiative of the individual was also released in temporal pursuits, and great incentive was given to social and economic aspirations. This, in the minds of liberal Puritans, was the order of Zion that led to the New Jerusalem that comes down from above.

For people living on this higher plane of human experience, there was very little need for law, for one who kept the Biblical Christian law had no need to break the law of the land. Though the American Founders, as political figures, were not directly involved in the enunciation and development of the truth and inner spiritual power related to this higher plane of life, they were nevertheless heirs of that greater heritage as it had emerged in the tradition that came to political fruition in the world of their day. They, therefore, sought to suppress the baneful effects incident to the first plane of human experience while idolizing the vision produced by the powerful elements incident to the second.

The vision of the American Founders was not limited to justice and equity as provided by the auxiliary precautions they built into the American republic but, in addition, one of liberty, open union, and progress. Set in the context of America's liberal Puritan tradition, their vision was a compound of Zion and the world; and while they were well aware of the challenges of the latter, they spoke and acted and centered their hopes in the former. In the Preamble of the Federal Constitution, they wrote, "We, the people of the United States, in order to form a more perfect union, establish justice, insure domestic tranquility, provide for the common defense, promote the general welfare, and secure the blessings of liberty to ourselves and our posterity, do ordain and establish this Constitution for the United States of America."

The foundation of this high order of society and government was living faith in Jesus Christ, with the spirit of free and open union that liberal reformers held flowed to the people from God. Washington's statement in his first inaugural address (1789), on the spirit of free and open union that he saw made manifest in the formation of the new nation, shows clearly that his basic view on the issue came from his observation and participation in this living moving Spirit, which (as shown later) had its roots in the elements of Biblical Christianity that liberal Puritans brought forth, and, above all, in the power of the Holy Spirit that they held was an active agent in their lives and communities.

It was an "Almighty Being," Washington declared to Congress and the American people, who worked by his "invisible hand…in the important revolution just accomplished in the system of their United Government." Speaking of events in which he was the central participant, the new president explained, "The tranquil deliberations and voluntary consent of so many distinct communities, by which the event has resulted, cannot be compared with the means by which most governments have been established, without some return to pious gratitude along with an humble anticipation of the future blessings which the past seem to presage." That these were not mere pious expressions is evident from his added statement, "These reflections, arising out of the present crisis, have forced themselves too strongly on my mind to be suppressed."

Based on this foundation, liberty in Christ and open union were the dominant ingredients of the new republic and the primary goals to be achieved by it. Said Washington in his first inaugural address, "I behold the surest pledges that as, on one side, no local prejudices or attachments, no separate views or party animosities will misdirect the comprehensive and equal eye which ought to watch over this great assemblage of communities and interests, so, on another, that the foundations of our national policy will be laid in the pure and immutable principles of private morality, and the pre-eminence of free government be exemplified by all the attributes which can win the affections of its citizens and command the respect of the world." And having sought to sustain this vision of government, while articulating its liberal principles of justice and individual rights, Jefferson declared one year after his retirement from the American presidency, "In a government like ours, it is the duty of the chief magistrate, in order to enable himself to do all the good which his station requires,...to unite in himself the confidence of the whole people. This alone, in any case where the energy of the nation is required, can produce a union of the powers of the whole and point them in a single direction, as if all constituted but one body and one mind." To him, the realization of this order of things comprised "the whole constitutional vigor" of the American Union, and because authority rested firmly on broad popular support, the American governmental system would become "the strongest on earth."

Though its central purpose was to guarantee the liberty of the individual, the American order of government was not based on faction or party spirit. Not merely liberty, but free and open union was the ideal of the new republic, the nature, character, and objectives of which can be seen by the fact that it was designed to operate above parties. Nothing more troubled and upset Washington, says Ketcham, "than the charges in the last two years of his presidency that he had...become the creature of a party." In his farewell address—his political testament to the nation—Washington levelled his "most solemn" admonition against "the baneful effects of the spirit of party generally." While faction might provide a check against improper use of power in monarchies, he declared that "in governments purely elective, it is a spirit not to be encouraged." "From their natural tendency," he explained, "it is certain there will always be enough of this spirit for every salutary purpose; and there being constant danger of excess, the effort ought to be by force of public opinion to mitigate and assuage it. A fire not to be quenched, it demands a uniform vigilance to prevent it bursting into a flame, lest, instead of warming, it should consume." Without the needed vigilance, Washington charged, "the alternate domination of one faction over another... has perpetuated the most horrid enormities, [and] is itself a frightful despotism."

"The greatest evil of faction and party was not its effect on public policy [though that was bad enough], but rather its narrowing and degradation of political motives, long regarded as the essence of corruption. Parties riveted public attention on partialities and self-interest, and the effect was nothing less than enslavement of the nation to sin and vice. Liberty for Washington as for John Winthrop [Note, this was Christian liberty.], was not doing what one pleased, if that meant satisfying selfish [factional] interests; rather, it was a positive act of rising above such enthrallment to understand and seek the public good."

"John Adams shared the ideal of disinterested leadership entirely, though his temperament, reputation, and circumstances made it even less achievable during his administration than it had been for his predecessor. In his inaugural address, Adams proclaimed his lack of sectional bias, his desire to love 'virtuous men of all parties and denominations,' and his 'wish to patronize every rational effort to encourage schools, colleges, universities, academies, and every institution for propagating knowledge, virtue, and religion among all classes of the people...as the only means of preserving our Constitution from its natural enemies, the spirit of sophistry, the spirit of party, the spirit of intrigue, the profligacy of corruption, and the pestilence of foreign influence, which is the angel of destruction to elective governments.'"

"Like Washington, Adams accepted in dead earnest that the role of the leader, standing above party, was critical to the preservation of liberty, which meant in effect the guidance of policy in the public interest. Adams expressed the ideal of leadership he shared with his predecessor [and, substantially, with his first four successors] when in the margin of his copy of [97–98] Bolingbroke's *The Spirit of Patriotism* he reflected on the meaning of the word patriotism. It comprehended, Adams noted, 'piety, or the love and fear of God; general benevolence to mankind; a particular attachment to our own country; a zeal to promote its happiness by reforming its morals, increasing its knowledge, promoting its agriculture, commerce and manufactures, improving its constitution, and securing its liberties: and all this without the prejudices of individuals or parties or factions, without fear, favor, or affection.'"

"In this view [that view in the paragraph above], liberty was not the absence of restraint or even the encouragement of diversity, but rather it was acting with the incorruptibility, the disinterested virtue, and the attention to the common good implicit in the Athenian conception of citizenship. Applied to one in a position of power and leadership, liberty meant above all shunning partisanship that is, avoiding the partial view or the alliance with faction that had defined corruption from the time of Cicero and Tacitus to that of the critics of Walpole whose words Adams had so taken to heart."

"A widespread morality, undergirded by Christianity, was a possible way, in Adams's view, to overcome faction in a government resting on consent."

Adams hoped that the public might be properly educated to where the people were wise enough to distinguish between "genuine liberty and its bastard offspring, faction."

In his inaugural address, Adams stated his desire "to patronize every rational effort to encourage schools, colleges, universities, academies, and every institution for propagating knowledge, virtue, and religion among all classes of the people...as the only means of preserving our Constitution from its natural enemies, the spirit of sophistry, the spirit of party, the spirit of intrigue, the profligacy of corruption, and the pestilence of foreign influence."

Model for nonpartisanship, says Ketcham, was "an ancient conception of leadership above party and without corruption." But a study of America's liberal Puritan tradition makes it very clear that the substantive elements upon which the order of liberty and open union rested were largely products of that tradition. When the conflicts of the Hamilton-Jefferson approaches to government had become somewhat submerged and peace established with the termination of the War of 1812, the aspiration of President James Monroe (1817–25) for this ideal of government became "the high-water mark of the republican intention shared by the first six presidents." Having been reared by the leading republican theorists in Virginia and the nation, especially George Wythe and Jefferson, and having served in governmental positions to the point that he became "the most widely experienced public servant" ever to come to the American presidency, Monroe won that office with 183 of 217 electoral votes in 1816, and he lost but one electoral vote four years later. In his first inaugural address, he stated that the American people constituted "one great family with a common interest." And he declared, "Discord does not belong to our system." In his second inaugural, Monroe again condemned party spirit and made reference to what Ketcham describes as "the unique circumstances in the United States that made party struggles unnecessary." As the last successor of the original American tradition of republican government under God, he hoped for the day when the demise of party spirit would be complete and America would attain to "the highest degree of perfection of which human institutions are capable," and that "the movement in all its branches" would exhibit "such a degree of order and harmony as to command the admiration and respect of the civilized world."

But even as Monroe spoke, the religio-spiritual elements that undergirded the liberal Puritan tradition and made the ideal of liberty and open union a viable base of political life by which American presidents could act above party aspirations and party control were being disregarded and their vital blessings began to slip away, and the forces of disunion and class conflict were beginning to make themselves manifest in American life. The subtitle of Ketcham's *Presidents Above Party: The First American Presidency, 1789–1829* (1984) indicates how long the original concept of American government lasted—forty years, which included the Era of Nationalism and the Era of Good Feelings, which were followed by the Era of Sectionalism that finally brought on the American Civil War. This was not merely an American phenomenon, and there appear to be different levels of effect. The loss of open union, coupled with the rise of interest in the rights of the common person, at first opened the way for the development of political parties. But especially in other areas of the West there was, on a deeper and more baneful level of effect, a shift toward the lust for power.

Viewing things from the vantage point of American's liberal Puritan heritage, the questions can and should be asked, What forces brought on the era of national union by which thirteen separate colonies were formed into a single national entity? And what forces (or lack of uniting forces), conversely, destroyed the original order of Christian republicanism that the American Founders established and idolized? Or, better stated, what caused the vital forces of free and open union that produced the original order to ebb away so that presidents controlled by party thereafter predominated in American politics? Though historians portray the American Founders as being somewhat naive; at the same time, they recognize that there was something about them—something truly great and inspired—that set them apart from most, if not all, other political figures on the American scene. It is hoped that this study will direction attention to neglected principles and areas of inquiry by which more accurate and meaningful answers can be given to the above questions.

There has never been such a group of political figures as the Founding Fathers of the American republic in this nation (or anywhere else) since there day simply because there has never been a foundation of living religio-spiritual truth and power upon which such a group could develop. And there has been no substantial progress toward higher political principles and forms of liberal government, by the hordes of public officials who fill America's public offices or the multitude of political scientists who fill America's colleges and universities, simply because the American nation is no longer travelling on the religio-spiritual path that leads to higher planes of liberty, open union, national purpose, and progress. While the Scientific Revolution that had its roots in the same elemental forces that brought about the age of modern liberty has moved on to a great flowering of truth, modern social, economic and political liberals have turned collectivists and are doubling back toward dependent society in their zealous quest for progress. It may, therefore, appear that the vision of Zion as a city upon a hill has been lost and that the present national and international trend is toward nuclear disarmament and the consolidation of a world order based on collectivism. This work has been written to give foundation for a viable alternative.

The aspiration of President James Monroe (1817–25) for this ideal of government became "the high-water mark of the republican intention shared by the first six presidents." Having been reared by the leading republican theorists in Virginia and the nation, especially George Wythe and Jefferson, and having served in governmental positions to the point that he became "the most widely experienced public servant" ever to come to the American presidency, Monroe won that office with 183 of 217 electoral votes in 1816, and he lost but one electoral vote four years later. In his first inaugural address, he stated that the American people constituted "one great family with a common interest." And he declared, "Discord does not belong to our system." In his second inaugural, Monroe again condemned party spirit and made reference to what Ketcham describes as "the unique circumstances in the United States that made party struggles unnecessary." As the last successor of the original American tradition of republican government under God, he hoped for the day when the demise of party spirit would be complete and America would attain to "the highest degree of perfection of which human institutions are capable," and that "the movement in all its branches" would exhibit "such a degree of order and harmony as to command the admiration and respect of the civilized world."

But even as Monroe spoke, the religio-spiritual elements that undergirded the liberal Puritan tradition and made the ideal of liberty and open union a viable base of political life by which American presidents could act above party aspirations and party control were being disregarded and their vital blessings began to slip away, and the forces of disunion and class conflict were beginning to make themselves manifest in American life. The subtitle of Ketcham's *Presidents Above Party: The First American Presidency, 1789-1829* (1984) indicates how long the original concept of American government lasted—forty years, which included the Era of Nationalism and the Era of Good Feelings, which were followed by the Era of Sectionalism that finally brought on the American Civil War. This was not merely an American phenomenon, and there appear to be different levels of effect. The loss of open union, coupled with the rise of interest in the rights of the common person, at first opened the way for the development of political parties. But especially in other areas of the West there was, on a deeper and more baneful level of effect, a shift toward the lust for power.

Viewing things from the vantage point of American's liberal Puritan heritage, the questions can and should be asked, What forces brought on the era of national union by which thirteen separate colonies were formed into a single national entity? And what forces (or lack of uniting forces), conversely, destroyed the original order of Christian republicanism that the American Founders established and idolized? Or, better stated, what caused the vital forces of free and open union that produced the original order to ebb away so that presidents controlled by party thereafter predominated in American politics? Though historians portray the American Founders as being somewhat naive; at the same time, they recognize that there was something about them—something truly great and inspired—that set them apart from most, if not all, other political figures on the American scene. It is hoped that this study will direction attention to neglected principles and areas of inquiry by which more accurate and meaningful answers can be given to the above questions.

Jefferson

"Despite the assumed party division of Congress from 1801 to 1809 between Federalists, who opposed the president, and Republicans, who supported him, Jefferson never made party itself the key to his leadership, nor would he have been pleased to have been classed with Andrew Jackson, Franklin Roosevelt, Lyndon Johnson, and other avowed masters of partisan politics.

"Jefferson saw party and leadership as antithetical and conducted his relationship with Congress generally according to that precept."

"Jefferson's administrations suggest that it might not be necessary under all circumstances for a president to depend on control of, or influence through, a political party in order to be an effective executive. His posture and performance as president indicate that, in important ways, good leadership can depend on a muted partisanship and that it may not be necessary for the president to be an active party leader while in office in order for the Constitution to 'work.'"

"Like many great leaders in the past, monarchical and other, and even like many later presidents who enhanced their effectiveness by appeals that transcended party, Jefferson capitalized on the perennial attraction of harmony and cooperation, as opposed to the incessant 'generation of conflict' often called for by partisan theories of leadership. Jefferson's presidency, and especially his skillful guidance of Congress, far from demonstrating that an effective president has to exert his will on Congress through the agency of party, proves on the contrary that legislative leadership can be achieved through persuasion, cultivation of supposed party opponents, and articulation of a program in the public interest that truly transcends party."

The Significance of 1829

"Why is 1829 such a turning point in the history of the [United States] presidency? What values and attitudes distinguished the Adams and Jackson presidencies? In what way did the leader [i.e.,

Jackson] of the first modern American political party embody a new conception of executive office?"

The Changing Temper: 1820-29

"Monroe knew, of course, as historians since have displayed in detail, that what a Boston newspaper during his visit [there in July 1817] had proclaimed as the 'Era of Good Feelings' was in fact a time of bitter personal and factional dispute perhaps better characterized as an era of bad feelings."

Note: Ketcham entitles his chapter on the presidencies of Monroe and John Quincy Adams "The Ebb of the Republican Presidency."

By the end of Monroe's administration, Jefferson had concluded "that great divisions over principle, especially over the question of whether mankind was capable of self-government, would always exist, although he also, perhaps inconsistently, never ceased to hope for the suppression of party."

"Madison accepted much of this belief [i.e., that which was held by Jefferson, above] that enduring differences over principle were inescapable and was sure as well that American pluralism would result always in the existence of factions and parties in the nation. He even thought some good came from 'making one party a check on the other,' as he had put it as early as 1792, but he quickly added, again perhaps inconsistently, that this was valuable only 'so far as the existence of parties cannot be prevented, nor their views accommodated.'"

Jefferson, Madison, and Monroe continued to the last "to believe parties were unwelcome and dangerous, and each conducted his presidency, as far as possible, according to that conviction.

"Fundamentally, each remained convinced that republicanism, to achieve its full, moral meaning, had to triumph over and exclude the spirit of faction and party... Although some politicians in the 1790s had begun to act in ways appropriate to a later era, and a few had even begun openly to accept the legitimacy of parties, [J. R. Sharp, "The 'Jeffersonian' Conception of Party: The Development of the idea of a Loyal Opposition" (paper delivered at the University of California, Berkeley, June 8, 1977)] such was by no means the common view."

A substantial change occurred "between the effective, almost idyllic leadership of Jefferson's first term and the factious disarray of Monroe's last term."

"Monroe's continued, earnest insistence on both the ancient antiparty ideology and the model of the patriotic leader leave little doubt that his aspiration remained the same as Jefferson's—and, quite self-consciously for Monroe, the same as Washington's. Indeed, the factional warfare, so distasteful to Monroe, served only to heighten his sense of the harm it did to the nation and to reinforce his determination to refuse to indulge or validate it."

The Changing Temper: John Quincy Adams

"John Quincy Adams was the last president, before the triumph under Jackson of a conception of leadership tied to a positive idea of party, who aspired to embody all the dimensions of the patriot leader."

So much had the temper of the times changed that, while it can be said that "no other public career in American history matches that of John Quincy Adams in either length or patriotic devotion," it is also true that "no other mind felt more excruciatingly the dilemmas of republic leadership."

In his inaugural address (1825), John Quincy Adams "proclaimed triumphantly that since 1815 the 'baneful weed of party strife' had been uprooted in the United States and that 'ten years of peace, at home and abroad, have assuaged the animosities of political contentions and blended into harmony the most discordant elements of public opinion.' [March 4, in Richardson, ed. *Messages of the Presidents*, II, pp. 862–5.] Thus, he viewed the feuds of the Monroe presidency as merely personal or at most sectional and as evidencing none of the profound disagreements in political theory or foreign policy that from 1790 to 1815 had divided the Federalists and the Republicans... He intended, if he could, to banish partisanship—just as Washington had intended."

"It is one of the great ironies of American history that even before [John Quincy] Adams delivered this [first inaugural] message, in fact from before his minority election by the House of Representatives, his presidency was embroiled in partisan strife of unparalleled bitterness...

"Even before Adams's inauguration, the supporters of three of his defeated opponents, Calhoun, W. H. Crawford, and Jackson, guided by Martin Van Buren and other regionally powerful politicians, were already forming a party, under Jackson's banner, to wreck vengeance on Adams and Clay [his vice president]." *Note*: It was charged that Adams struck a deal with Clay that, in exchange for Clay's vote in the House, Adams would appoint him Secretary of State, which appointment Adams made.

The administration of John Quincy Adams reveals "the profound cultural changes surrounding his paradoxical effort at national leadership." But while his "own values and public philosophy remained" the same as that of his predecessors, Adams "lived in a world of political parties."

"Perhaps the most revealing aspect of John Quincy Adams's presidency, then, is its subsequent perception as 'unreal,' or 'lurid,' or 'futile,' or 'archaic.' To students aware of the later history of American politics [and making judgments favoring the change], the Adams presidency has seemed perverse at best: the president proclaiming the most high-minded ideas of public service amid the most outraged cries against his own corruption; the president repudiating party as an intensified party system took shape before his eyes; the president urging a strongly nationalistic program as sectional feelings burgeoned, and so on. If one believed the new directions were the irresistible wave of the future, the conscience-bound chief executive could seem only blind or antiquated [139–140]. He offered grand plans that bore no relationship to either the mood of the nation or the possibility of support in Congress. He kept ardently Jacksonian partisans in office, even at the cabinet level. He acted as though party organization did not exist, and he refused to use his high office to aid in his reelection. Meanwhile, Adams's opponents articulated programs attuned to popular sentiment, built party organization, electioneered assiduously, fused coalitions, and made clear their intent to use patronage to punish foes and reward friends, with the expected result: the Jacksonian movement acquired a force that swept the self-righteous president from office in 1829. Beginning in that year, 'the rising spirit of democracy...simply took possession of the system through the instrumentality of the political party,' [Leonard D. White, *The Jacksonians: A Study in Administrative History, 1829–1861* (New York 1954), p. 552] thus virtually requiring a president to be a leader of party in order to be effective."

CHAPTER 6

The Bible And America

Most early Americans believed that the Bible was "infallible on all possible questions," says Hall, "even of science, history, and government." They believed in heaven, hell and a personal devil, in "rude conceptions of atonement, and a judgment yet to come." Among the American Founders, men like Benjamin Franklin and Thomas Jefferson "knew their Bibles well," and in this, they were no different from the "great body of their educated contemporaries." The Bible was the chief "political textbook of the fathers of the Republic." Their political writings between 1760 and 1805 show that 34 percent of their quoted sources came from Scripture, with Deuteronomy (which contains God's law to ancient Israel) as the dominant source. "In America," Tocqueville explained, "religion is the road to knowledge, and the observance of the divine laws leads man to civil freedom." Thus, the system of constitutional republicanism that the Founders established has an "indispensable theological" base.

These facts, by themselves, do not fully reveal how and in what ways the Bible was the foundation of the free order of society and political government that emerged in America. Two other basic points must be considered as foundation for such understanding. First, from the religious groups that arose from the Bible Revolution in England and were planted in America, two "contending types" of Protestantism are evident: what Hall calls the Continental type, with Calvin as its "chief inspiration," and an older "primitive English Protestant type of which Wyclif and the Lollards were the main teachers." Each placed a different emphasis on the Bible, which resulted in a different outlook on society and government. By contrast to Calvinistic Puritans, the several groups within the primitive English tradition had no external central authority. Nor did they need one. "The Bible, together with the Holy Spirit to interpret it, was all they really needed." These were the groups from whom modern liberty was born.

As early as 1570, advance reformers within this tradition began to promote liberal views derived solely from the Bible, particularly the New Testament—the basic position Wyclif took much earlier. These liberal principles, concepts, and societal forms were then expanded and developed to a point of great fruition in the period of the Puritan Revolution and Commonwealth, the modern axial hub, where many advocates gave birth to liberty. On the same basic religio-spiritual foundations, but under conditions of colonial life, a similar rise of liberal sentiment and thought took place in America, supplemented, enlarged, and refined by the liberal thought of men like Milton, Sidney, Locke, and the English Commonwealth men, who took the spirit of liberty and its basic principles and societal forms from vestiges of Biblical Christianity and advance reformers who gave birth to liberty in the modern axial hub.

Second, within the setting of the ongoing clash between the two contending Protestant types of religious life and society mentioned above, Americans were increasingly influenced by the views and attitudes of the English Commonwealth men, whose genuine desire was to build on true Biblical Christian faith, principles, and democratic forms while repudiating in strident terms arbitrary religion and the ecclesiastical systems of the Continental Calvinistic type. This in no way meant that they were anti-religious, humanists or secularists, though they greatly contributed to the decline of organized religion that was very evident when the American Revolution began.

By failing to see the American Founders in this vital historical setting, historians have often portrayed them as rationalists, humanists, and even secularists. But it is much more logical and historically accurate to see them taking the same basic approach to religion as the English Commonwealth men, who made Jesus Christ, the New Testament Church, and the Holy Spirit the foundation of life, society, and republicanism. Voicing the same dislike that the Commonwealth men felt toward "outgrown dogmas and outworn creeds," John Adams asked bluntly, "Where do we find a precept in the gospels requiring ecclesiastical synods, conventions, and whole carloads of trumpery that we find religion encumbered with these days?") Jefferson was no less discerning, committed, and forthright when he declared that those who called him "infidel and themselves Christians and preachers of the Gospel…draw all their characteristic dogmas from what its Author never said nor saw." Said Jefferson, "They have compounded from the heathen mysteries a system beyond the comprehension of man, of which the great Reformer of the vicious ethics and deism of the Jews, were He to return to earth, would not recognize one feature." All this had devastating effects. "Their blasphemies," Jefferson charged, "have driven thinking men into infidelity, who have too hastily rejected the supposed Author himself with the horrors so falsely imputed to Him."

The scriptural basis of America's law of liberty, justice, and democratic society and republicanism began with such early legal and political documents as the Mayflower Compact of 1620. On May 31, 1638, Thomas Hooker delivered a sermon in the First Church of Hartford. His text was Deuteronomy 1:13: "Take you wise men, and understanding, and known among your tribes, and I will make them rulers over you." Based on God's declarations to Moses, Hooker taught that the selection of public officials belonged to the people, by the Lord's allowance, and that it was God's will that they make this choice. Eight months later, his sermon became the basis of the fundamental orders of Connecticut—the first written constitution in modern times and a forerunner to American Constitutionalism. Continuing this tradition, the American Founders "invoked God in their civil assemblies, called upon their chosen teachers of religion for counsel from the Bible, and recognized its precepts as the law of their public conduct." And while asserting that government "protects all in their religious rights," Washington added, "True religion affords to government its surest support." When Americans embarked on the revolution, they did so, not "as soldiers of fortune but, like [Oliver] Cromwell and the soldiers of the Commonwealth, with the Word of God in their hearts and trusting in him." And the spiritual life they derived from Christ gave them the moral energy that "sustained the Republic in its material weakness against superior numbers, and discipline, and all the power of England."

Early Americans being educated in the Bible judged matters by the Bible. Equally important, from it, they developed sensitivity to principle and a positive character that caused Daniel Webster to state that the American "fathers accomplished the revolution on a strict question of principle." In New England, Governor Thomas Hutchinson remarked, men took sides on "mere speculative points in government, when there was nothing in practice that could give any grounds for forming parties." This tendency in American education, Edmund Burke pointed out, was a major factor that fostered the spirit of liberty that promoted resistance to England. It made the people "acute, inquisitive, dexterous, prompt in attack, ready in defense, [and] full of resources." The result was that Americans augured "misgovernment at a distance" and snuffed the "approach of tyranny in every tainted breeze." The English Parliament asserted the right to tax the colonies in all cases whatever, Webster explained, and accordingly levied a "trifling" tax. But the "claim itself was inconsistent with liberty." So the colonists "poured out their treasures and their blood like water, in a contest in opposition to an assertion, which those less sagacious, and not so well schooled in the principles of civil liberty, would have regarded as barren phraseology, or mere parade of words."

Having cited Burke and Webster, Thornton explains, "It is in this habitual study of political ethics, of 'the liberty of the gospel'—perhaps the principle feature in New England history—that we discern the source of that earnestness that consciousness of right begets, and of those appeals to principle that distinguished the colonies, and that they were ready to vindicate with life and fortune... The church polity of New England begot like [democratic] principles in the state.

The pew and the pulpit had been educated to self-government. They were accustomed 'to CONSIDER.' The highest glory of the American Revolution, said John Quincy Adams, was this, 'It connected, in one indissoluble bond, the principles of civil government with the principles of Christianity.'" This was but logical; the former were born of the latter.

Sharpness of analysis, coming from attention to principle and the enlightening power of the Holy Spirit, produced many Puritan sects in the seventeenth century, with a significant impact on the formation of American life and society. While such diversity at times induced conflict, it also promoted toleration and liberty. And given the tendency of organized religion to exert arbitrary power, some liberal minds saw diversity in faiths as better suiting free society. In *Common Sense*, Thomas Paine wrote, "I fully and consciously believe that it is the will of the Almighty that there should be a diversity of religious opinions among us. It affords a larger field for our Christian kindness... On this liberal principle, I look on the various denominations among us to be like children of the same family, differing only in what is called their Christian names." "The United States will embosom all the religious sects or denominations in Christendom," exclaimed Ezra Stiles. "Here they may all enjoy their whole respective systems of worship and church government complete." Of the American order, he said, "The example of a friendly cohabitation of all sects in America, providing that men may be good members of civil society and yet differ in religion—this precedent, I say, which has already been intently studied and contemplated for fifteen years past by France, Holland, and Germany, may have already had an effect in introducing moderation, lenity, and justice among European states."

The idea of Christian republicanism toward which liberal thought within the Puritan movement had been moving for generations drew two dominant elements from the Bible. The first consisted of liberal features that were taken from Biblical Christianity—the spirit of liberty, the spirit of free and open union, private and public virtue, and the ideas of covenant, consent, individual rights, etc.—that provided the dynamic, idealistic, free, and open features of Christian Republicanism. The second was the biblical concept of man under the power of the fall that Adam and Eve instituted by their transgression in Eden. Unregenerate man in his fallen mortal state is often inclined to pride, greed, self-aggrandizement, insensitivity to the interests of others, and the lust for power. The realization of these basic facts of human nature gave the Founders practical reason to design the machinery of the republic so that government could preserve itself against the ambitions of unregenerate interests and power.

By taking positive elements of life and society from Biblical Christianity and the biblical vision of Zion, liberal minds who emerged from the Puritan movement sought to build a new order of life and society based on the free and open union of people in Christ, spiritually, economically, and politically that would lead to their ideal of the New Jerusalem. Meanwhile, the baneful forces within fallen man made it necessary to build precautionary devises into the republican system, including a vertical and horizontal separation and balance of power. Thus, Christian ensigncies and the doctrine of the fall combined to give positivism and realism to American theo-republicanism. While the latter showed the need for auxiliary precautions to be built into the system, dynamic elements of Biblical Christianity in the hands of liberal minds promoted the spirit and substance of liberty, virtue, open union, and individual rights within the republican concept that emerged in the New World. Reasoning from the vantage point of the free society that was planted in America from congregational principles born of Biblical Christianity, Thomas Paine stated in *Common Sense* that society and political government "are not only different but have different origins." Said Paine, "Society is produced by our wants and government by our wickedness; the former promotes our happiness positively by uniting our affections, the latter negatively by restraining our vices... Society in every state is a blessing, but government, even in the best, is but a necessary evil." Like the clothing we wear, he explained, "government...is the badge of lost innocence... Were the impulses of conscience clear, uniform, and irresistibly obeyed, man would need no other lawgiver."

Here can be seen the Biblical Christian idea of the open society as it arose in modern times. In his *Discourses Concerning Government*,

Algernon Sidney declared a basic assumption on which the political order of America was built. "To depend upon the will of a man," he said, "is slavery." The statement had distinct meaning to liberal minds, which held that true society must rest on a divine order of renewing truth and life above mortal man. Nor was it right to depend solely, or primarily, on the will of the people. The American idea was not that of a popular secular or humanistic order of government. Nor was it, strictly and accurately speaking, a mere republic. Sovereignty was centered, first, in God, second, in the people under God's law. The American order was a government based on the law of God, primarily in Scripture and, also, in Nature. It was a theo-republic, or a representative theodemocracy. Having repudiated monarchy by appealing to Scripture, Thomas Paine wrote in *Common Sense*, "Where, say some, is the king of America? I'll tell you, friend, he reigns above and does not make havoc of mankind like the Royal Brute of Great Britain. Yet that we may not appear to be defective even in earthly honors, let a day be solemnly set apart for proclaiming the Charter. Let it be brought forth placed on the divine law, the Word of God. Let a crown be placed thereon, by which the world may know, that so far as we approve of monarchy, that in America THE LAW IS KING."

Liberal minds who gave birth to free society and government insisted that their democratic theory was subject to a fundamental law that the people had "no power to change." God's law of liberty, justice, and individual rights, not merely the representative principle of government, was fundamental. Such a view of democracy was "far from any believe in parliamentary sovereignty," and it "assumed constitutionalism" as a "natural consequence" of their liberal view of life and society. The basic reason had to do with the nature and influence of the inner forces that gave birth to liberal Puritan thought. From these elements, a societal concept—a soul-set more than a mind-set, though it included the latter—arose that was "fundamentally federal" in nature. Indeed, federalism describes the "system of theology" that came to full bloom in New England. Given this essential nature, it followed that a federal government had to "have a constitution." And based on their experience with the spiritual power of the Word, liberal minds in mid-seventeenth-century England solved the problem of "the relation between religious and political organizations" by limiting the scope and power of each. This was done by "limiting, by constitutional instrument, the sphere of the political body."

As the new order of society started to rise on the western hemisphere, Americans looked upon the continent as an asylum for afflicted people in all parts of Europe, who began to grasp the ideas of liberty, justice, and equality that emerged from the Revolution of Life and Liberty. Thomas Paine perceived the great scenario to be the central feature of God's design in the world. Arguing that the "blood of the slain" in the rise of liberty and the "weeping voice of nature cries 'TIS TIME TO PART"—to separate from England, he reasoned in *Common Sense*: "The time...at which the continent was discovered adds weight to the argument, and the manner in which it was peopled increases the force of it. The Reformation was preceded by the discovery of America, as if the Almighty graciously meant to open a sanctuary to the persecuted in future years, when home should afford neither friendship nor safety." Having argued that the Almighty "implanted in us" the desire for the vital elements of true Christian society—truth, liberty, justice, etc.—that emerged and were planted in America, Paine exclaimed, "O ye that love mankind! Ye that dare oppose not only tyranny but the tyrant, stand forth! Every spot of the Old World is overrun with oppression. Freedom has been hunted round the globe. Asia and Africa have long expelled her. Europe regards her like a stranger, and England has given her warning to depart. O receive the fugitive and prepare in time an asylum for mankind." The idea of asylum was part of America from the beginning, rooted in a sense of divine providence and God's order of things for mankind as revealed in the Bible. "The new world," said Paine, "has been the asylum for the persecuted lovers of civil and religious liberty from every part of Europe. Hither have they fled, not from the tender embraces of the mother but from the cruelty of the monster. And it is so far true of England, that the same tyranny which drove the first emigrants from home pursues their descendants still." The appeal was to nationalize, not only the liberty and justice but the compassion of Christ.

"Faith gives a man fellowship in the Invisible Church," said John Cotton of this central fact, "and in all the inward spiritual blessings of the Church."

The Role of the American Clergy

Quite naturally, the power of the Bible Revolution—the Revolution of Life and Liberty—was reflected in the role American clergymen played in society and government, especially in New England from the beginning of colonial times. Liberal Puritans in England and America gave birth to the spirit, principles and forms of liberty, while men like Roger Williams, Thomas Hooker, and William Penn did much to establish American governmental theory on a liberal foundation. Should not the clergy, therefore, be involved in cradling the infant which was coming to birth by the genius of the biblical spirit and principles?

Before, during, and after the American Revolution, Smylie explains, Congregational, Presbyterian, and Baptist clergymen were "deeply…involved in American political life," as well as many Anglican clergymen. The American clergy comprised one of the most influential—if not the most influential—groups, in the colonies in the period leading up to the revolution and the establishment of the United States Constitution. "Practically all the Puritan clergy had been educated at Harvard or Yale," says Cole, "the most influential of them having their master's or doctor's degree." Being as a general rule the best educated person in his community, the minister exercised leadership over its elementary school and fostered interest in higher education, and members of the clergy "superintended the education of many of the nation's leaders in colleges spread across the country." Institutions of higher learning over which ministers presided included Harvard, Yale, Queen's College, College of New Jersey (now Princeton), William and Mary, and Hampden-Sydney College in Virginia. "Practically to a man, these educators were sympathetic to the American cause during the revolution."

As intellectual leaders, many clergymen were close friends, confidants, and associates of the American Founders. John Adams ranked Jonathan Mayhew equal with James Otis and Samuel Adams as a patriot statesman. Mayhew, also a friend of Otis and Samuel Adams, is credited with suggesting to Otis the idea of Committees of Correspondence that played a vital role in the revolution. The Reverend Samuel Cooper, elected president of Harvard in 1774, was a close friend of Benjamin Franklin, John and Samuel Adams, John Hancock, and George Washington. The Reverend William Smith of Weymouth was the father-in-law of John Adams. And Charles Chauncey of Boston, a highly influential force in the cause of independence, was a friend of John and Samuel Adams and other revolutionary leaders. Thus, the idea that the writers of the United States Constitution were isolated from the religious thought and climate of the day and that they found primary sources in the writings of ancient philosophers for doctrines that were commonplace, indeed hackneyed, in their own country is wholly false and unacceptable. To the contrary, Ahlstrom observes that "the Declaration of Independence is almost a theological document," and that "patriotic idealism in the United States, as well as the prevailing rationale for democratic institutions, has always been invested with elements of enlightened religion—whether with the Federalist accents of John Adams or the Republicanism of Jefferson."

The clergy made an important contribution by building a foundation for the American Revolution. As early as about 1633 in Massachusetts and 1674 in Connecticut, the practice arose of having a prominent minister preach a sermon at each election. On such occasions, political topics were discussed in their natural biblical setting within the Puritan tradition, with distinct scriptural flavor. This practice, when viewed within the Puritan experience, seems not to have been a mere adjunct to the political process, but a natural outgrowth of the Puritan experience, where the principle of private and public virtue, the doctrine of higher law, the spirit and principle of Christian liberty, the idea of right reason, the concept of unalienable rights, and the congregational principle of consent that had their origin largely in the New Testament were transferred to the political sphere and applied to create a new order of political thought. To the Puritan fathers (especially to liberal minds), the root elements—the religio-spiritual elements leading to human dignity and responsible liberty under God—underlying all these principles and concepts were more basic and fundamental than the external or practical principles that they had extended from the religious and ecclesiastical to the political sphere. This gave knowledgeable ministers grounds to offer sage counsel, in theory and admonition, as a means of keeping political ideology and practice pure and properly grounded. The practice of Election sermons was simply the Puritan way of reminding the political child to which it gave birth of its true place, purpose, and responsibilities under God.

The basic idea was grounded in the Puritan view that all law centers in God, and this was also true for liberal Puritans in the separatist tradition, who wanted to separate the church (as a body of spiritually regenerated people) from the state. But the state too was subject to divine law, which governed it in its sphere. Religious authorities had the responsibility to teach and admonish the people in their religious, spiritual, and ecclesiastical duties. And by means of the Election sermon, political figures were reminded of the principles of their civil faith that was grounded in the moral and ethical principles of the Bible and the civil law found therein.

Year after year, these sermons were delivered before the governor, assembly, and other public officers. Frequently, they were printed and discussed throughout the country, often from the pulpit by local ministers. William Gordon, a historian contemporary with the American Revolution, explained that the participating clergymen being mostly from the congregational order were for that reason "more attached and habituated to the principles of liberty than if they had spiritual superiors to lord it over them, and were in hopes of possessing, in their turn, through the gift of government, the seat of power." Of their teachings and their influence, he said, "They oppose arbitrary rule in civil concerns from the love of freedom, as well as from a desire of guarding against its introduction into religious matters. The patriots, for years back, have availed themselves greatly of their assistance... As the patriots have prevailed, the preachers of each sermon have been the zealous friends of liberty; and the passages most adapted to promote the spread and love of it have been selected and circulated far and wide by means of newspapers, and read with avidity and a degree of veneration on account of the preacher and his election to the service of the day."

In Baldwin's *The New England Clergy and the American Revolution*, where she analyzed the contents of the Elections sermons of New England ministers, she describes the intimate relationship of the clergy to the thought and life of eighteenth-century America. Consistent with the emphasis many clergymen placed on the role of Israel in the economy of God, some Election sermons "discussed the government of the ancient Hebrews and its excellency." Many sermons were "theoretical, concerned with the origin and the end of government." And some dealt "more particularly with their own charters and the dearly won rights of Englishmen." The diaries, letters, and pamphlets of New England ministers, as well as their sermons, reveal that the primary source of their beliefs was the Bible. "The New Testament," Baldwin reports, "gave authority for the liberties of Christians, for the relation of Christians to those in authority over them, and for the right of resistance." "Systematically, the clergy called for the overthrow of tyrants who subverted the liberty of the people. Many, such as Samuel Cook of Arlington (a friend of some of the Founders), emphasized the right derived from their Saxon-Israel heritage to limit the power of rulers. As early as 1750, Jonathan Mayhew courageously repudiated the doctrine of unlimited submission and nonresistance to political power, showing clearly that tyranny in any form was contrary to the laws of God, and in his Election sermon of 1763, he described true love of liberty and true love of religion as being synonymous. Consistent with the fact that the spirit of American liberty originated among liberal elements of seventeenth-century Puritanism, he and other New England clergymen were convinced that civil liberty was a direct outgrowth of religious faith. In the gospel of Christ, as the apostle James had written, one could find "the perfect law of liberty." Taking his cue from the biblical declaration that "where the Spirit of the Lord is, there is liberty," and that Christians are truly "called unto liberty," the Reverend B. Stevens declared in his Election sermon of 1761, "Liberty both civil and religious is the spirit and genius of the sacred writings."

In his study of the American clergy during the period the United States Constitution was written and adopted, Smylie deals with the authorities they cited on political thought. "The men hailed as greatest and cited most often," he reports, "were Newton, Locke, and Montesquieu." Nevertheless, they "rested the case for their political opinions and decisions, not simply upon the political writers with whom they were acquainted in some way, but upon the three keys of political knowledge: reason, revelation, and experience." Says Smylie, "The Bible was the most important single source of political knowledge cited, and as such, it must be included seriously and integrally in any analysis of clerical thought." This was consistent with Baldwin's findings that there was an unmistakable similarity "of Puritan theology and fundamental political thought." In all this, "the New England clergy preserved, extended, and popularized the essential doctrines of political philosophy, thus making familiar to every churchgoing New Englander long before 1763, not only the doctrines of natural rights, the social contract, and the right of resistance but also the fundamental principle of American constitutional law that government, like its citizens, is bounded by law, and when it transcends its authority, it acts illegally." Using Baldwin's study as a basis of his statement, Sweet stated, "In these sermons...the whole political philosophy of the American Revolution is set forth many years before the opening of the war. They preached the doctrine of Civil Liberty as taught by Sidney, Locke, and Milton. Civil government, they claimed, was of divine origin; rulers were God's delegates and derived their power from Him, not directly but through the people. They emphasized fundamental law and its binding quality. God and Christ, they claimed, always governed by fixed rules, by a divine constitution. There are certain great rights given us by nature and nature's God, and no rulers may violate those rights; and rulers as well as people are strictly limited by law. Thus the Congregational ministers 'gave to the cause of the colonies all that they could give of the sanction of religion.'"

Clerical advocacy continued through the Revolutionary and Constitutional eras, including clergymen who presided over institutions of higher learning. "Practically to a man," the clergy, having been patriotic propagandists before hostilities began, "remained ardent supporters of the American cause as citizens or chaplains during the conflict." This was true especially of Congregational, Baptist, and Presbyterian clergymen. If the principles embodied in the Declaration of Independence had become commonplace among the people by 1776, the American clergy must be given primary credit. The principles and ideals of freedom and resistance to tyranny did not come to the average American by a direct route from ancient or contemporary philosophers of the Old World but substantially from the American pulpit and from domestic experience. It is unthinkable to suppose that the American Founders, who, after all, were fully integrated into a society where religion was predominant, were not knowingly or unknowingly influenced, and singularly so, by the religious climate in which they most all grew to manhood. "Even the technically nonsectarian College of Philadelphia, founded by Franklin," Ketcham insisted, "gave its students the usual training in Christian morality and was presided over by a zealous Anglican minister."

The Relevance of Biblical Christian Origins

This book focuses on the causative factors and forces that produced a distinct kind of people, society, and republicanism in the New World. The American Founders, as an example, are without peer in modern history, in political talents, goodness, and commitment to public interest. And James Madison wrote, "They accomplished a revolution which has no parallel in the annals of human society. They reared the fabrics of [state and federal] governments which have no model on the face of the globe"? These were distinct monumental achievements. "How did it happen," asks Henry Steele Commager, "that every major political and constitutional institution which we now have was invented before the year 1800, and that not one of comparable importance has been invented since?" Again, "how did it happen that two young men [John Jay and Alexander Hamilton] in their thirties [with the occasional assistance of an old man (James Madison) in his forties!] were able to dash off, in the midst of exacting political duties, eighty-five *Federalist Papers*, probably the greatest political treatise since Montesquieu, while the thousands of highly trained scholars at two-score advanced institutions of government today have produced nothing comparable?"

Commager suggests only partial explanations which, with his probing questions, imply that, since the time of the Founders, Americans have neither clearly understood nor built substantially on their tradition of liberty under God. Conclusive evidence presented in this and other studies that are cited make it clear that answers to the questions of origin lie primarily in the religio-spiritual realm, not merely in the intellectual or ideological spheres. Early Americans had more than a distinct ideological mind-set; whether churched or unchurched, many had a vital soul-set. Based on historical studies and evidence, the central thesis of this volume is that religio-spiritual factors centering in Christ gave birth to the ecclesiastical and political principles and forms that the colonists espoused, and that the combined spiritual and ideological thrust played the dominant role in producing the American systems of church, society, and state on the basis of a reactivated Anglo-Saxon heritage. This vital reform Christian foundation was largely lost to the country after the passing of the Founding Fathers. They were a rare breed, and their rarity consists not fundamentally in their political ideology and philosophy but in the degree to which enlivening religio-spiritual elements, extending back to liberal Puritan roots and beyond to Christ were the basis of their lives and thought.

Not only did America's Founding Fathers produce the institutions of American freedom, but they also initiated a unique revolution of limited violence, the philosophy and goals of which were not betrayed in the events that followed. Theirs was a special kind of dissent and revolution that can be understood only in light of the religio-spiritual elements that emerged in the Puritan Revolution more than a hundred years earlier. "Above all," wrote University of North Carolina Professor of History Don Higginbotham, "the revolutionists were constructive statesmen; they were not haters and negativists." Nor were they "guerrilla chieftains." "If they broke up a relationship characterized by colonialism and monarchy, this was about the extent of their destructive activity." "We cannot fail to see," said Robert Nisbet, "the restraint, responsibility, and wisdom of such men as John Adams, Jefferson, Madison, Dickinson, Franklin, Hamilton, and others, and I would not for a minute dismiss the importance of this factor. It is crucial."

Commager calls the American episode "a constructive revolution," and, noting that restraint marked the disturbances which occurred between 1765 and 1775, Higginbotham observes, "Violence and intimidation were usually confined to specific objects and carried out with no bloodshed." Says Kristol, "This was a revolution which, unlike all subsequent revolutions, did not devour its children: the men who made the revolution were the men who went on to create the new political order, who then held the highest elected positions in this order, and who all died in bed." Moreover, Kristol concludes, "Alone among the revolutions of modernity, the American Revolution did not give rise to the pathetic and poignant myth of 'the revolution betrayed.' It spawned no literature of disillusionment; it left behind no grand hopes frustrated, no grand expectations unsatisfied, no grand illusions shattered."

To see such a revolution in light of its religio-spiritual roots and still call it a humanistic or secular affair is ignoramus to the ninth degree.

CHAPTER 7

The American Christian Israel

"I felt on his death with my countrymen," Jefferson said of Washington's passing, "that 'verily a great man has fallen this day in Israel.'" The idea prevailed that the new nation on the western hemisphere was an American Israel, and that its life, society, and political law were based on biblical principles and images. When Ephraim and Manasseh—sons of the ancient patriarch Joseph—were given separate tribal status in the biblical kingdom of Israel, the number of its tribes was increased to thirteen. Similarly, modern Israel left spiritual and temporal bondage to form thirteen colonies in the New World, and the formation of the American Israel was consummated when the federal constitution united the thirteen original American states into a common union. The basic moral order that many early Americans envisioned and the idea of the general welfare that incorporated the principles of private and public virtue, covenant, consent, individual rights, etc. was the foundation of the American Israel. It was "'a due form of government' that was as close to the example of Mosaic Israel as circumstances would allow," and many early Americans saw their polity as collectively "in covenant with the Lord for a special corporate task in the world."

Bible-reading Americans saw ancient Israel as a rudimentary type of free society and government, with the greater ideal being a true Christian Israel. As the Spirit of Christ, as the spirit of liberty, and New Testament principles, concepts and societal forms were developed, many liberal minds came to view the Old Testament, or old covenant, as capable of being transformed and perfected by the power of Christ's Gospel to become the new covenant that Paul said was "written, not with ink, but with the Spirit of the living God" and "not in tables of stone but in fleshy tables of the heart." This view was not a denial but a fulfillment of the old covenant and an upgrading of it to the higher spiritual plane of Christ's Gospel, which gave the people much greater liberty in the Son of God, with a more perfect free and open union in him. The federation that God gave to ancient Israel through Moses was a rudimentary form of the greater religio-spiritual religious and political covenant they hoped for in Christ. And within this envisioned relationship, liberal minds, such as Jefferson and Franklin, drew on the Old Testament for "examples and patterns to a much greater degree than was customary for writers such as Calvin." The result was the idea of an American Christian Israel.

Many American clergymen were deeply involved in developing social and political institutions in the New World. At times, they spoke in generalities of the American Israel. But more often, they selected illustrative texts that described specific incidents in which the God of Israel delivered his ancient people from dangers, "similar to those from which he…delivered America." Looking with hope to the future, the eighty-four-year-old Increase Mather stated in the foreword of *Elijah's Mantle* (1722), "If it may please God to incline the hearts of the rising generation to continue in those right ways of the Lord wherein their fathers walked before him, this will be such a happy sign and token that he will be with us as he was with them and will not leave us nor forsake us, as all that wish well to our ISRAEL will greatly rejoice in."

The image of the American Israel was also applied in the Revolutionary War and to its results. In his fiery tract, *Common Sense*, Thomas Paine bluntly declared that he "rejected the hardened, sullen-tempered Pharaoh of England." Such metaphor was based on the idea of an American Israel in bondage. "The Lord, the God of this American Israel," recalled John Marsh, "strengthened us in our weak, feeble and unproved condition." In *A Memorial of the Lexington Battle, and of Some Signal Interpositions of Providence in the American Revolution*, Samuel Phillips Payson wrote, "The finger of God has indeed been so conspicuous in every stage of our glorious struggle that it seems as if the wonders and miracles performed for Israel of old were repeated over anew for the American Israel in our day. The hardness that possessed the heart of Pharaoh of old seems to have calloused the heart of the British king; and the madness that drove that ancient tyrant and his hosts into the sea appears to have possessed the British court and councils, and to have driven them and their forces to measures that, in human view, must terminate in their own confusion and ruin." Speaking of opposition raised against America in the war, Rozel Cook said, "So far, God suffered the wrath of our enemies to rise, and so far, their wrath shall praise him, by laying a foundation for the display of his power and goodness, in shielding and defending his American Israel." And of the outcome of the revolution, George Duffield declared, "The earth has indeed brought forth, as in a day. A nation has indeed been born, as at once... Almost as soon as our American Zion began to travail; and without experiencing the pangs and pains that apprehensive fear expected, she brought forth her children, more numerous than the tribes of Jacob, to possess the land."

Bible-reading colonists saw an example of free government under God in the federation Moses set up in ancient Israel, which markedly differed in popular principles from other systems. Though monarchy was supreme in Egypt where Moses grew to manhood, he established a system of divine law under judges who were ratified by the people.[12] This earliest known order of popular government, based on the principle of consent, continued for nearly five hundred years before it was replaced by a system of kings that eventually brought on national ruin. In the Israelite federation, judges served the interests of the people, who could appeal hard cases to a chief judge. Being divinely endowed, these public officials were charged with the task of upholding liberty and justice and adjudicating conflicts among the people by the standard of God's law.

The republican order was suggested to Moses by his father-in-law, Jethro, who said of the people, "You shall teach them ordinances and laws, and shall show them the way in which they must walk, and the work that they must do. Moreover, you shalt provide out of all the people able men, such as fear God, men of truth, hating covetousness; and place such over them... And let them judge the people at all seasons: and it shall be that every great matter they shall bring unto you, but every small matter they shall judge." Moses, therefore, stated to Israel, "How can I alone bear your cumbrance, and your burden, and your strife? Take you wise men, and understanding, and known among your tribes, and I will make them rulers over you." The ancient lawgiver later said, "I took the chief of your tribes, wise men, and known, and made them heads...and officers among your tribes. And I charged your judges at that time, saying, hear the causes between your brethren, and judge righteously between every man and his brother, and the stranger that is with him." Moses emphasized, "You shall not respect persons in judgment, but you shall hear the small as well as the great. You shall not be afraid of the face of man, for the judgment is God's: and the cause that is too hard for you, bring it unto me, and I will hear it." Judges had no right to be partial, for only God had the right to judge, and they were but instruments of his will.

The Israelites had a representative government, under God, in which they freely sustained divine law and counsel. The "men of Judah" anointed David to be their king. Later, "all the congregation" made Solomon king. When Solomon's son, Rehoboam, threatened arbitrary rule, the northern tribes rejected him. The Israelite commonwealth forbade all caste and class distinctions; and the people, as individuals, were held to be equal before the law. The system avoided ecclesiastical aristocracy by making the priesthood dependent on voluntary contributions from the people. In the Israelite code of justice, reparation was made to the victim, not in fines paid to the state. But for first-degree murder, where the willful offender could not give "satisfaction," the penalty was death.

When worldly pride crept in, the ancient Israelites finally tired of their system of liberty and chose to be ruled by kings. Many centuries later, the scriptural record of their fateful decision had a powerful influence on the American mind in the years leading to the American Revolution. Thomas Paine made much of it in *Common Sense*, which was published as an appeal for separation from England early in 1776 and was credited by Washington with having "worked a powerful change in the minds of many men." The tract "literally propelled America into the revolution."

"Government by kings," Paine charged in his argument against George III, "was first introduced into the world by the heathens, from whom the children of Israel copied the custom." The original political system of Israel "was a kind of republic, administered by a judge and the elders of the tribes. Kings they had none, and it was held sinful to acknowledge any being under that title but the Lord of Hosts." But Paine explained, "Laying hold of the misconduct of Samuel's two sons who were entrusted with some secular concerns, they came in an abrupt and clamorous manner to Samuel, saying, 'Behold thou art old, and thy sons walk not in thy ways, now make us a king to judge us like all the other nations.'" Said Paine, "Here we cannot but observe that their motives were bad, viz. that they might be like unto other nations [i.e., the heathens], whereas their true glory lay in being as much unlike them as possible."

The request caused Samuel to seek counsel from God. Paine continued, "And the Lord said unto Samuel, 'Hearken unto the voice of the people in all that they say unto thee, for they have not rejected thee, but they have rejected me, THAT I SHOULD NOT REIGN OVER THEM. According to all the works which they have done since the day that I brought them up out of Egypt even unto this day, wherewith they have forsaken me, and served other Gods: so do they also unto thee. Now therefore, hearken unto their voice. Howbeit, protest solemnly unto them and show them the manner of the king that shall reign over them.'"

The Lord, Paine explained, did not speak of "any particular king but the general manner of the kings of the earth whom Israel was so eagerly copying after." "And," he added, "notwithstanding the great distance of time and difference of manners, the character is still in fashion."

Returning to the biblical text while interpolating his views parenthetically, Paine quoted, "Samuel told all the words of the lord unto the people that asked of him a king. And he said, 'This shall be the manner of the king that shall reign over you. He will take your sons and appoint them for himself for his chariots and to be his horsemen, and some shall run before his chariots [this description agrees with the present mode of impressing men], and he will appoint them captains over thousands and captains over fifties, will set them to ear his ground and to reap his harvest, and to make his instruments of war and instruments of his chariots. And he will take your daughters to be confectionaries, and to be cooks, and to be bakers [this describes the expense and luxury as well as the oppression of kings], and he will take your fields and your vineyards, and your olive yards, even the best of them, and give them to his servants. And he will take the tenth of your seed, and of your vineyards, and give them to his officers and his servants [by which we see that bribery, corruption, and favoritism are the standing vices of kings], and he will take the tenth of your men servants, and your maid servants, and your goodliest young men, and your asses, and put them to his work: and he will take the tenth of your sheep, and ye shall be his servants, and ye shall cry out in that day because of your king which ye shall have chosen, AND THE LORD WILL NOT HEAR YOU IN THAT DAY.'"

Paine reasoned, "This accounts for the continuation of monarchy. Neither do the characters of the few good kings which have lived since either sanctify the title or blot out the sinfulness of the origin. The high encomium given to David takes no notice of him officially as a king, but only as a man after God's own heart."

Yet Paine reported, citing the biblical text, "The people refused to obey the voice of Samuel, and they said, 'Nay but we will have a king over us, that we may be like all the nations, and that our king may judge us, and go out before us and fight our battles.'" So a monarchy replaced the system of judges in ancient Israel, and later, generations were left to ponder the warning of the prophet Samuel.

Paine was not content with this recitation of the evils of monarchy and the role the Bible played in revealing correct views on political economy. Having installed Saul as the first king of Israel, Paine wrote, the prophet Samuel continued to reason with the Israelites, "but to no purpose. He set before them their ingratitude, but all would not avail. And seeing them fully bent on their folly, he cried out, 'I will call unto the Lord, and he shall send thunder and rain [which was then a punishment, being in the time of wheat harvest] that you may perceive and see that your wickedness is great which you have done in the sight of the Lord IN ASKING YOU A KING. So Samuel called unto the Lord, and the Lord sent thunder and rain that day, and all the people greatly feared the Lord and Samuel. And all the people said unto Samuel, 'Pray for thy servants unto the Lord thy God that we die not, for WE HAVE ADDED UNTO OUR SINS THIS EVIL, TO ASK A KING.'"

The evidence was clear. "These portions of scripture are direct and positive," Paine emphasized in his charge against George III. "They admit of no equivocal construction. That the Almighty has here entered his protest against monarchical government is true, or the scripture is false."

To the evil of monarchy was added that of "hereditary succession." The first, said Paine, was "a degradation and lessening of ourselves," and the second was "an insult and imposition on posterity." It was the case of parents saying to given person, "Your children and your children's children shall reign over ours forever." Said Paine, "One of the strongest natural proofs of the folly of hereditary right in kings is that nature disapproves it; otherwise, she would not so frequently turn it into ridicule by giving mankind an ass for a lion."

Paine again turned to the Bible for arguments against the hereditary succession of kings. When the Israelite judge Gideon routed the oppressing Midianites, his fellow Israelites, elated with his success, proposed to make him their king, saying, "Rule thou over us, thou and thy son, and thy son's son." Said Paine, "Here was temptation in its fullest extent; not a kingdom only, but a hereditary one." But with true piety, Gideon replied, "I shall not rule over you, neither shall my son rule over you. THE LORD SHALL RULE OVER YOU." Said Paine, "Words need not be more explicit. Gideon does not decline the honor but denied their right to give it. Neither does he compliment them with invented declarations of his thanks, but in the positive style of a prophet charges them with disaffection to their proper sovereign, the king of heaven."

With knowledge of ancient Israel's theo-republic and of the subsequent activities of her kings, as well as the example of English kings, it was little wonder that Washington refused to be king over the American Israel. The Founders of the new nation consistently set up a system of law under God as their form of government. And following the precedent of the early Israelites, they placed the supreme court, with its judges, to determine law and to be the final appellate body, superior in this function to the president and his Cabinet, the Senate and Congress, and the military order of the nation.

Franklin and Jefferson made clear their view that the new nation was God's American Israel by proposing that scenes from Israelite history be portrayed on the Great Seal of the United States of America. Franklin proposed a scene depicting God's great intervention for Israel at the Red Sea. Jefferson described the scene: "Pharaoh sitting in an open chariot, a crown on his head and a sword in his hand passing through the divided waters of the Red Sea in pursuit of the Israelites: rays from a pillar of fire in the cloud, expressive of the divine presence and command, reaching to Moses who stands on the shore and, extending his hand over the sea, causes it to overwhelm Pharaoh." Franklin suggested the caption, "Rebellion to tyrants is obedience to God," to be engraved under the scene.

Jefferson based his proposal for the Great Seal on another important aspect of Israelite history, with a scene from America's Saxon heritage for the reverse side. In a letter to his wife, Abigail, John Adams wrote, "Mr. Jefferson proposed the children of Israel in the wilderness, led by a cloud by day and a pillar of fire by night." "On the other side," Adams continued, "Hengist and Horsa, the Saxon chiefs, from whom we claim the honor of being descended, and whose political principles and form of government we have assumed. "That Jefferson was deeply sincere in his proposal is evident from his second inaugural address [March 4, 1805], where he supplicated the aid of "that Being...who led our forefathers, as Israel of old, from their native land, and planted" them in the New World.

The learned Ezra Stiles saw America as a fulfillment of Moses' vision of Israel in the last days. "Taught by the omniscient Deity," Stiles began his Election sermon on the future glory of the United States, "Moses foresaw and predicted the capital events relative to Israel, through the successive changes of depression and glory, until their final elevation to the first dignity and eminence among the empires of the world." This was the millennial kingdom of Christ that Stiles and many contemporaries held the American order of liberty would help introduce on earth.

Stiles briefly reviewed Moses's prophetic vision from ancient to modern times with its predictions of a mighty latter-day kingdom of Israel. This Stiles did as a basis for his discussion of "the political welfare of God's American Israel and…allusively prophetic of the further prosperity and splendor of the United States," as the precursor of the peaceful kingdom of Jesus Christ.

Of Moses's vision of Israel, the learned president of Yale College said, "He foresaw, indeed, their rejection of God and predicted the judicial chastisement of apostasy—a chastisement involving the righteous with the wicked. But, as well to comfort and support the righteous in every age, and under every calamity, as to make his power known among all nations, God determined that a remnant should be saved." Accordingly, "Moses and the prophets, by divine direction, interspersed their writings with promises that when the ends of God's moral government should be answered in a series of national punishments, inflicted for a succession of ages, he would, by his irresistible power and sovereign grace, subdue the hearts of his people to a free, willing, joyful obedience; turn their captivity; recover and gather them 'from all the nations whither the Lord had scattered them in his fierce anger; bring them into the land that their fathers possessed; and multiply them above their fathers, and rejoice over them for good, as he rejoiced over their fathers.'"

Speaking of "God's American Israel," Stiles explained, "Then the words of Moses, hitherto accomplished but in part, will be literally fulfilled, when this branch of the posterity of Abraham shall be nationally collected, and become a very distinguished and glorious people, under the great Messiah, the Prince of Peace. He will then 'make them high above all nations that he has made, in praise, and in name, and in honor, and they shall become a holy people unto the Lord their God.'"

On this premise, Stiles proposed to consider the reasons that made it "probable that the United States will, by the ordering of heaven, eventually become this people." Since America was Christian Israel, he anticipated that they could "expect that, by the blessing of God, these states may prosper and flourish into a great American Republic and ascend into high and distinguished honor among the nations of the earth."

Not only was America Christian Israel, but the newborn nation was the birthright son, Joseph, who was cast out and sold by his brethren into Egyptian bondage but rose to be a savior to his father's family. The patriarch Joseph's life and the prophecies concerning him were aptly fulfilled in America. "Who can tell how extensive a blessing this American Joseph may become to the whole human race," Stiles exclaimed, "although one despised by his brethren, exiled, and sold into Egypt? How applicable that in Genesis 49:22, 26 [it states]: 'Joseph is a fruitful bough, even a fruitful bough by a well; whose branches run over the wall. The archers have sorely grieved him and shot at him and hated him. But his bow abode in strength; the arms of his hands were made strong by the arms of the mighty God of Jacob.'" "The blessings of your father," Jacob said of himself to Joseph, "have prevailed above the blessings of my progenitors [that is, Abraham and Isaac, who were given the land of Palestine for an inheritance] unto the utmost bound of the everlasting hills [that is, the land with hills and mountains extending interminably from the north to the south pole]: they shall be on the head of Joseph, and on the crown of the head of him that was separated from his brethren."

Modern Joseph as a branch of Israel run over the wall into the land of the everlasting hills would finally be revealed to the world in a true light. "Little would civilians have thought ages ago," Stiles continued, "that the world should ever look to America for models of government and polity. Little did they think of finding this most perfect polity among the poor outcasts, the contemptible people of New England, and particularly in the long despised civil polity of

Connecticut—a polity conceived by the sagacity and wisdom of a Winthrop, a Ludlow, Haynes, Hopkins, Hooker, and the other first settlers of Hartford, in 1636." And relying on the principle of progressive insight into the meaning and the fulfillment of Scripture that liberal reformers espoused in earlier generations, Stiles continued, "While Europe and Asia may hereafter learn that the most liberal principles of law and civil polity are to be found on this side of the Atlantic, they may also find the true religion here depurated from the rust and corruption of ages and learn from us to reform and restore the church to its primitive purity. It will be long before the ecclesiastical pride of the splendid European hierarchies can submit to learn wisdom from those whom they have been inured to look upon with sovereign contempt. But candid and liberal disquisition will, sooner or later, have a great effect. Removed from the embarrassments of corrupt systems, and the dignities and blinding opulence connected with them, the unfettered mind can think with a noble enlargement, and, with an unbounded freedom, go wherever the light of truth directs." Stiles, therefore, suggested, "Religion may here receive its last, most liberal, and impartial examination."

John Hancock wrote after the Boston Massacre, in *The Tremendous Bar of God*, "Surely you will never tamely suffer this country to be a den of thieves. Remember, my friends, from whom you sprang. Let not a meanness of spirit, unknown to those whom you boast as your fathers, excite a thought to the dishonor of your mothers. I conjure you, by all that is dear, by all that is honorable, by all that is sacred, not only that ye pray, but that ye act, that, if necessary, ye fight, and even die, for the prosperity of our Jerusalem. Break in sunder, with noble disdain, the bonds with which the Philistines have bound you."

CHAPTER 8

The Idea of American Republicanism

The American Spirit of Free Christian Society

Based on the democratic principles that Separatists took from the New Testament Church and extended to the state as early as 1582, the new order of free Christian society and government that emerged in America came from two major sources. They were, says A. D. Lindsay, first, the spirit and principles of democracy that arose with the separatist movement, on the basis of which advance English and American Reformers originally gave birth to liberty in the first half of the seventeenth century; and, second, the social changes produced by the Industrial Revolution, which studies by Max Weber, R. H. Tawney, and others clearly demonstrate emerged in the West by the influence of religio-spiritual elements coming from the Bible.

Nowhere are the character and power of these basic life- and liberty-giving elements more clearly revealed in their various effects and ramifications than in America. "On my arrival in the United States," Tocqueville wrote, "the religious aspect of the country was the first thing that struck my attention, and the longer I stayed there, the more I perceived the great political consequences resulting from this new state of things." Said the noted Frenchman of the American colonists, "They brought with them into the New World a form of Christianity which I cannot better describe than by styling it a democratic and republican religion. This contributed powerfully to the establishment of a republic and a democracy in public affair; and from the beginning, politics and religion contracted an alliance which has never been dissolved."

Tocqueville compared the unique society he saw in America with that in his own land. "In France," he said, "I had almost always seen the spirit of religion and the spirit of freedom marching in opposite directions. But in America, I found they were intimately united and that they reigned in common over the same country." This was not to say that religious influence was exerted directly "on the laws and...details of public opinion." Instead, Tocqueville explained, "it directs the customs of the community, and, by regulating domestic life, it regulates the state."

Advance Reformers in America saw their faith in Christ and the spirit, principles, and societal forms they took from the New Testament as the basis of their life and society and of the revolutionary movement in which they were participants. To the Pilgrim leader William Bradford, the overthrow of the Anglican bishops and of King Charles I in the English Civil Wars was "the Lord's doing." While Bradford gave credit to liberal Puritan reformers, ultimate credit went to Christ," he that sits on the white horse, who is called faithful and true, and judges and fights righteously (Rev. 19:11)." This was he "whose garments are dipped in blood," said Bradford, "and his name was called the Word of God, for he shall rule with a rod of iron."

In the context of the progressing Revolution of Life and Liberty in America, John Adams wrote to Jefferson, "I think with you that it is difficult to say at what moment the [American] Revolution began. In my opinion, it began as early as the first plantation of the country. Independence of church and parliament was a fixed principle of our predecessors in 1620, as it was of Samuel Adams and Christopher Gadsen, in 1776... The hierarchy and parliamentary authority ever were dreaded and detested even by a majority of professed Episcopalians." In America, even Anglican colonists partook of the basic spirit of liberty and independence.

The rise of free society from the Revolution of Life and Liberty implied that before there could be a lasting republican form of government, there had to be a republican populace. And before there could be a republican populace, there had to be a republican ideology, which, in turn, had to be accompanied by a republican spirit as an expression of deep feelings and sentiments in the lives of spiritually enlivened Christians. John Wise, thus, wrote that man's liberty "under the conduct or right reason," being equal with his trust, could be "considered, internally as to his mind, and externally as to his person." The first implied "a faculty of doing or omitting things according to the direction of his judgment," not "an unbounded license of acting" but freedom "guided and restrained by the ties of reason and laws of nature." As for the second, said Wise, "Every man must be conceived to be perfectly in his own power and disposal, and not to be controlled by the authority of any other" but to judge for himself "what shall be most for his…happiness and well-being."

A restless energy and drive in economic enterprise, an inquisitiveness toward life and the natural world, a desire for equality and open union in covenant and contractual relationships—all these characterized life in British America. A strong "spirit of levelism," says Odegard and Helmes, made war against older aristocratic forms of society that had gained a foothold in the New World. The "rising spirit," Parrington explains, was expressed "in individualism." It "exalted liberty and hated tyranny—a spirit that had for its ultimate purpose the reduction of the powers of the political state."

Tocqueville called the American zeal for liberty, equality, open union, and economic enterprise a "democratic revolution" that glowed with heat and displayed a "strong spirit of independence." John Stuart Mill described it as "that go-ahead spirit; that restless, impatient eagerness for improvement in circumstances; that mobility; that shifting and fluctuating—now up, now down, now here, now there; that absence of classes and class-spirit; that jealousy of superior attainment; that want of deference for authority and leadership; that habit of bringing things to the rule and square of each man's understanding."

Emphasizing the role of the American frontier in bringing forth these traits and characteristics, Frederick Jackson Turner described the expressions of the existing revolution as "that coarseness and strength combined with acuteness and inquisitiveness; that practical inventive turn of mind, quick to find expedients; that masterful grasp of material things, lacking in the artistic but powerful to effect great ends; that restless, nervous energy; that dominant individualism working for good and evil, and with all that buoyancy and exuberance which comes from freedom."

Tocqueville concluded that equality and the desire for equality were so much the cause of the "moral and social phenomena" he witnessed in America that he characterized the ultimate ascendancy of the democratic principle as a law of nature. Turner, on the other hand, concluded that the "striking characteristics" of the new age were "traits of the frontier."

Mill discredited Tocqueville's conclusion, stating that an equality of conditions could not be "the exclusive or even the principal cause" of the dynamic American spirit. French Catholics in Lower Canada enjoyed a relative degree of equality, yet no such revolutionary spirit existed among them. The same argument discredits Turner's position on the influence of the frontier. The broad historical picture of the Revolution of Life and Liberty that extends back in the West to a time before America was colonized makes it clear that neither the quest for equality nor the frontier was the primary factor in the phenomena Tocqueville observed.

In the rise of the spirit of liberty and enterprise in America, the frontier did play an influential role. By its leveling power, each person could recognize his own importance. As the new country developed into a land of builders and producers, largely devoid of landed gentry and the idle rich, labor tended to unify rather than to divide, classes, and create social status. Freed from the aristocracy and class distinctions of the Old World, the frontier released the spirit of liberty and enterprise that early colonists brought to the New World. The harshness of the frontier developed physical strength, ruggedness, and independence in character, and the closeness of nature had a sobering, stabilizing influence on dwellers in the new land.

Finally, in the frontier setting, the colonists were able to duplicate many democratic features of England's early Saxon heritage. Some Americans, like Jefferson, idealistically compared the colonization of America to the colonization of England—by the Angles, Saxons, and Jutes—in the fifth century AD.

The British statesman Edmund Burke recognized the influence of the intangible spirit of liberty or the Revolution of Life and Liberty in America. The cause of the mounting conflict between America and England, he said in his *Speech on Conciliation with America* before the English Parliament in 1775, was that a "fierce spirit of liberty" had arisen in America. "It has grown with the growth of the people in your [that is, Parliament's] colonies," he explained, "and increased with the increase of their wealth: a spirit, that, unhappily meeting with an exercise of power in England, which, however lawful, is not reconcilable to any idea of liberty, much less with theirs, has kindled this flame that is ready to consume us."

Burke explained that this spirit of liberty was not found so much in the American people's "tenets as in their history," which was essentially that of liberal reform in the seventeenth century. During that early period, the spirit of liberty "was high," he said, and in the American immigrants, it was "the highest of all." "It is the spirit that has made the country," Burke declared. To him, the primary cause of conflict was the country's "temper and character." He observed, "In this character of the Americans, a love of freedom is the predominating feature which marks and distinguishes the whole… The fierce spirit of liberty is stronger in the English colonies, probably, than in any other people of the earth." It was not Burke's intent to commend either that spirit or the "moral causes" that produced it. But he exclaimed, "What in the name of God, shall we do with it?"

Burke identified five specific reasons for the mounting conflict between America and England. The first of these was "descent"—the nature and character of the people who went to America as English colonists. He spoke of "the stubborn spirit, attached to liberty" of their "Gothic ancestors," and declared, "An Englishman is the most unfit person on earth to argue another Englishman into slavery." To Parliament, he explained, "The colonists emigrated from you [beginning in the seventeenth century] when this part of your character was most predominant, and they took this bias and direction the moment they parted from your hands. They are, therefore, not only devoted to liberty but to liberty according to English ideas and on English principles."

Since liberty was not merely an abstract principle but inhered "in some sensible object," the great contests for freedom in England from earliest times centered chiefly in the question of taxation. "They took infinite pains," said Burke, "to inculcate, as a fundamental principle, that in all monarchies the people must in effect themselves, mediately or immediately, possess the power of granting their own money, or no shadow of liberty could subsist." The American colonists drew from England, "as with their lifeblood, these ideas and principles," and their love of liberty was "fixed and attached on this specific point of taxing."

The second reason for the American spirit of liberty was the "form of government" among the colonists, which, essentially, was a combination of congregational principles and forms taken from the teachings of Scripture, the liberal benefits of their commerce with the Holy Spirit and the congregational forms of the New Testament Church that were applied to political life, on the chassis of England's democratic Saxon heritage, which English Whigs sustained in some degree. These latter principles and forms, as shown later, were identical with (and very possibly derived from) the societal concepts and political forms that Moses set up among the ancient Israelites. Americans were convinced of the correctness of these principles, which they incorporated into "their provincial legislative assemblies." Said Burke, "Their governments are popular in an high degree:…in all, the popular representative is the most weighty; and this share of the people in their ordinary government never fails to inspire them with lofty sentiments, and with a strong aversion from whatever tends to deprive them of their chief importance."

The third reason for America's dynamic spirit of liberty was the religions of their northern provinces. "If anything were wanting to this necessary operation of the form of government," said Burke, "religion would have given it a complete effect. Religion, always a principle of energy, in this new people is no way worn out or impaired; and their mode of professing it is also one main cause of their free spirit." Here, the American spirit of liberty was an expression of a particular type of religion. "The people are Protestants," Burke emphasized, of "that kind" that was the "most adverse to all implicit submission of mind and opinion." Indeed, theirs was a persuasion, "not only favorable to liberty but built upon it."

The spread of Roman Catholicism had "generally gone hand in hand" with political systems and had "received great favor and every kind of support" from them. The Church of England had also been "formed from her cradle under the nursing care of regular government." But of early New England faiths, Burke said, "The dissenting interests have sprung up in direct opposition to all the ordinary powers of the world and could justify that opposition only on a strong claim to natural liberty." He explained, "All Protestantism, even the most cold and passive, is a sort of dissent. But the religion most prevalent in our northern colonies is a refinement of the principle of resistance: it is the dissidence of dissent, the Protestantism of the Protestant religion."

Religious dissent by people coming from countries other than England was also an important factor in the colonization of America and in giving rise to the idea of America as a great asylum for the oppressed. "Even that stream of foreigners which has been constantly flowing into these colonies," said Burke, "has, for the greatest part, been composed of dissenters from the establishment of their several countries and have brought with them a temper and character far from alien to that of the people with whom they mixed."

The fourth reason Burke identified for America's spirit of liberty was the "manners" of the people in the Southern colonies. Admixed to the "spirit of liberty" in Virginia and the Carolinas was the institution of slavery, which made zeal for liberty "more high and haughty" than among northern people. Burke called the Southern temper "the high aristocratic spirit of Virginia and the Southern colonies." Anglicanism was the predominant faith, and slavery was a determining factor molding the Southern spirit. "Where this is the case in any part of the world," Burke said of slavery, "those who are free are by far the most proud and jealous of their freedom. Freedom is to them not only an enjoyment, but a kind of rank and privilege." Thus, people in the Southern colonies were "much more strongly, and with a higher and more stubborn spirit, attached to liberty than those to the northward." "Such will be all masters of slaves," Burke concluded, "who are not slaves themselves. In such a people, the haughtiness of dominion combines with the spirit of freedom, fortifies it, and renders it invincible."

The fifth reason for America's spirit of liberty, to which reference has previously been made, was in the realm of education. This was an effect and a cause of the spirit of liberty that emerged in the seventeenth century. "Education," said Burke, "contributes no mean part towards the growth and effect of this intractable spirit." This was true in the study of law, particularly divine and natural law [the second being one expression of the first] and English Common Law.

"In no country, perhaps, in the world is the law so generally a study," said Burke. "The profession itself is numerous and powerful, and in most provinces it takes the lead." He explained, "The greater number of the deputies sent to the Congress were lawyers. But all who read, and most do read, endeavor to obtain some smattering in that science." Of the effect of legal studies, combined with the emerging spirit of liberty and sharpness of intellect derived from religio-spiritual elements operating in America, he said, "This study renders men acute, inquisitive, dexterous, prompt in attack, ready in defense, full of resources. In other countries, the people, more simple, and of a less mercurial cast, judge of ill principle in government only by an actual grievance." But not so in British America. Burke emphasized, "They anticipate the evil and judge of the pressure of the grievance by the badness of the principle. They augur misgovernment at a distance and snuff the approach of tyranny in every tainted breeze." This they did, it may be added, by the power of right reason that arose in the Revolution of Life and Liberty, their national life was blessed by the benefits of Advance Reform Christianity.

To these five reasons for the spirit of liberty in America, Burke added that of "the remoteness of the situation from the first mover of government." Distance played a major role in "weakening government." "Seas roll," he reminded his colleagues, "and months pass, between the order and the execution; and the want of a speedy explanation on a single point is enough to defeat a whole system... This is the immutable condition, the eternal law, of extensive and detached empire."⁾ The result was frustration. Men like Thomas Paine, in *Common Sense*, made the distance at which "the Almighty has placed England and America...a strong and natural proof that the authority of the one over the other was never the design of heaven." The need to run "three or four thousand miles with a tale or petition," then wait "four or five months for an answer" that, when obtained, required "five or six more to explain it in" was beginning to be seen as "folly and childishness." To this adolescent awareness, Paine added, "There is something absurd in supposing a continent to be perpetually governed by an island. In no instance has nature made the satellite larger than its primary planet."

The American system of free constitutional theo-republicanism embodied the several characteristics of the moving spirit of the new age. And the combined traits, characteristics, and fruits of that moving spirit distinguished American republicanism from all past republican systems and made American society a unique religio-ecclesiastical, social, economic, and political organism in the history of the world. The spirit of the emerging nation was further advanced by the genius of the American Founders, which, with very few individual exceptions, has been superior to all other political figures on the American scene since their day.

Burke's observations, as the American Revolution loomed large on the horizon, made clear the issues at hand and the general reasons why the spirit of American liberty stood in defiance to British authority. Except for the influence of slavery on the Southern libertarian temper and the factor of distance from the center of English rule as causes of the breach, the American spirit of liberty that perplexed the English Parliament had its origin in liberal reform groups in seventeenth-century England, where the dynamic forces of the Age of the Spirit gave birth to liberal principles, concepts, and societal forms on the foundation of England's Saxon heritage of freemen, including the common law. Burke's statement indicates that, primarily, the dynamic spirit of liberal Puritanism and England's Anglo-Saxon heritage were the root elements that created the American spirit of liberty and incited revolt against the arbitrary regulations of English government.

As indicated in volume 1, the life and character of the quickening spirit of the Western Awakening that promoted the new age had no prior equivalents in the contemporary world. This awakening arose from no like antecedents, while the new Christian civilization that finally emerged and gave birth to the United States of America reached back to the New Testament for its basic formula of renewing life and truth. This order differed markedly from that of Traditional Christianity, the Classical World, and later Reform Christianity; and more arbitrary man-made forms of Christianity were gradually modified over the years by liberal influences coming from the Single Tradition so that the American varieties finally became altogether different in free character than the original systems formulated by Luther, Calvin, John Knox, and Queen Elizabeth, with some similar transformations in Roman Catholicism. As a case in point, Ignatius of Loyola (1491–1556), the Spanish founder of the "Society of Jesus," made the new individual-type Christianity that arose the basis of the Jesuit Order that went forth and won many Protestants back to the Catholic Church.

Since historians have neglected to give insightful attention to the religio-spiritual foundations of early British America, John Dewey points out that mere legal emphasis has been placed on key elements in the Declaration of Independence, and for this reason, the basic "nature of Jefferson's political philosophy is concealed from us." Says Dewey, "The 'self-evident truths' about the equality of all men by creation and the existence of 'inherent and unalienable rights' appear today to have [but] a legal…meaning… [Yet] in Jefferson's own mind, the words had a definitely ethical import, intimately and vitally connected with his view of God and Nature… [As] a sincere theist,…he was convinced…of the existence of a divine righteous Creator who manifested his purposes in the structure of the world, especially in that of society and the human conscience. The natural equality of all human beings was…intrinsically moral, as a consequence of the equal moral relation all human beings sustained to their Creator—equality of moral claims and of moral responsibilities... The word 'faith' is thus applied advisedly to the attitude of Jefferson toward the people's will, and its right to control political institutions and policies. The faith had a genuinely religious quality. The forms of government and law, even of the Constitution, might and should change. But the inherent and unalienable rights of man were unchangeable, because they express the will of the righteous Creator of man embodied in the very structure of society and conscience."

Jefferson sensed that the free enlivening spirit that underlaid the new nation he helped bring forth, that consisted of society founded on "voluntary associations," differed markedly and intrinsically from classical culture. Of the Greeks, Jefferson, thus, said, "So different was the style of society then, and with those people, from what it is now and with us, that I think little edification can be obtained from their writings on the subject of government." Said the Sage of Monticello, "They had just ideas of the value of personal liberty, but none at all of the [inner] structure of government best calculated to preserve it. They knew no medium [of voluntary life and open union] between a democracy [the only pure republic, but (to them it was) impracticable beyond the limits of a town] and an abandonment of themselves to an aristocracy or a tyranny independent of the people." Greek life and culture were lacking in the quickening elements of liberty and enlightened cohesion and union that later arose in the Revolution of Life and Liberty and in an inwardly motivated volunteerism which is the genius of America.

The living Bible-Christian Spirit and principles that were built into American minds, hearts, and, especially, souls brought the people to see and feel why and how they had "the right to choose" and sustain "a republican, or popular, government" that could be "exercised over any extent of country." Said Jefferson of the decisive incentive, "The introduction of this new [inwardly motivating] principle of representative democracy has rendered useless almost everything written before on the structure of government; and, in a great measure, relieves our regret, if the political writings of Aristotle, or of any other ancient, have been lost, or are unfaithfully rendered or explained to us." The author of the Declaration of Independence who voiced the spirit and idea of a new order of individualistic sociopolitical life, dignity, and human rights saw no real need to consult neither the Greeks nor the Romans on matters of government.

Instead, Jefferson urged, "My most earnest wish is to see the [inwardly animating] republican element of popular control pushed to the maximum of its practicable exercise." Given the life factor that he sensed to be the basis of his ideal order of republicanism—which instilled private and public virtue, the spirit of liberty, free and open union, right reason, etc. into the people—Jefferson added, "I shall then believe that our government may be pure and perpetual."

Jefferson's views reveal him to be a leading mind who promoted the fruits of the Single Tradition of Liberty that emerged in America. The concept of free spontaneous republicanism that he envisioned was a system of self-governing republics—federal, state, county, and local units called "wards"—that would form, he explained, "the keystone of the arch of our government," where each man would be a participating member. Said he, "The elementary republics of the wards, the county republics, the state republics, and the republic of the union would form a gradation of authorities, standing each on the basis of law, holding everyone its delegated share of powers, and constituting truly a system of fundamental balances and [vertical as well as horizontal] checks for the government. Where every man is a sharer in the direction of his ward republic, or of some of the higher ones, and feels that he is a participator in the government of affairs, not merely at an election one day in the year but every day."

Said Jefferson of the complete design, "The full experiment of a government democratically, but representative, was and is still reserved for us [to establish]. The idea [taken, indeed, from the little specimen formerly existing in the English constitution (that is, from the free order of early Saxon society vitalized by the Word/Spirit), but now lost (to the West)] has been carried by us, more or less, into all our legislative and executive departments." "But," he stressed, "it has not yet, by any of us, been pushed into all the ramifications of the system, so far as to leave no authority existing not responsible to the people." To Jefferson, the new emerging democratic order had to be fully extended and applied to make a true and complete republic.

President Ezra Stiles of Yale College, in whose heart civil and religious liberty "kindled at the altar" of Christian faith were "animating and vivid, "stressed that Jefferson 'poured the soul of the continent'" into the Declaration of Independence. American liberty had a definite inner life that burned, not merely in the minds but in the souls of people and provided a unique and distinct base for all facets of American society. Tocqueville, therefore, noted, "Religion in America takes no direct part in the government of society, but it must be regarded as the first of their political institutions; for if it does not impart a taste for freedom, it facilitates the use of it… Americans combine the notions of Christianity and of liberty so intimately in their minds that it is impossible to make them conceive the one without the other; and with them this conviction does not spring from that barren, traditional faith which seems to vegetate rather than to live in the soul." The distinct belief in a divine Creator, the doctrine of higher law, to which the people could appeal, the self-evident truths that all men are created equal and are endowed by their Creator with certain unalienable rights, the principles of self-determinism under God and of government by the consent of the people, and the right to resist tyranny—all these were born of a Bible-type Christian faith and, in the understanding of early Americans, were infused by the living Spirit of Christ into the hearts of men.

CHAPTER 9

The American Sense of Divine Mission

"God sifted a whole nation that he might send choice grains over into this wilderness," William Stoughton soberly declared in his Election sermon of 1668. "The Lord hath measured out an inheritance for a precious remnant of his people in this wilderness." The sturdy advocate of the Puritan cause explained, "This we must know that the Lord's promises and expectations of great things have singled out New England, and all sorts and ranks of men among us, above any nation or people in the world; and this hath been and is a time and season of eminent trial to us. If I should say that the very world or common ordinary professors expect great things from us at this day, there is a great deal of weight in it."

Stoughton was voicing "the American mission"—a deep spiritually inspired sense of national purpose, destiny, and responsibility founded in the religious faith and the sense of divine union which many people in the New World had with God. It was a simple but profound conviction—"comprehensible, viable, and endlessly serviceable." The idea, Rossiter explains, assumed that a living and active God had, "at the proper stage in the march of history, called forth certain hardy souls from the old and privilege-ridden nations; that he carried these precious few to a new world and presented them and their descendants with an environment ideally suited to the development of a free society; and that in bestowing his grace he also bestowed a peculiar responsibility for the success of popular institutions." This gave America a "divinely appointed mission," and their "vision was a conspicuous arrow in the well-filled quiver of the great revolutionaries," so much so that some scholars conclude that the doctrine of divine mission "ranks with the fundamental law and the free individual as one of the three leading articles of our democratic faith."

In his preface to Cotton Mather's *Magnalia Christi Americana*, Higginson spoke of the "wonderful works of God in this last age"; the "time they lived" was "portentous." By the power of the Holy Spirit, as stated earlier, God wrought upon "many thousand" people to migrate to the new land, as a thing "marvelous in our eyes"—a divine drama aimed at "the establishment of God's kingdom on earth." "And the 'historical way' towards that consummation," Bercovitch quotes Higginson as saying, "leads forward through 'all ages' with an ever-enlarging sense of fulfilment: Israel, the church of Christ, the Reformation, and now ('what hath the Lord wrought!') this 'desert land of America.'"

In the work of deducing present and future reality from the revelations of God in the Bible, the early American Puritans "had not quite charted their voyage to the end of time," and they filled in the outlines gradually. Yet, as Bercovitch observes, John Winthrop's great sermon, *A Model of Christian Charity*, which he preached on board ship before arriving in the New World, "shows that they carried their vision with them on the Arbella." And the "model, in accordance with exegetical tradition, is at once social, christic, and figural." Anchoring "their meaning in prophecy, they felt secure that the future would vindicate them." In applying the idea of Christian ensigncies voiced by earlier reformers to the Puritan venture in the New World—the idea that the true Christian order of society was to be an ensign and a standard to the world—Winthrop based the American mission on Christ's statement to his disciples, "Ye are the light of the world. A city that is set on a hill cannot be hid." In his sermon to his fellow Puritans, Winthrop voiced the anticipation, "We shall be as a City upon a Hill, the eyes of all people are upon us. So that if we shall deal falsely with our God in this work we have undertaken, and so cause him to withdraw his present help from us, we shall be made a story and a by-word through the world."

The American sense of divine mission is seen in the correlations that were made between American and Old Testament personalities. Cotton Mather entitled his life of Winthrop, *Nehemias Americanus*. Winthrop was the "American Nehemiah." When Cyrus, the ancient Persian emperor, allowed captive Jews in Babylon to return to Jerusalem in 538 BC, Nehemiah led his people out of their captive state, restored their theocracy in Jerusalem, inspired them to resume their covenant obligations with God, revived their sense of national and cultural destiny, organized further migrations from Babylon to Judea, reformed their society by a divine standard, and directed the reconstruction of Jerusalem as a city upon a hill. "Nehemiah," says Bercovitch of the New England view of the ancient leader, "was a 'personal type' of Jesus, and the Israelites' exodus from Babylon a 'national type.'" To understand Winthrop, one must "see him simultaneously as a saint, as a latter-day Nehemiah, and as the representative of a new chosen people." In the correlation of the past, present and future, Bercovitch writes, "Christology equated the saint with the heroes of scripture; typology merged the saint's life with scripture history." Thus, it was not by chance "that Nehemiah became the favorite ministerial as well as magisterial exemplum of the colonial clergy." The Israelite leader stood for the "succession of exoduses" that, though repetitive, were developmental in the divine program of human life and would eventually "culminate in the exodus from history itself." Noah abandoned a doomed world, Abraham set forth from idolatrous Ur, the Israelites under Moses fled their Egyptian persecutors, and the primitive Christians left heathen Rome. So it was only natural for early Americans to conclude that the ancient flight of the Jews from Babylon "applied with special force to their own departure, in due time, from the deprivations of Europe." Mather began the *Magnalia Christi Americana* by assuming that departure to be "the last and greatest of the premillennial migrations."

Bercovitch sees the Puritan "vision of history" clearly expressed in Mather's *Magnalia Christi Americana*, where the term *American* first appears in its modern usage, and Mather was "the first major writer to infuse it with the imaginative power it has carried ever since." While the term *Englishman* in the idea of national election became, by Puritan influence, "a metaphor for the temporary conjunction of sainthood and nationality," the term *Americanus* became and remained a "symbol of their fusion," carrying a federal identity that was not merely associated with the work of redemption but that was "intrinsic to the unfolding pattern of [biblical] types and antitypes, itself a prophecy to be fulfilled."

The New England sense of identification and union with God in history, Bercovitch explains made "the norms of the good life... eschatological, not institutional." In the colonial mind, Christ, "the 'antitype,' stood at the center of history," and he cast his "shadow forward to the end of time, as well as backward across the Old Testament." Through Christ, Puritanism gave the individual identity, genealogy, present status, and perpetuity, which enabled Cotton Mather to deduce the providential meanings of the New World "from the preordained scheme of redemption." The identification with God in history also gave American Puritanism what Bercovitch calls "sheer ideological persistence." The Pilgrim and Puritan colonization was a major effort to apply the whole of scriptural truth, history, and prophecy to the establishment of a biblical order of society in the New World. "Many things that literally concerned the Jews," declared Richard Mather, "were types and figures, signifying the like things concerning the people of God in these latter days."⁾ So it was that Cotton Mather had an "overriding emphasis on history." In ancient times, Jerusalem, Babylon, and Israel were the great "landmarks of the scheme of salvation." "So too," says Bercovitch, "are New England and America, insofar as they represent [as Mather says they do]...the mighty works of Christ."

Such views, Bercovitch points out, "represent the process of the creation of the symbol of America." That emerging symbol, embodying optimistic enterprise and progress, was the result of the science and art of scriptural interpretation, "rather than...mere spiritualizations or hyperboles." It was a "titanic effort" to apply the kind of scriptural insight wherein one had "to identify with the divine meaning of the New World" in order to correctly understand one's environment. Asserting that "our eyes have seen our Sion," and calling upon a deaf or unbelieving Europe to look upon their "towns and fields," their "habitations and shops and ships," to behold the "great increase in the blessings of the land and sea," an early American declared, "There is not only a spiritual glory, visible only to a spiritual eye but also an external, and visible glory." God had promised in ancient times, "I will make the wilderness a pool of water, and [in] the dry lands, I will plant a cedar." This divine decree was being fulfilled, literally, "before our eyes," and Christian ensigncies, as the essence of their vision, presaged greater things to come in the unfolding providential design of the new continent. God intended "some great thing when he planted these heavens and laid the foundations of this earth." And that which he designed was "a Scripture pattern that shall in due time be accomplished the whole world throughout."

With biblical truth and prophecy as the basis of their enterprise, New England Puritans elevated the mundane to the plane of the divine, Bercovitch explains, thereby "transforming secular into sacred identity." Personifying the New World "as America microchrista," they combined the style and form of "political and spiritual exhortation" while equating "public and personal welfare"; and thereby, they "invented a colony in the image of a saint," in which they merged "private, public, and prophetic identity." Even colonial histories "read like spiritual biographies of an elect land," and Joseph Morgan's *History of the Kingdom of Basaruah* (1715) portrayed the Puritan colonization of the New World as a preliminary work to the eventual millennial reign of Jesus Christ on earth.

The narrative sections of Cotton Mather's *Magnalia Christi Americana* mark the high point in applying the style, form, and content of scriptural writings to the New England experience. And to such a degree did the hand of providence direct the work of the colonists that Thomas Hooker made the "distinguishing mark of the saint" the ability to "see God in all things." New England was the renewal of the ancient biblical relationship between God and man in the accomplishment of divine purpose. "To see God in all," says

Bercovitch, "is to have experienced and understood New England's part in the divine plan."

Thus, Bailyn observation is important, that, of all the strains of thought which combined to make up the American Revolutionary mind, New England Puritanism contained "the broadest ideas of all," in that it "offered a context for everyday events nothing less than cosmic in its dimensions." This broad view carried on into the eighteenth century, where revolutionary thought were imbued with the idea, originally worked out in the sermons and tracts of the settlement period, that "the colonization of British America had been an event designed by the hand of God to satisfy his ultimate aims." These views and assumptions, which were "everywhere in the eighteenth-century colonies," built confidence in the assumption "that America had a special place, as yet not fully revealed, in the architecture of God's intent." Whatever that place was, its essence was the dignity and liberty of the individual. "Great and extensive will be the happy effects of this warfare," said Stiles of the American Revolution, "in which we have been called in Providence to fight out not the liberties of America only, but the liberties of the world itself."

Given this elevated view of things, the American assumption that a true Christian Israel could become an ensign and standard to the world was, perhaps, the most advanced ideological development within the Bible Revolution, which, from earliest times, fostered the urge to bring forth a new order of society and carried with it a sense of obligation to all people. "If America preserves her freedom," said Simeon Howard in a Massachusetts' Election sermon in 1780, "she will be an asylum for the oppressed and persecuted of every country; her example and success will encourage the friends and rouse a spirit of liberty through other nations... So that our contest is not merely for our own families, friends, and posterity but for the rights of humanity, for the civil and religious privileges of mankind. "Were Americans to fail their mission [which increasingly took on the character of an experiment in self-government], says Rossiter, "they would fail not only themselves, but all men wanting and deserving to be free."

This deep spiritually based sense of national election as a chosen people, "as strong in seventeenth-century Boston as it had been in ancient Israel," was molded by men like Jonathan Mayhew, Jonathan Edwards, John Adams, George Washington, and Thomas Jefferson into the doctrine of the American Mission, which many "great and remembered men," as well as numerous "small and forgotten men," voiced with much feeling and conviction. In a religious age when such an idea born of profound spiritual conviction had great power to take hold of the minds and hearts of the people, it was no small thing for a commanding figure like Edwards to declare solemnly that America was called of God to be "the glorious renovator of the world." Stiles saw the American mission as an opportunity to point the way to a new political order. "All the forms of civil polity have been tried by mankind, except one," he declared at the conclusion of the Revolutionary War, "and that seems to have been reserved in Providence to be realized in America... A democratical polity for millions, standing upon the broad basis of the people at large, amply charged with property, has not hitherto been exhibited."

In their expansive view of divine mission, the American Founders envisioned a universal application of the principles of the Declaration of Independence and the United States Constitution. Morgan observes that they knew they were "on the threshold of a great experience not only for themselves but perhaps for the whole world." To this end, John Jay affirmed, in the "Federalist 2," that Providence had blessed the new nation with bounteous natural resources and had brought forth "one united people—a people descended from the same ancestors, speaking the same language, professing the same religion, attached to the same principles of government, and who have nobly established their general liberty and independence."

Paine declared in *Common Sense* that "the cause of America is, in great measure, the cause of all mankind." He explained, "The present time...is that peculiar time which never happens to a nation but once, viz. the time of forming itself into a government... We have every opportunity and every encouragement before us to form the noblest, purest constitution on the face of the earth. We have it in our power to begin the world over again... The birthday of a new world is at hand." John Adams assured his wife, Abigail, that July 4 would become "the most memorable" day in the history of America. But he warned that if America failed in her divinely appointed mission, it would be "treason against the hopes of the world." He, with hundreds of patriots, held that "the defeat of the colonies would mean the defeat of liberty everywhere." Thus, Madison observed that, since it was "more than probable" that the American Founders were designing a plan that would "decide forever the fate of republican government," they ought to not only to "provide every guard to liberty that its preservation could require" but be "equally careful" to avoid the defects which their own experience had pointed out.

Based on their sense of union with the divine, many Americans described their role in history as a distinct feeling of identity with all mankind in their day and in all generations to come. "Look forward...to distant posterity," Provost Smith challenged. "Figure to yourselves millions and millions to spring from your loins, who may be born freemen or slaves, as heaven shall now approve or reject your councils. Think, that on you it may depend, whether this great country, in ages hence, shall be filled and adorned with a virtuous and enlightened people; enjoying liberty and all its concomitant blessings, together with the religion of Jesus, as it flows uncorrupted from his holy oracles; or covered with a race of men more contemptible than the savages that roam the wilderness." Voicing similar views, Jefferson wrote to Dr. Joseph Priestley in 1802: "We feel that we are acting under obligations not confined to the limits of our own society. It is impossible not to be sensible that we are acting for all mankind; that circumstances denied to others, but indulged to us, have imposed on us the duty of proving what is the degree of freedom and self-government in which a society may venture to leave its individual members." Still looking to the future, Jefferson wrote of the Declaration of Independence, ten days before his death on July 4, 1826: "May it be to the world, what I believe it will be [to some parts sooner, to others later, but finally to all] the signal of arousing men to burst the chains under which monkish ignorance and superstition had persuaded them to bind themselves, and to assume the blessings and security of self-government."

Thus, it was that Abraham Lincoln later explained that not only were the American Founders giving liberty "to the people of this country but hope to the entire world for all future time. It was that which gave promise that in due time, the weight would be lifted from the shoulders of all men and that all should have an equal chance." In the words of Walt Whitman, "All the pulses of the world, falling in, they beat for us." In his first inaugural address, Washington voiced the conviction that "the preservation of the sacred fire of liberty and the destiny of the republican model of government are justly considered, perhaps, as deeply, as finally, staked on the experiment entrusted to the hands of the American people." And in his farewell address, he expressed the hope that government under the "free Constitution" would so function in the United States that it would recommend itself "to the applause, the affection, and the adoption of every nation which is yet a stranger to it."

The Founders translated their views of Christian ensigncies and divine mission into hope of great blessings for their posterity. "If there be anything which may justly challenge the admiration of all mankind," Supreme Court Justice Joseph Story declared, "it is that sublime patriotism, which, looking beyond its own time, and its own fleeting pursuits, aims to secure the permanent happiness of posterity by laying the broad foundations of government upon immovable principles of justice. There is a noble disinterestedness in that [attitude] which disregards present objections for the sake of all mankind, and erects structures to protect, support, and bless the most distant generations. He who founds a hospital, a college, or even a more private and limited charity is justly esteemed a benefactor of the human race. How much more do they deserve our reverence and praise, whose lives are devoted to the formation of institutions, which, when they and their children are mingled in the common dust, may continue to cherish the principles and the practice of liberty in perpetual freshness and vigor!"

The emphasis on family, free Christian republicanism, and posterity that commenced among liberal Puritans years before the colonization of America is evident in many statements by the Founders. "'Tis not the affair of a city, a county, a province, or a kingdom; but of a continent—of at least one-eighth of the habitable globe," Paine wrote in *Common Sense*. "'Tis not the concern of a day, a year, or an age; posterity are virtually involved in the contest, and will be more or less affected even to the end of time by the proceedings now." To the veterans at Valley Forge, he made a similar statement. Commager notes that, similarly, Washington "invoked Posterity in all his public addresses." And as events moved toward the Declaration of July 4, 1776, John Adams solemnly stated that "objects of the most stupendous magnitude, and measures in which the lives and liberties of millions yet unborn are intimately interested, are now before us." Adams wrote the word posterity "into the Constitution of Massachusetts five times," and to Abigail, after signing the Declaration of Independence, he said, "Through all the gloom, I can see the rays of ravishing light and glory; posterity will triumph, even though we should rue it." With the same view and disposition, the New York House of Representatives proclaimed in December 1776: "We do not fight for a few acres of land, but for freedom—for the freedom and happiness of millions yet unborn."

The American Sense of Guiding Providence

"Many have been the interpositions of divine providence on our behalf," said Samuel West in his Election sermon of May 29, 1776, "both in our father's days and ours; and…can we think that he who has thus far helped us will give us up into the hands of our enemies?… Can we suppose that the God who created us free agents, and designed that we should glorify and serve him in this world that we might enjoy him forever hereafter, will suffer liberty and true religion to be banished from off the face of the earth?" Having played the leading role in the events of the American Revolution and the formulation of the United States Constitution, Washington declared, "To the manifest interposition of an overruling Providence, and to the patriotic exertions of united America, are to be ascribed those events which have given us a respectable rank among the nations of the earth." And speaking of the world in his day, Franklin wrote, "I see so much wisdom in what I understand of its creation and government that I suspect equal wisdom may be in what I do not understand. And thence have perhaps as much trust in God as the most pious Christian."

The sense of guiding providence that many Americans relied on in bringing about a new order of republican government was based on faith in God as a positive principle. Being what William Barrett calls "the openness of the whole man toward God," it was trust before it was belief, and it was belief before it was union in power with God. Assurance of the truth of Biblical Christianity gave Americans a foundation for faith that, in action, was essentially rational and consistent. The idea of natural rights as a corollary to divine and/or natural law was perfectly reasonable to the man of faith. If, by study, one came to the conclusion (as did some Greek philosophers) that only a moral people may enjoy the blessing of liberty, the discovery merely confirmed the prior acceptance of that point through religious instruction. If Newton revealed an ordered universe, his work substantiated the existing belief in divine creation. And if England violated natural law and natural rights, the course of action that faith made clear was to return to the original bestowal of such gifts and withdraw allegiance from the tyrannical system. In all these things, God was the source, and he would guide and sustain those who trusted in him in their effort to apply them.

Evidences of guiding Providence were clear to many Americans, as shown by the numerous references in Election sermons to "Providence" and the "Finger of God." The sense of guiding Providence was not merely present; it was conspicuous among the American Founders. And as events led to the Declaration of Independence, the revolution, and the formation of the federal constitution, they spoke in the positive terminology of faith of their assurance of America's divine mission and destiny. "When I consider the dispensations of Providence towards this land ever since our fathers first settled in Plymouth," West declared, "I find abundant reason to conclude that the great Sovereign of the universe has planted a vine in this American wilderness which he has caused to take deep root, and it has filled the land, and that he will never suffer it to be plucked up or destroyed."

Nor, Mead points out, was the sense of providential care "a specialized notion, nor a propositional truth subject to the judgment of being true or false." Even deists, with their faith in an autonomous mechanical universe, entertained it, which is no doubt one reason why American adherents differed in a Biblical Christian way from European deists. All classes accepted the idea. It was a presupposition, Mead writes, "which Franklin...placed among the things he 'never doubted.'" Being an assertion of the obvious, it was a feeling "that purpose pervaded the universe and every discrete event found its meaning only in relation to that purpose." As Lincoln would later say, it was "confidence that 'we cannot but believe that he who made the world still governs it.'"

One great evidence of divine blessing and providence was the free and open union that emerged, at the crisis with England, among the several independent colonies. "I cannot but take notice," West continued, "how wonderfully Providence has smiled upon us by causing the several colonies to unite so firmly together against the tyranny of Great Britain, though differing from each other in their particular interest, forms of government, modes of worship, and particular customs and manners, besides several animosities that have subsisted among them. That, under these circumstances, such a union should take place as we now behold, was a thing that might rather have been wished than hoped for."

There was a spirit of free and open union that many liberal Puritans derived from Biblical Christianity and which they sought to develop and foster as religio-spiritual foundation for their covenant associations. No doubt it was this principle of union or a direct ramification of it, to which West referred. When tensions mounted toward revolution, the British Parliament suspended the formal functions of law in the colonies, which revealed the spiritual substance of union and prompted West to ask, "Who could have thought that, when our charter was vacated, when we became destitute of any legislative authority, and when our courts of justice in many parts of the country were stopped, so that we could neither make nor execute laws upon offenders, who, I say, would have thought that in such a situation the people should behave so peaceably and maintain such good order and harmony among themselves? This is a plain proof that they, having not the civil law to regulate themselves by, became a law unto themselves, and by their conduct, they have shown that they were regulated by the law of God written in their hearts. This is the Lord's doing, and it ought to be marvelous in our eyes." This evidence of a divine factor governing the practical affairs of American life prompted West to say, "I cannot help hoping, and even believing, that Providence has designed this continent for to be the asylum of liberty and true religion." And his conclusion, as the colonists stood on the verge of independence, was "that Providence seems plainly to point to us the expediency, and even necessity, of our considering ourselves as an independent state."

Such views, mingling the divine with the practical, were deeply rooted in the spiritual senses of many people. Looking back from 1795, Samuel Miller asserted that God had guided all the major developments that led to the establishment of the Constitution of the United States of America. Nor were such views mere afterthought. During the founding era, public discourses contained statements like Oliver Hart's Thanksgiving Day sermon in 1789, on the "great, unexpected and marvelous things" that God had "wrought for America." "We shall begin with the discovery of America," said Hart; "in this, the providence of God was visibly displayed. God raised up CHRISTOPHER COLUMBUS, to make the discovery... By means of COLUMBUS, God discovered to the enlightened nations this vast continent...intended in Providence, no doubt, for a theater of great and marvelous events."

Likewise, Bishop James Madison of Virginia called attention to "those manifold displays of divine providence which the history of America exhibits," including the guidance and support given to "the bold navigator" who first visited "these distant regions of the earth," then added, "Providence seems to have thrown a veil over this portion of the globe, in order to conceal it from the eyes of the nations of the east until the destined period had arrived for the regeneration of mankind in this new world, after those various other means which the wisdom of the Almighty had permitted to operate in the old had proved ineffectual."

Tocqueville made a similar observation, when he suggested that in the discovery of America, it was as if the western hemisphere "had been kept in reserve by the Deity and had just risen from beneath the waters of the [Noachian] Deluge." Quoting the early Puritan historian Nathaniel Morton that God had "guided his people by his strength to his holy habitation and planted them in the mountain of his inheritance in respect to precious gospel enjoyments." Tocqueville commented, "In our eyes, as well as in his own, it was not merely a party of adventurers gone forth to seek their fortune beyond seas, but the germ of a great nation wafted by Providence to a predestined shore." Tocqueville saw "the destiny of America embodied in the first Puritan who landed on those shores, just as the whole human race was represented by the first man." To him, the "newness" of America, her isolation from other powers, and the heritage the colonists brought with them combined with a "thousand circumstances independent of the will of man [to] facilitate the maintenance of a democratic republic in the United States."

As events moved toward the breaking point with England, there were those who saw need for greater reliance on Providence. In a Massachusetts' Election Day sermon, in May 1775, Samuel Langdon admonished, "May we be truly a holy people, and all our towns' cities of righteousness! Then the Lord will be our refuge and strength… He can command the…elements to wage war with his enemies. He can destroy them with innumerable plagues, or send faintness into their hearts, so that the men of might shall not find their hands."

The hand of Providence was to many especially conspicuous in the events of the American Revolution and in the establishment of the federal constitution. As the revolution began, Chauncey Whittelsey observed, "In the rise and in the whole progress of the unnatural controversy between Great Britain and the now United Independent American States the hand of God has been, I must think, very conspicuous." As a case in point, Charles Chauncey explained that it was under God's "all-wise overruling influence that a spirit was raised up in all the colonies nobly to assert their freedom as men and English-born subjects." Stiles called attention to several providential acts, in 1783, then said of the appointment of Washington to lead America's military forces: "Posterity, I apprehend, and the world itself, inconsiderate and incredulous as they may be of the dominion of heaven, will yet do so much justice to the divine moral government as to acknowledge that this American Joshua was raised up by God, and divinely formed, by a peculiar influence of the Sovereign of the universe, for the great work of leading...this people through the severe, the arduous conflict, to liberty and independence." William Rodgers was not, therefore, addressing uninitiated listeners when he stated that the Constitution of the United States had emerged under the guidance of Providence, and when the Reverend Ashbel Green publicly thanked God, on July 4, 1789, for the guidance given to those who founded the republic and sealed its glory with the federal constitution, his statement was but another affirmation of consensus.

During the whole era, the American Founders operated within the framework of a deep sense of awareness of divine providence. They "worked prudently," says Kirk, "with the material they felt had been given to them by Providence: the American colonial experience of parliamentary government and local rights; the English legacy of common law and checks upon power; the Christian theories of natural law and natural rights; the classical ideal of a Republic; the Old Testament morality which was the fundamental educational discipline of eighteenth-century Americans." Paine saw Providence intervening in American affairs even before the Declaration of Independence. When the decision to announce their independence was made, John Adams wrote to his wife, Abigail, that the political order they contemplated would "require a purification from our vices, and an augmentation of our virtues," to establish the blessings of liberty. "But," he concluded, "I must submit all my hopes and fears to an overruling Providence, in which...I firmly believe." Franklin held to a similar view. "In the beginning of our contest with Great Britain," he stated to the Philadelphia Convention, "when we were sensible of danger we had daily prayers in this room for the divine protection. Our prayers...were heard, and they were graciously answered... To that kind Providence, we owe this happy opportunity of consulting in peace on the means of establishing our future national felicity." Out of the background of his personal experience, he then declared, "The longer I live, the more convincing proofs I see of this truth—which God governs in the affairs of men... I also believe that without his concurring aid, we shall succeed in this political building no better than the builders of Babel."

Reliance on divine providence continued through the constitutional era. In *Letters of Caesar and Cato*, Hamilton said of the federal constitution, "For my part, I sincerely esteem it as a system, which, without the finger of God, never could have been suggested and agreed upon by such a diversity of interests." Writing in the context of belief in divine providence, he said of the reason for divine aid, in the introductory paragraph of the "Federalist 1": "It has been frequently remarked that it seems to have been reserved to the people of this country, by their conduct and example, to decide the important question, whether societies of men are really capable or not of establishing good government from reflection and choice, or whether they are forever destined to depend for their political constitutions on accident and force." A wrong decision on their part, he warned, "may, in this view, deserve to be considered as the general misfortune of mankind." But having written in the "Federalist 20" of political deficiencies in other systems, Hamilton and Madiston admonished, "Let us pause...for one moment over this melancholy and monitory lesson of history; and with the tear that drops for the calamities brought on mankind by their adverse opinions and selfish passions, let our gratitude mingle an ejaculation to heaven for the propitious concord which has distinguished the consultations for our political happiness."

For himself, Madison wrote, in the "Federalist 37," of the founding of the new nation: "It is impossible for the man of pious reflection not to perceive in it a finger of that Almighty hand which has been so frequently and signally extended to our relief in the critical stages of the revolution." As the editor of Madison's *Papers*, Robert A. Rutland insisted that his chief interest in life was to prove that America had been chosen by Providence for an experiment to test man's capacity for self-government.

Washington, in playing the central role in the birth of the new nation, was equally convinced that American liberties were "the object of divine protection." Repeatedly, he expressed belief on this point, to the degree that he could write, "I reiterate the profession of my dependence upon heaven as the source of all public and private blessings." So aware was he of an overruling Providence and the need to acknowledge the many divine interventions that he stated soberly in his first inaugural address: "No people can be bound to acknowledge and adore the invisible hand, which conducts the affairs of men, more than the people of the United States. Every step, by which they have advanced to the character of an independent nation, seems to have been distinguished by some token or providential agency." He then added, "These reflections, arising out of the present crisis, have forced themselves too strongly on my mind to be suppressed."

In the Second Virginia Convention, at Richmond, Virginia, March 23, 1775, as the American Revolution loomed on the horizon, Patrick Henry declared, "We shall not fight our battle alone. There is a just God who presides over the destinies of nations; and who will raise up friends to fight our battle for us. The battle…is not to the strong alone; it is to the vigilant, the active, the brave."

Speaking to the Second Virginia Convention on March 23, 1775, Patrick Henry listed the efforts of the colonists James Madison made perhaps the classic statement of the role of God in the Constitutional Convention of 1787. The whole of his "Federalist 37" is a prelude leading up to his testimony of the role of God in the creation of the United States Constitution. As one reads the "Federalist 37," the picture of Madison seated at his desk intently engaged in the activities of the convention comes forcible to mind. During those daring days, he seriously contemplated the challenges confronting that body of men. "Many allowances ought to be made," he explained, "for the difficulties inherent in the very nature of the undertaking referred to the convention." The Articles of Confederation were "founded on principles which were fallacious," he wrote, and it was necessary to "change this first foundation…and with it the superstructure resting upon it." Other systems of government had been plagued by "the same erroneous principles and can therefore furnish no other light than that of beacons, which give warning of the course to be shunned, without pointing out that which ought to be pursued."

"Among the difficulties encountered by the convention," Madison explained, "a very important one must have lain in combining the requisite stability and energy in government with the inviolable attention due to liberty and the republican form." Said he, "Without substantially accomplishing this part of their undertaking, they would have very imperfectly fulfilled the object of their appointment or the expectation of the public... Energy in government is essential to that security against external and internal danger and to that prompt and salutary execution of the laws which enter into the very definition of good government. Stability in government is essential to national character and to the advantages annexed to it, as well as to the repose and confidence in the minds of the people, which are among the chief blessings of civil society."

"The people of this country," Madison continued, "enlightened as they are with regard to the nature, and interested, as the great body of them are, in the effects of good government, will never be satisfied till some remedy be applied to the vicissitudes and uncertainties which characterize the State administrations" combined under the Articles of Confederation. Said he, "On comparing, however, these valuable ingredients with the vital principles of liberty, we must perceive at once the difficulty of mingling them together in their due proportions. The genius of republican liberty seems to demand on one side, not only that all power should be derived from the people, but that those entrusted with it should be kept in dependence on the people by a short duration of their appointments; and that even during this short period the trust should be placed not in a few but a number of hands. Stability, on the contrary, requires that the hands in which power is lodged should continue for a length of time the same,...whilst energy in government requires not only a certain duration of power, but the execution of it by a single hand."

This was not all. He explained, "Not less arduous must have been the task of marking the proper line of partition between the authority of the general and that of the state governments." He continued, "A still greater obscurity lies in the distinctive characters by which the objects in each of these great departments of nature have been arranged and assorted... Experience has instructed us that no skill in the science of government has yet been able to discriminate and define, with sufficient certainty, its three great provinces—the legislative, executive, and judiciary; or even the privileges and powers of the different legislative branches. Questions daily occur in the course of practice which prove the obscurity which reigns in these subjects and which puzzle the greatest adepts in political science."

History verified his statement. "The experience of ages," he noted, "with the continued and combined labors of the most enlightened legislators and jurists, has been equally unsuccessful in delineating the several objects and limits of different codes of laws and different tribunals of justice. The precise extent of the common law and the statute law, the maritime law, the ecclesiastical law, the law of corporations, and other local laws and customs remains still to be clearly and finally established in Great Britain, where accuracy in such subjects has been more industriously pursued than in any part of the world."

There were also the weaknesses and inadequacies of language. "All new laws, though penned with the greatest technical skill and passed on the fullest and most mature deliberation," Madison wrote, "are considered as more or less obscure and equivocal until their meaning be liquidated and ascertained by a series of particular discussions and adjudications." To illustrate, he cited the greatest example possible. "When the Almighty himself condescends to address mankind in their own language," he said, "his meaning, luminous as it must be, is rendered dim and doubtful by the cloudy medium through which it is communicated." There were "three sources of vague and incorrect definitions: indistinctness of the object, imperfection of the organ of conception, inadequateness of the vehicle of ideas." Said he, "Any one of these must produce a certain degree of obscurity. The convention, in delineating the boundary between the federal and state jurisdictions, must have experienced the full effect of them all."

Added to these and other challenges were those that arose in the course of the convention. There was "the interfering pretensions of the larger and smaller states." Said Madison, "We cannot err in supposing that the former would contend for a participation in the government, fully proportioned to their superior wealth and importance; and that the latter would not be less tenacious of the equality at present enjoyed by them. We may well suppose that neither side would entirely yield to the other, and consequently that the struggle could be terminated only by compromise." And after the ratio of representation had been adjusted, this compromise "produced a fresh struggle between the same parties to give such a turn to the organization of the government and to the distribution of its powers as would increase the importance of the branches, in forming which they had respectively obtained the greatest share of influence."

Every state was divided into districts and its citizens into different classes, which gave birth "to contending interests and local jealousies," Madison wrote. And so too "the different parts of the United States are distinguished from each other by a variety of circumstances, which produce a like effect on a larger scale." Thus, he stated, "everyone must be sensible of the contrary influence…experienced in the task of forming" the constitutional foundations of the new government.

Pressures could have forced the convention "into some deviations" from the required symmetry that characterized the Constitution. Given all these and other factors, Madison wrote, "The real wonder is that so many difficulties should have been surmounted, and surmounted with unanimity almost as unprecedented as it must have been unexpected. It is impossible for any man of candor to reflect on this circumstance without partaking of the astonishment. It is impossible for the man of pious reflection not to perceive in it a finger of that Almighty hand which has been so frequently and signally extended to our relief in the critical stages of the revolution."

The trauma of the Netherlands, an important area where early seeds of liberty sprouted, stood in contrast to the above scene of union. Repeated trials "have been unsuccessfully made in the United Netherlands for reforming the baneful and notorious vices of their constitution," Madison stressed. "The history of almost all the great councils and consultations held among mankind for reconciling their discordant opinions, assuaging their mutual jealousies, and adjusting their respective interests is a history of factions, contentions, and disappointments, and may be classed among the most dark and degrading pictures which display the infirmities and depravities of the human character." All this, he finally stated, lead to two important conclusions regarding the United States Constitution: "The first is that the convention must have enjoyed, in a very singular degree, an exemption from the pestilential influence of party animosities—the disease most incident to deliberative bodies and most apt to contaminate their proceedings. The second conclusion is that all the deputations composing the convention were either satisfactorily accommodated by the final act, or were induced to accede to it by a deep conviction of the necessity of sacrificing private opinions and partial interests to the public good, and by a despair of seeing this necessity diminished by delays or by new experiments" (Camp Hill, PA, 1991, pp. 131–5).

CHAPTER 10

The American Sense of Destiny

The principle of progressive insight that the Pilgrims and other Advance Reformers brought to America contributed largely to the building of an American sense of destiny, religiously and politically. While the Mayflower carried furniture and other items to the New World that are greatly valued, the "most precious thing it took was that expectant spirit that God has more truth to break forth and the free democratic idea of the nature of the Christian Church." "We have but few principles from which we can argue with certainty, what will be the state of mankind in future ages," Samuel Williams declared in 1775. "But if we may judge of the designs of Providence, by the number and power of the causes that are already at work, we shall be lead to think that the perfection and happiness of mankind is to be carried further in America than it has ever been in any place."

Williams was one of many Americans from the beginning who combined a sense of divine providence with sentiments of liberal reform thought and prophetic elements taken from the Bible to create a dynamic sense of meaning and destiny that was shared by political and religious leaders alike. The founding generation, especially, believed that God had done great things. Theirs was "an age of wonders," said Stiles in 1783, in which more marvelous things were accomplished in eight years than were usually "unfolded in a century," all that suggested that God had "greater blessings in store for this vine which his own right hand has planted, to make us high among the nations in praise, and in name, and in honor."

By the practical blessings of Providence, Stiles saw "numerous weighty and conclusive" reasons to anticipate future greatness for America. "In our civil constitutions," he said, "those impediments are removed which obstruct the progress of society toward perfection, such, for instance, as respect the tenure of estates, and arbitrary government." By the combination of elements that had never before been combined to that degree, a new foundation was established for society which also presaged great things to come. "Liberty, civil and religious, has sweet and attractive charms," Stiles observed. "The enjoyment of this, with property, has filled the English settlers in America with a most amazing spirit, which has operated, and still will operate, with great energy. Never before has the experiment been so effectually tried of every man's reaping the fruits of his labor and feeling his share in the aggregate system of power." The growth of population suggested that within a century of the American Founding, there could be as many as fifty million people in the new nation, and "before the millennium," it could rival in number the greatest nations on earth. "Should this prove a future fact," he concluded, "how applicable would be the text, when the Lord shall have made his American Israel high above all nations which he has made, in numbers, and in praise, and in name, and in honor!"

The American sense of destiny focused, fundamentally, on two points: (1) the spread of civil and political liberty, justice, and equity from the new nation to other parts of the earth, and (2) the progressive renewal of the human family and of society by the continuous unlocking, by divine inspiration or revelation, of the truth and spiritual power of Bible Christianity. "It seems no unnatural conclusion from ancient prophecy, and from present appearances," David Austin explained in 1794, "that in order to usher in the [universal] dominion of our glorious Immanuel, as predicted to take place, and usually called the latter-day glory, TWO GREAT REVOLUTIONS are to take place; the first outward and political; the second inward and spiritual." Said he, "The first is now taking place; its happy effects we, in this country, already enjoy; and O that the Lord would graciously put it into the hearts of his ministers and churches, nay, of all now under the dominion of civil and religious liberty, to begin the second revolution, that which is inward and spiritual, even the revolution of the heart... Behold the first revolution, [through the agency of the hero of America (that is, of Christ)] in this country, already began, nay, already accomplished!—Why not then now begin the second?"

In connection with the second of the two anticipated revolutions, many, if not most, religious thinkers in America envisioned an eventual establishment of Bible Christianity in America in its original purity and power, and the growth of that system as a means of fulfilling the purposes of God in ushering in the millennial reign of Christ. Said Ebenezer Baldwin of the prevailing view, "That Christ will set up his kingdom upon earth in a more glorious manner than it has ever yet appeared, before the end of the world, is generally believed by divines." To this end, the work to be accomplished in the first, or political revolution, was important and preliminary. Said Baldwin, "Whenever this glorious state of the church takes place, civil liberty must be enjoyed, for religion cannot subsist in this flourishing state under tyranny and despotism."

This vision of destiny, on the broad scale of American experience, had been and was being expressed in various ways and to various degrees. In the more direct and visible sense (with negative connotations for the prevailing Christian order), it was made manifest in the hopes and aspirations of the Seekers, who were among the leaders of Advance Reform Christianity in mid-seventeenth-century England where the spirit, principles, and concepts of Anglo-American liberty were born. Having established a new settlement at Providence, Rhode Island, in 1636, based on separatist views Roger Williams moved in this direction in his thought. "Puritan logic," Brockunier explains, "brought Williams to the dilemma of those who insisted on an uncorrupted apostolic succession and upon church ceremonies in their original purity but who were forced to derive the one through the channel of the medieval church and the other from the welter of contradictory precedents of the Bible and early church writings. Facing this dilemma with all the honesty and logic of a trained and critical intellect, he...groped his way through to the ultimate scruple which was the key to all the others. His difficulties, he realized at last, revolved upon this one point: all churches, all ordinances, all true apostolic succession had been lost in the apostasy of the Roman church, by the accretions through the ages of man-made rites and articles of belief—'inventions of men.'" Thus, Sweet explains, "Williams repudiated all visible churches, holding that there was no true church left in the world; therefore, there was nothing to do but await the reestablishment of the true church by some divine intervention."

Williams had established a Baptist Church at Providence, in 1639; but, Winthrop reported, he then questioned his baptism, "not being able to derive the authority of it from the apostles, otherwise than by the ministers of England [whom he judged to be ill authority], so as he conceived God would raise up some apostolic power.") And in renouncing the Baptists, said colonial historian John Callender, Williams "turned Seeker, [i.e., to wait for new Apostles, to restore Christianity]." Only "prophecy" remained, as a foundation upon which to build.) This, says Brockunier, "was the ultimate logic to which his principles carried him." In Williams's way of thinking, the new revelation and commission could take place in America.

The Webb family gave what may be a unique example within the general stream of anticipation that began on the continent of Europe, then England, and was finally transplanted to the New World to become part of the American sense of destiny. William Webb (1675–1746) wrote in his will: "There is a legacy left me by my father who was left it by his father to be passed on to my heirs... We believe with others that man should be free to worship his Maker in a manner pleasing to himself... My father, John, a righteous, just, forgiving man, was told in a dream that the time was nearing when Jesus Christ would return to set up his kingdom. It will not happen during my lifetime, nor that of my children, and perhaps not my grandchildren. But the time will come, soon, when believers may become members in the kingdom of Jesus Christ." Three generations later, Samuel Webb (1776–1822) wrote in his will: "I am mindful of the tradition spoken of by my forbearers that the time will soon come when our Savior, Jesus Christ, will establish his kingdom on earth. Believing that time is nigh, I desire that my beloved wife, Sarah, and my William and daughter Lydia will accept and enter that kingdom."

The view that the birth of the American republic was preparatory to the kingdom of Christ that would usher in the millennial reign was a unique "millennial anticipation." Not that the reign of Christ was expected immediately, but that the achievements of the revolutionary and constitutional era in America were preparatory to its dawn in a time to come. To William Linn, God, by establishing the Constitution of the United States, was "preparing the way for the introduction of a glorious scene upon earth," and the Baptists of the Warren Association proclaimed "that America is reserved in the mind of Jehovah to be the grand theater on which the divine Redeemer will accomplish glorious things."

Like other colonial leaders, the clergy were amazed at the extraordinary virtue and valor displayed by Americans in 1774 and 1775. They, therefore, asked themselves, said Wood, "Was it possible that this was 'the time, in which Christ's kingdom is to be thus gloriously set up in the world?'" Like many others, the clergy felt "the country 'to be on the eve of some great and unusual events' and their language, ecstatic but not uniquely religious, took on a millennial tone." Prior evidence of God's hand in American affairs, said John Woodhull, gave cause to "look out for the glory of the latter day."

This vision of America as an elect nation was a transfer of millennial hope that focused at first on England so that it gave men like Stiles reason to address the mother country: "How have I been wont to glory in the future honor of having thee for the head of the Britannico-American empire for the many ages till the millennium, when thy great national glory should have been advanced in then becoming a member of the universal empire of the Prince of Peace!... But now, farewell—a long farewell—to all this greatness!"

Such expectations were not new or unique to the period of the American Revolution. Smylie speaks of the ministers of that era as "revitalizing the vision of earlier colonists." Long before America's break with England, there were many who had a vision of the Lord of history "providentially involved in the destiny of America," as the land designed to be a "final theater of God's latter-day activities." This vision "gave unity" to those who shared it; and it greatly contributed to the "tremendous American vitality" that produced "'freedom's ferment,' the 'benevolent empire,' and the throbbing life of the century ahead," which was looked upon as "the next to the last century before the promised millennium."

The two revolutions of the future, it was held, would witness the establishment of the perfected Zion, the New Jerusalem, in America, in preparation for the return of Christ. John Bunyan, whose writings were popular in the New World, asserted that the existence of the heavenly city would witness a glorious outbreaking of Christian truth. Knott explains that, in the biblical description of the New Jerusalem, Bunyan saw "compelling evidence of the triumph of the Word." When the gospel finally burst forth in its "primitive glory with the fall of Antichrist," it would convert multitudes, including the Jews. The New Jerusalem would also witness the full development of the true and harmonious order of the Christian Church. The church's "disordered parts" would be "brought into 'exact form and order' by this realization of the rule of the New Testament," Knott explains. The people would then believe in the true and full doctrine of the apostles "rather than a popish, and a Quaker, and a Presbyterian doctrine."

From the earliest times, those who saw America as the home of the New Jerusalem gave that vision of anticipated glory a prominent place in their hearts. Edward Johnson, a first-generation Puritan layman, claimed that God would erect "Mt. Zion in the wilderness." This would realize Winthrop's vision of the city upon a hill, and like him, many "looked forward to the coming of the New Jerusalem." Yet this would not immediately be realized. Smylie speaks of the clergy, after the establishment of the federal constitution, "peering deep into the future" to see its fulfillment. Timothy Dwight wrote, "Here Empire's last, and brightest throne shall rise; and peace, and right, and freedom, greet the skies." And of the end result, Samuel Cooper said, "Thus will our country resemble the new city which St. John saw 'coming down from God out of heaven adorned as a bride for her husband.'"

Bercovitch observes that no less a figure than Samuel Sewall, chief justice of the Massachusetts Supreme Court, in exclaiming "how 'wonderfully suited' was 'the coming of Christ into America' in these latter days," makes reference to the "New Jerusalem as 'the Heart of America,' and of 'America's plea' for the Second Coming as 'the strongest' now being raised to God." Cotton Mather was equally positive. Repeatedly, he stated that America stood "as the first among Christ's beloved,...the most beautiful of his brides." In view of the "glorious nuptials" that were to be consummated in the New World, with Christ's coming to receive his people—his adorned bride, Mather foresaw "the 'Holy City, in AMERICA,' as 'America,' a city the streets whereof will be pure fold.'" This was not considered to be wishful thinking; it was a view based on "a long study of scriptural texts" pertinent to the covenant of grace and the work of redemption portrayed in the Word. They all led to the "same inescapable significance: 'AMERICA is legible in these [biblical] promises.'" Like his grandfather John Cotton (in 1640), Mather paraphrased Isaiah's enraptured song for "the marriage of heaven and earth," found in Isaiah 52:1: "'Awake, Awake, put on thy strength, O New-English Zion, and put on thy beautiful garments, O American Jerusalem,' 'Put on thy beautiful garments, O America, the holy City!'" He reasoned, "If God have a purpose to make here a seat for any of those glorious things, which are spoken of thee, O thou City of God; then even thou, O New-England art within a very little while of better days than have ever yet dawn'd upon thee. Our Lord Jesus Christ shall have the uttermost parts of the earth for his possession, the last [shall] be first, and the Sun of Righteousness come to shine brightest, in climates which it rose latest upon!"

The goal of Zion for which many Americans sought during the Revolutionary and Constitutional Periods increasingly envisioned a political order as part of the full divine system but with its spiritual principle supreme. Samuel Langdon and Samuel West headed their Election sermons (delivered May 31, 1775, and May 29, 1776, respectively) with the prophetic declaration in Isaiah 1:26, concerning the redemption of latter-day Israel, which they applied to America: "And I will restore thy judges as at the first, and thy counselors as at the beginning; afterward thou shalt be called the City of Righteousness, the Faithful City." Speaking in the same vein, Stiles said in 1783, "While Europe and Asia may hereafter learn that the most liberal principles of law and civil polity are to be found on this side [of] the Atlantic, they may also find the true religion here depurated from the rust and corruption of ages, and learn from us to reform and restore the church to its primitive purity. It will be long before the ecclesiastical pride of the splendid European hierarchies can submit to learn wisdom from those whom they have been inured to look upon with sovereign contempt. But candid and liberal disquisition will, sooner or later, have a great effect. Removed from the embarrassments of corrupt systems, and the dignities and blinding opulence connected with them, the unfettered mind can think with a noble enlargement, and, with an unbounded freedom, go wherever the light of truth directs." On this foundation of progressive insight by revelatory means, Stiles contended, "Religion may here receive its last, most liberal and impartial examination."

Stiles did not limit true Christianity, based on progressive revelatory insight, to a support position to the civil and/or political order. "If...we defend and plead for Christianity from its secular and civil utility only," he said, "and leave it here, we dishonor religion by robbing it of half, nay, its greatest glories." True Christianity, as a living program of personal revelation and life, was designed to enlighten and bless people in all spheres of human activity, including the political. "Shall the Most High send down truth into the world from the world of light and truth," he challenged, "and shall the rulers of this world be afraid of it? Shall there be no intrepid Daniels—great in magistracy, great in religion?" Divine light and truth being the foundation of true Christian life and society ought to be the end of human endeavor. And a righteous state should help promote this goal, not by union with the church but by recognition of the ultimate purpose of human life. "We err much," Stiles argued, "if we think the only or chief end of civil government is secular happiness. Shall immortals, illuminated by revelation, entertain such an opinion? God forbid! Let us model civil society with the adoption of divine institutions so as shall best sub serve the training up and disciplining innumerable millions for the more glorious society of the church of the firstborn. Animated with the sublime ideas which Christianity infuses into a people, we shall be led to consider the true religion as the highest glory of a civil polity. The Christian institution so excelled in glory, that the Mosaic lost all its glory. So the most perfect secular polity, though very excellent, would lose all its glory when compared with a kingdom wherein dwells righteousness, a community wherein the religion of the divine Jesus reigns in vigor and perfection."

The vision of America, with the anticipated political and spiritual revolution, gave great scope and dimension to the new nation's political purpose. Even before the revolution was over, Samuel Cooper stated that the war of liberation had as a "laudable" objective "to lay the foundation of our Republic with extended views." Jefferson's words to John Adams reveal the feeling of both political and religious destiny that many held. "The flames kindled on the Fourth of July 1776," he wrote, "have spread over too much of the globe to be extinguished by the feeble engines of despotism."

Yet more was to be achieved than the extension of political liberty throughout the world. After forcefully criticizing distortions of Christ's doctrine, Jefferson added in another letter, "We may hope that the dawn of reason, and freedom of thought in these United States, will do away all these artificial scaffolding and restore to us the primitive and genuine doctrines of this the most venerated Reformer of human errors." Said Jefferson, "The genuine and simple religion of Jesus will one day be restored: such as it was preached and practiced by himself."

John Adams entered the Revolutionary Era filled with anticipation for the future. "America," he declared in 1765, "was designed by Providence for the theater on which man was to make his true figure, on which science, virtue, liberty, happiness, and glory were to exist in peace." To George Wythe of Virginia, he wrote early in 1776, "You and I, my friend, have been sent into life at a time when the greatest lawgivers of antiquity would have wished to live. How few of the human race have ever enjoyed an opportunity of making an election of government, more than of air, soil, or climate, for themselves or their children!" In the original draft of *A Dissertation on the Canon and the Feudal Law* that he recorded in his diary, Adams wrote, "I always considered the settlement of America with reverence and wonder, as the opening of a grand scene and design in Providence for the illumination of the ignorant, and the emancipation of the slavish part of mankind all over the world." In this statement, Tuveson saw a suggestion that the American settlements might "be destined to be the nucleus not only of a holy but a millennial people." Of the American view, Tuveson says, "Is it possible that the Reformation was the beginning of a process, within history, which is to lead to the establishment of God's kingdom in the entire world? If so, it seems almost as if the 'finger of prophecy' must point to this, the last, the best child of the Reformation. Why, many were to wonder, did Providence hold back the discovery of this vast part of the earth until the very time when the mystical Babylon began to suffer her death pangs?" In later years, Adams wrote to Jefferson, "Our pure, virtuous, public spirited, federative republic will last forever, govern the globe, and introduce the perfection of man."

Like others, Ebenezer Baldwin projected the year AD 2000 as the time when the era of liberty being inaugurated in 1776 would begin its consummation in the kingdom of Jesus Christ. "Other kingdoms have enjoyed their season of liberty," he said. "It remains for America to enjoy hers. And since it is in the last ages of the world that America is to enjoy this prosperous state, and as this is the time in which Christ's kingdom is to be thus gloriously set up in the world, I cannot think it chimerical to suppose, America will largely share in the happiness of this glorious day, and that the present scenes are remotely preparing the way of it." With like anticipation, Samuel Buell concluded an address by inviting the people to pray "that the whole 'earth may be full of the knowledge of the Lord,' that Jews and Gentiles may all know Him, 'from the least to the greatest;' that there may be, as it were, 'a new heaven and a new earth'—a new world, a young world, a world of countless millions, all in the fair bloom of piety, training up for final fixation, in the state of immortal youth, glory and felicity at the right hand of God."

Looking to future preparations for the millennium, President Stiles declared that there were three major events to take place: "the annihilation of the pontificate, the reassembling of the Jews, and the fullness of the Gentiles." America would play a major role in the first of these events—the fall of spiritual Babylon, by the further unfolding of scriptural truth and the development of the kingdom of God among the people of the new nation. "That liberal and candid disquisition of Christianity which will most assuredly take place in America," he said, "will prepare Europe for the first event." And with the return of the latter-day descendants of ancient Israel to the Holy Land, he added, "There will burst forth a degree of evidence hitherto unperceived, and of efficacy to convert a world." He explained, "Heaven put a stop to the propagation of Christianity when the [original New Testament] church became corrupt with the adoration of numerous deities and images, because this would have been only exchanging an old for a new idolatry." But when the true and full Christian system was finally established in America, a new thrust would be given to foreign missions. "It may be of the divine destiny," he opined, "that all other attempts for gospelizing the nations of the earth shall prove fruitless, until the present Christendom itself be recovered to the primitive purity and simplicity; at which time, instead of the Babel confusion of contradicting missionaries, all will harmoniously concur in speaking one language, one holy faith, one apostolic religion, to an uncontroverted world. At this period, and in effecting this great event, we have reason to think that the United States may be of no small influence and consideration." This would, in very deed, bring in the "fullness of the Gentiles"—their full opportunity to hear and receive the fullness of the Gospel of Jesus Christ.

With the American Revolutionary War over and the Constitution of the United States established, views of America's millennial destiny were voiced with even greater confidence and a more complete doctrine—the glorious vision of "heaven's Last Wondrous Acts." In 1793, Samuel Hopkins appended *A Treatise on the Millennium* to the second volume of *The System of Doctrines*. The following year David Austin published *The Millennium*, and William Linn *Discourses on the Signs of the Times*. As "an Almanac of Prophecy," the Bible was seen as a "sacred calendar," pointing the way to the "long-wished-for promised day."

Morgan Edwards explained "that this world is to last seven thousand years, and that at the end of the sixth thousand the millennium will begin." In his vision on Patmos, John was shown a book with seven seals, each representing a thousand years of the earth's temporal state, which began with the fall of Adam, implying that the millennium would commence after the opening of the seventh seal or near the year AD 2000. This was "time little enough to bring forth the events we have already mentioned," said Edwards, "viz. the destruction of the Ottoman empire; the restoration of the Jews, and their rebuilding Jerusalem and the temple; the exploits of Antichrist towards the mastery of the world, &c. Therefore, we may expect soon to see the fig tree budding and putting forth its leaves."

The immediate significance of these biblical calculations centered on the Constitution of the United States. The years from 1776 to 1789 "had been rich in preparatory events" for the millennium, Smylie explained, the "first event of importance" being the establishment of the federal constitution. "From the rise and present exaltation of America," Daniel Foster declared, "we conclude she is to be the theater, where the latter-day glory shall be displayed; and the medium through which religion, liberty, and learning shall be handed round creation." In the words of David Tappan, "The rapid progress of knowledge, and a spirit of free inquiry, of late years, over the earth—these and other familiar events form a grand chain of Providence, in which the American Revolution is a principle link—a chain, which is gradually drawing after it the most glorious consequences of mankind; which is hastening on the accomplishment of the scripture—prophecies relative to the millennial state, the golden age of the church and the world in the latter days." In his statement, made more than four years before the Constitution of the United States of America was written, he exclaimed, "How magnificently great the works of Jehovah toward America appear, when viewed in this light! What complicated, extended, lasting advantages seem to be wrapped up in them, not only to many millions in the Western world but to countless multitudes, as we trust, in various parts of the globe!"

A major feature of millennial doctrine was the assertion that the American republic, which institutionalized civil and religious liberty, was a forerunner of the universal kingdom that would extend those principles throughout the earth. In *The Millennial Door Thrown Open, or, the Mysteries of the Latter-Day Glory Unfolded*, Austin explained that the day the Declaration of Independence was signed "was an important day, both in relation to the benefits which it brought in its train, in a national point of view, and in reference to the foundation of that national edifice from which is yet to beam forth the light and glory of the world." He suggested, "Let…the day be celebrated as the hour which gave birth to the mighty events which of necessity were needful to prepare the way for the peaceful empire of the Prince of Peace."

The colonist's sense of American destiny was based in part on the prophecies of Daniel and John. The prophet Daniel portrayed the beginning of the universal order as being like a stone "cut out of the mountain without hands" that would roll forth and finally fill "the whole earth," and John likened the political order of the divine system to a "man child" who would "rule all nations with a rod of iron." Austin, therefore, exclaimed, "Behold the regnum montis, the kingdom of the mountain, began on the Fourth of July, 1776, when the birth of the MAN CHILD—the hero of the civil and religious liberty took place in these United States… He was to rule all nations with a rod of iron,…supported by an omnipotent arm… Behold, then, this hero of America wielding the standard of civil and religious liberty… See the votaries of the tyrants; of the beasts; of the false prophets, and serpents of the earth, ranged in battle array, to withstand the progress and dominion of him, who hath commission to break down the usurpations of tyranny—to let the prisoner out of the prison house; and to set the vassal in bondage free from his chains—to level the mountains—to raise the valleys, and to prepare an high way for the Lord!"

The course of human events in past ages had witnessed a successive shift of empire from east to west, which American students of the Bible saw portrayed in Daniel 2. There, the Hebrew prophet spoke of a succession of kingdoms—the Babylonian, Medo-Persian,

Greco-Macedonian, and Roman empires, respectively, onward to the anticipated kingdom of God to be set up in the last days, which would roll forth like a stone cut out of a mountain without hands to fill the whole earth. In the work of establishing the Constitution of the United States of America, with the building of Zion on the western hemisphere, preparations would take place for the last great shift of empire to the millennial kingdom. Fifty years before the American Revolution, the English philosopher and bishop, George Berkeley, who lived from 1728 to 1731 in Rhode Island, voiced this grand vision of the destined kingdom of Daniel America for which America would prepare the way:

> There shall be sung another golden age,
> The rise of empire and of arts...
> Westward the course of empire takes its way.
> The four first acts already past,
> A fifth shall close the drama with the day;
> Time's noblest offspring is the last.

American spokesmen were not slow to catch this vision of the new nation's role in the divine drama of human affairs. While anticipating that Christ would "set up his kingdom upon earth in a more glorious manner," Baldwin emphasized, "Liberty, as well as learning and religion, has from the beginning been travelling westward." To William Smith, nature was a type and shadow of God's divine plan. As the sun pursues a western course, he explained, so God "appears to call upon us, and to have preserved us, as chosen instruments for planting and disseminating a 'new empire of sound religion and liberty, wisdom, virtue, arts and science to the utmost ends of the New World; at a time when they are drooping or dead in most countries of the Old World, which once enjoyed their brightest splendor." The task of diffusing "heavenly knowledge, and liberty, and arts and science into the extremist bounds of America" was to him the "first and greatest work" that American colonists had come to the New World to accomplish—to make "the 'wilderness and the solitary places glad through us, and the desert to rejoice and blossom as the rose.'" All this was preparatory to the rise of Zion, the building of which would be consummated by the coming of the Lord in glory. "To look forward to that glorious era," Smith explained, "when heavenly wisdom and virtue, and all that can civilize, adorn, and bless mankind, shall cover this whole continent, as the waters cover the sea—to attend to the times and the seasons, and to dwell upon the many prophecies which predict its near approach—to contribute my share towards the advancement of it, and to possess the minds of the rising generations of youth, who are to be principal actors in the work, with the great animating idea, that heaven has yet mighty blessings in store for the inhabitants of this land, of every clime and every color—this hath been my joy, and this my labor from my earliest years."

Speaking of the "almost-boundless" prospects of the "future glory of America" and quoting Berkeley on the westward course of empire, Samuel Stillman said in an oration at Boston, "The sun of the old world is setting; of the new just beginning to rise. Hail! My country, the glorious theater, perhaps, of heaven's last wondrous acts! That divine personage [Christ], who made his entrance in the east, will ride in triumph through this western world, and upon all the glory shall be a defense."

In concluding that the millennial glory "will commence when the two thousand years of the Christian era shall close, which will be six thousand years from the creation," Thomas Brockway declared in a Thanksgiving sermon at the end of the American Revolution and before the Constitution was written, "God has given us the victory and ratified the peace and independence of America: but we are not to conceive this the ultimate object in the divine plan: he has done it in subservience to the glorious scheme of the gospel of redemption." Brockway explained, "Empire, learning and religion have in past ages been traveling from east to west, and this continent is their last western stage; and the great Pacific Ocean which bounds the western part of the continent, will bound their further progress in this direction. Here then is God erecting a stage, on which to exhibit the great things of his kingdom, the stage is spacious, the territory extensive, such as no other part of the globe can equal; and here from the analogy of reason, and the usual course of divine providence, we may expect

God's greatest works. And no doubt this interesting revolution of American independence is a leading step; the world is far advanced in age, from prophecy it is apparent that the latter day glory is at no great distance. And when we consider above three thousand miles of western territory, the most fertile part of America, yet uninhabited: Can we suppose this vast region designed merely for beasts of prey? Or may we not rather suppose, this is the wilderness and the solitary place that shall be glad, and the desert that shall blossom as the rose."

American Sense of Destiny

In their origins among liberal Puritans, the idea of the free political state and the quest for greater religio-spiritual truth were directly correlated. In discussing the early application of covenant principles to the political sphere to give birth to constitutional governments, particularly in America, Woodhouse observes that "the Puritan belief in the progressive interpretation of truth...was written into the covenant of the Pilgrims' church." But while this was not the case with the Agreements of the People, he continues, "It is recognized in the fact that, as issued by the Levelers, and perhaps also by the Independents, they were designed to furnish a basis for discussion, and to serve as explorations leading to truth and consent."

As a prominent American who was solidly in this prophetic tradition, President Ezra Stiles of Yale College could see the New World saga as the fulfillment of prophecy voiced by the patriarch Noah, concerning his posterity in the latter days. "Can we contemplate their present and anticipate their future increase," said Stiles of Americans, "and not be struck with astonishment to find ourselves in the midst of the fulfillment of the prophecy of Noah? May we not see that we are the object which the Holy Ghost had in view four thousand years ago, when he inspired the venerable patriarch with the visions respecting his posterity? How wonderful the accomplishments in distant and disconnected ages!"

"An idea—strange as it is visionary—has entered into the minds of the generality of mankind that empire is traveling westward; and everyone is looking forward with eager and impatient expectation to the destined moment, when America is to give the law to the rest of the world."

Jonathan Edwards said, "God presently goes about doing great things in order to make way for the introduction of the church's latter-day glory—which is to have its first seat in, or is to rise from [this] new world."

The general thrust of the Revolution of Life and Liberty promoted two optimistic undertakings: (1) the quest for a free society and a representative government to embody and to protect the spiritual life in Christ that Advance Reformers on the highest plane achieved, and (2) the eventual restoration of Bible Christianity and the New Testament Church.

To see the full ideal of American destiny, one must view things in the eyes of the Seeker: (1) the return of the New Testament Church and the building of Zion; (2) the spread of a free government throughout the world based on the constitutional system set up by the Founding Fathers.

Sense of Destiny

The words of Julia Ward Howe's "The Battle Hymn of the Republic" combine the American sense of faith and destiny; or, perhaps better stated, the sense of Christian faith and destiny of a nation grounded in the doctrines, spirit, and prophetic vision of the Bible. Her verses were designed to provide more worthy words to the militant Civil War melody, "John Brown's Body," and they first appeared in print in the *Atlantic Monthly*, February 1862. Therein, she voiced the faith and yearnings of America's Christian heritage and the vision of the Christian nation's destiny, whose people were then being sorely chastened by the throes of a fratricidal conflict. Howe wrote,

> Mine eyes have seen the glory of the coming of
> the Lord
> He is trampling out the vintage where the grapes
> of wrath are stored

He hath loosed the fateful lightning of His terrible swift sword
His truth is marching on, His truth is marching
Glory, glory, Hallelujah! Glory, glory, Hallelujah!
Glory, glory, Hallelujah! His truth is marching on
I have seen Him in the watch fires of a hundred circling camps
They have builded Him an altar in the evening dews and damps
I can read His righteous sentence by the dim and flaring lamps
His day is marching on
Hallelujah, Hallelujah!
In the beauty of the lilies, Christ was born across the sea
With a glory in His bosom that transfigures you and me
As He died to make men holy, let us live to make men free
While God is marching on
Glory, glory, Hallelujah! Glory, glory, Hallelujah!
Glory, glory, Hallelujah! His truth is marching on!
His truth is marching on! And on and on and on and on and on

Jefferson's Sense of American Destiny

Very often, Jefferson used the phrase "an empire of liberty" to bring the principle of dominion within the framework of the Declaration of Independence. "In sending George Rogers Clark to secure the Illinois country in 1778, in drafting the Northwest Ordinance in 1784, in purchasing Louisiana and in dispatching the Lewis and Clark expedition in 1803, in supporting the War of 1812, and in favoring the liberation of Spain's Latin American colonies in the 1820s, Jefferson had in view always the enlargement of the 'empire of liberty.' He had urged Clark in 1779 to respect the religion and customs of the people of the Illinois country so that there might be added 'to the empire of liberty an extensive and fertile country, thereby converting dangerous enemies into valuable friends.' He hoped that later the world would witness in the continental United States 'such an extent of country under a free and moderate government as it has never yet seen,' where 'range after range' of new, equal, and self-governing states would cover the Mississippi Valley, and that in the whole American hemisphere European tyranny would be expelled and this vast area become filled with free nations."

Benjamin Franklin spoke of his hope that "not only the love of liberty but a thorough knowledge of the rights of man may pervade all the nations of the earth."

In anticipating a great democracy in the New World, the Reverend Mason L. Weems said, "Perhaps, God may be about to establish here a mighty empire, for the reception of a happiness unknown on earth, since the days of blissful Eden."

Roger Williams and the Seekers are another example of the underlying power of the Bible Revolution. Seekerism, like the principle of progressive insight into scriptural truth from which it apparently took its origin, rose primarily from the New Testament, not from a given human expositor. It was, Brockunier says of Williams, "but the ultimate logic to which his principles carried him." Motivated as Williams was by the power of the Bible Revolution, "it was the solution of his intellectual dilemma." And it gave birth to his vision and hope for America. In the final analysis, Williams came to rely on "prophecy," as the basis of that hope, and here he made a significant contribution that fostered the idea of the mission and prophetic destiny of America.

Drawing upon sentiments from Psalms, Isaiah, and Zechariah, Cotton Mather exclaimed, "Awake, Awake, put on thy strength, O New-English Zion, and put on thy beautiful garments, O American Jerusalem," then reasoned, "If God have a purpose to make here a seat for any of those glorious things, which are spoken of thee, O thou City of God; then even thou, O New-England art within a very little while of better days than have ever yet dawn'd upon thee. Our Lord Jesus Christ shall have the uttermost parts of the earth for his possession, the last [shall] be first, and the Sun of Righteousness come to shine brightest, in climates which it rose latest upon."

Liberty, progress, and glory had arisen from Christ, who was to be the center of the higher and more glorious developments yet to come. President Ezra Stiles of Yale University, therefore, stated, "Let us model civil society with the adoption of divine institutions so as shall best sub serve the training up and disciplining innumerable millions for the more glorious society of the Church of the Firstborn [which must finally come]. Animated with the sublime ideas which Christianity infuses into a people, we shall be led to consider the true religion as the highest glory of a civil polity. The Christian institution so excelled in glory, that the Mosaic lost all its glory. So the most perfect secular polity, though very excellent, would lose all its glory when compared with a kingdom wherein dwells righteousness, a community wherein the religion of the divine Jesus reigns in vigor and perfection."

Tocqueville's study of America's free, progressive society led him to contemplate the possible union of liberty and equality in America. Based on his observation of dynamic religio-spiritual elements operating in the lives of early Americans, with their thrust toward liberty, equality, and open union—the tradition Colet and Erasmus helped establish—Tocqueville concluded that Americans had progressed a long way toward realizing the age-old goal of social justice. Assuming a continuation of their progress, he opined, "It is possible to imagine an extreme point at which freedom and equality would meet and blend."

Looking at the enormous prospects of the new nation in light of his understanding of the prophetic picture portrayed in the Bible, George Duffield said in a Thanksgiving sermon preached at the conclusion of the Revolutionary War, "Here…shall our Jesus go forth conquering and to conquer; and the heathen be given him for an inheritance, and these uttermost parts of the earth, a possession. Zion shall here lengthen her cords, and strengthen her stakes; and the mountain of the house of the Lord be gloriously exalted on high.

Here shall the religion of Jesus, not that, falsely so called, which consists in empty modes and forms, and spends its unhallowed zeal in party names and distinctions, and traducing and reviling each other, but the pure and undefiled religion of our blessed Redeemer: here shall it reign in triumph, over all opposition. Vice and immorality shall yet here become ashamed and banished; and love to God and benevolence to man rule the hearts and regulate the lives of men. Justice and truth shall here yet meet together, and righteousness and peace embrace each other: And the wilderness blossom as the rose and the desert rejoice and sing. And here shall the various ancient promises of rich and glorious grace begin their complete divine fulfilment, and the light of divine revelation diffuse its beneficent rays, till the Gospel of Jesus have accomplished it's day, from east to west, around our world. A day, whose evening shall not terminate in night, but introduce that joyful period, when the outcasts of Israel and the dispersed of Judah shall be restored; and with them the fullness of the Gentile world shall flow to the standard of redeeming love: And the nations of the earth become the kingdom of our Lord and Savior. Under whose auspicious reign holiness shall universally prevail, and the noise and alarm of war be heard no more. Nor shall there be anything to hurt or destroy, or interrupt the tranquility of men, through all the wide dominions of this glorious Prince of Peace. How pleasing the scene! How transporting the prospect!"

CHAPTER 11

The Extension of the English Revolution to America

The main connecting link between the English revolutions of the seventeenth century and the American Revolution was the philosophy of the English Commonwealth men. Though of limited impact in England, their writings, says Robbins, "served to maintain a revolutionary tradition and to link the histories of English struggles against tyranny in one century with those of American efforts for independence in another." Because he saw the basic correlation between the seventeenth- and eighteenth-century revolutions (the first two in England and the last in America) as episodes rising out of the Puritan movement, one historian suggests "that when the British government forced the [Puritan] Dissenters to leave England and flee to America [in the seventeenth century], it simply put off for one hundred fifty years, and removed to another land, the final struggle between those who represented the established church, feudal practice and tradition, the king's prerogative, landed property and privilege on the one side; and other opponents on the other side, the radicals and liberals in church and state, with antagonistic ideas as to church and secular government." Much earlier, John Adams arrived at a similar conclusion. "I think with you," he wrote to Jefferson in 1818, "that it is difficult to say at what moment the [American] Revolution began.

In my opinion, it began as early as the first plantation of the country. Independence of church and parliament was a fixed principle of our predecessors in 1620, as it was of Samuel Adams and Christopher Gadsden, in 1776; and independence of church and parliament was always kept in view in this part of the country, and, I believe, in most others."

Though there was a direct filial connection between the American Revolution and the English revolutions of the previous century, active colonial dissent against the British government that led to the American Revolution did not begin until after the Treaty of Paris in 1763 in which France, after the Seven Years' War, renounced to England all the mainland of North America east of the Mississippi, except for New Orleans and its environs. A new British policy then began to be enacted that disregarded the rights of British citizens in the New World; and Americans started to assert the principles of "freedom under God," which their progenitors had championed in the seventeenth century, and to take the position of dissent which their fathers had taken. Early American Puritans were the same sort of people, religiously and politically, as those Puritans who rose against Charles I and later James II; and it was natural for them to reassert the Christian principle of dissent that brought their fathers to the New World and to give heed to those writers in England and America who carried on the spirit and ideology of liberty that were born in the Puritan Revolution.

The American Revolution was, therefore, an extension and an updating of the Puritan Revolution and the Glorious Revolution of 1688. The original advance Puritan emphasis on the rights of the individual and the need to arrange governmental forms to establish and preserve those rights and the principle of consent was far from consummated in the Glorious Revolution. These objectives still awaited their more complete realization in the American Revolution. Locke's Two Treatises on Government, an advance Puritan work founded on the principles of individual liberty and covenant/contract that emerged in the milieu of the Puritan Revolution and justified the Glorious Revolution, then became a major source of American thought and justified the revolt of the American patriots.

And the same was true of the writings of the English Commonwealth men. Trenchard and Gordon "wrote expressly to justify the Glorious Revolution," Jacobson points out, and from their attacks on the doctrine of divine right, the colonists could find arguments to reject the authority of George III. "The after-the-fact defense of one revolution thus easily provided arguments in support for another and later revolution by a people who, in 1776, believed they had kept the Whig tradition purer than the old country and that they were, to a large extent, simply maintaining and continuing that heritage of ideals and liberties."

This was the American "mind-set" in the period that led to the American Revolution. "When the colonists thought historically," says R. A. Humphreys, "they did not merely think in terms of Mayflower compacts, charters, and covenants, but they thought of the great constitutional struggles of the seventeenth century, of the arguments which common lawyers used against prerogative, of the idea for which their ancestors suffered, of the Great Rebellion and the Glorious Revolution, of Milton, and of Locke. History, indeed, became philosophy teaching by examples. Aristotle, Cicero, Vattel, what Jefferson called the 'elementary books of public right'—and there were many of them—these were familiar enough to the colonists. But it was English ideas and English history of the seventeenth century which they particularly cherished." A study of sermons and literature in Colonial America makes this fact clear. Colonial America's mission was to "carry a political tradition to conclusion," says Rossiter, "not to create a tradition of its own." Colonial political thought was "a proudly conscious extension" of thought initiated in England. "The more independent and self-assertive the colonists became, the more anxious they were to sound like trueborn Englishmen."

"The American Revolution," Hans Kohn confirms, "innovated upon the English." At the time of the Revolution, at least seven in ten people were English in blood," says Rossiter, and "virtually all their traditions, ideas, and laws were English in origin and inspiration." Having canvassed the major sources of colonial thought, Wilson O. Clough concludes that "American colonials were British from the outset." Students of the period read predominantly from great English writers of literature and political thought.

The American Revolution began in Puritan New England, and in taking action, American patriots were, in effect, reasserting their Puritan heritage of opposition to arbitrary rule by the British government. Thus, says Commager, the American Revolution "repudiated eighteenth-century political practices but vindicated those of the seventeenth century. To the question of the origin of the institutions that Americans devised during the Revolutionary generation—how to explain "the crystallization, in a single generation, of four or five of the most valuable institutions of modern politics"—he said, "The explanation is to be found in English history, chiefly seventeenth century; as [Andrew C.] McLaughlin says, in our history we never get too far from the seventeenth century. It is an old story, this, that the American Revolution reasserted in the New World political principles that the English had asserted during the Puritan Revolution, and then repudiated or abandoned."

When the Continental Congress began to meet in September 1774, John Adams wrote to his wife, Abigail, describing the effect of the opening prayer on that body of men who had just "heard the horrible rumor of the cannonade of Boston," which included the reading of the Psalm 35. Said Adams of the latter, "I never saw a greater effect upon an audience. It seemed as if heaven had ordained that Psalm to be read on that morning... I must beg you to read that psalm." David wrote, quoting the Psalm,

> In the wake of other national movements—the French, Russian, and Chinese revolutions, as well as the multiple movements for national independence in Africa, Asia, and Latin America—the leadership class of the successful revolution proceeded to decimate itself in bloody reprisals that frequently assumed genocidal proportions. But the conflict within the American revolutionary generation remained a passionate yet bloodless affair in which the energies released by national

independence did not devour its own children. The Burr-Hamilton duel represented the singular exception to this rule.

Said Isaac Baskus in 1773, "The present contest between Great Britain and America is not so much about the greatness of the taxes already laid as about a submission to their taxing power."

In 1773, when opposition to oppressive policies of the English government was mounting, John Allen wrote to the Right Honorable Earl of Dartmouth in "An Oration upon the Beauties of Liberty," to ask, "How your lordship would like to have his birthright, liberty, and freedom, as an Englishman, taken away by his king, or by the ministry, or both?" Said he, "Would not your lordship immediately say, it was tyranny, oppression, and destruction by a despotic power? Would not your lordship be ready to alarm the nation and point out the state upon the brink of destruction?" Allen then inquired, "My lord, are not the liberties of the Americans as dear to them as those of Britons?"

The "oration" went through seven printings and five editions within two years, and it became very popular in the four cities of New England, where it was reprinted. In his published works Allen urged readers to "engrave the motto! 'May it be thus: Liberty, Life, or Death!'"

Allen explained, "I reverence and love my king, but I revere the rights of an Englishman before the authority of any king upon the earth. I distinguish greatly between a king and a tyrant. A king is the guardian and trustee of the rights and laws of the people, but a tyrant destroys them."

"The inhabitants of America know as well," he added, citing a familiar document, "'as the people of England, that the people are the right and foundation of power and authority, the original seat of majesty—the authors of laws, and the creators of officers to execute them.'" He, thus, declared, "My lord, as this is according to the laws of England, the liberty, privilege, and power of his majesty's subjects in Great Britain, why not then the privilege of his majesty's subjects in America?" He then warned, "But it may be meet to let your lordship know, that if the Americans unite [as there seems a good prospect of it] to stand as a band of brethren for their liberties, they have a right, by the law of God, or nature, and of nations, to reluctant, and even to resist any military and marine force… But suppose, my lord, that this should be the bloody intent of the ministry, to make the Americans subject to their slavery, then let blood for blood, life for life, and death for death decide the contention… The Americans will not submit to be slaves."

The rising impasse rested on a sure foundation. "The parliament of England cannot justly make any laws to oppress, or defend the Americans," Allen wrote, "for they are not the representatives of America, and therefore, they have no legislative power either for them or against them." Basing his statements on the truth of eternal principles centering in God and nature, Allen declared, "It is not rebellion, I declare it before GOD, the congregation, and all the world, and I would be glad if it reached the ears of every Briton and every American; that it is not rebellion to oppose any king, ministry, or governor, that destroys by any violence or authority whatever, the rights of the people." Said he, "Shall a man be deemed a rebel that supports his own rights? It is the first law of nature, and he must be a rebel to GOD, to the laws of nature, and his own conscience, who will not do it. A right to the blessing of freedom we do not receive from kings, but from heaven, as the breath of life, and essence of our existence, and shall we not preserve it, as the beauty of our being?"

Religious Liberty

Isaac Backus ranks with Roger Williams, John Leland, Thomas Jefferson, and James Madison as a preeminent figure in establishing freedom of conscience in America. His chief intellectual attainment centered on the idea that "religion is ever a matter between God and individuals." And his major institutional accomplishment was the promotion of the religious sphere as being outside the jurisdiction of civil magistracy. In traveling and preaching as an evangelist, he calculated that he made 918 trips more than ten miles in length with a total of sixty-eight thousand miles, mostly on horseback. He was a trustee of Brown University and conferred with the delegates to the First Continental Congress in Philadelphia in 1774.

Backus began *An Appeal to the Public for Religious Liberty, Against the Oppressions of the Present Day* with "a few thoughts concerning the general nature of liberty and government, and then show wherein it appears to us, that our religious rights are encroached upon in this land." Said he, "The true liberty of man is, to know, obey and enjoy his Creator, and to do all the good unto, and enjoy all the happiness with and in his fellow creatures that he is capable of; in order to which the law of love was written in his heart, which carries in its nature union and benevolence to being in general, and to each being in particular, according to its nature and excellency, and to its relation and connection to and with the supreme Being, and ourselves. Each rational soul, as he is part of the whole system of rational beings, so it was and is, both his duty and his liberty to regard the good of the whole in all his actions."

Said Backus, "Who can hear Christ declare that his kingdom is not of this world and yet believe that this blending of church and state together can be pleasing to him?"

CHAPTER 12

One historian called our Founding Fathers "the most remarkable generation of public men in the history of the United State or perhaps of any other nation."

Another historian added, "It would be invaluable if we could know what produced this burst of talent from a base of only two and a half million inhabitants."

Note: The point in the last quote is the all-important one. What produced America and the display of substantial talent in the genuine tradition of liberty and constitutional government? This is the critical issue.

The American Revolution

"The Stamp Act was a fact that Americans had to face, and it touched off a long series of incidents that reached a climax on the Lexington green. Yet if the British had not tinkered with the old colonial system, George Mason might have lived out his days as a gentleman planter, taking only occasional notice of colonial politics. But the tinkering began. As clumsy men often do, the British leaders stepped on so many toes that instead of isolated outcries, they soon had to face the wrath of thirteen colonies. After the year 1763, British policy leaped from crisis to crisis, generating colonial unity in a way that would have seemed incredible a few years earlier.

"No matter how Boston radicals may have welcomed the friction with England, Mason and most other Virginians did not. So the peaceful days prior to 1763 were soon a precious memory, replaced on the one hand by growing American talk about self-rule, and on the other by determined ministers in London who shook with rage at American impertinence.

"It began innocently enough. British officials, failing to see that they were in fact sharply reversing old policies, had sought new sources of tax revenue. To the colonial American, Mother England seemed suddenly to have turned into a grasping and greedy scold. Moreover, colonial pocketbooks that had been reasonably obese became flabby, convincing Americans that the shift in policy, far from being shrewd statesmanship, was merely common, ordinary rapacity.

"The Stamp Act was the first symbol of the power struggle. In Virginia, Patrick Henry and Richard Henry Lee were the foremost spokesmen of resistance. Henry supplied the fiery oratory while Lee represented the rising element that in a decade would be called the radical patriot group. If these two men occupied the center of the stage, Mason was close by in the wings, or often in the prompter's box. During the opening scenes of this developing drama, he became a close friend of Lee and may have been the coadjutor when Lee wrote a bold address to Governor Fauquier in 1765."

"Specie-poor Virginians, having passed a paper currency act that British ministers promptly struck down, complained that Americas had the right to be governed by 'laws made with our own consent.' A copy of the address in Mason's handwriting further declared that Americans gloried in their British connection 'as our only security; but this is not the dependence of a people subjugated by the victorious arms of a conqueror.'

"The stamp tax that soon followed quickly raised American hackles. Coming on the heels of the Currency Act, it was to men of Mason's circle a clear case of an illegal levy that had to be resisted. He actively joined the patriots by drafting a plan for the Fairfax county burgesses that would permit certain classes of debtors and landlords to sidestep the use of stamped paper. Then abruptly, the whole stamp dispute took an embarrassing personal turn for Mason. His naive cousin George Mercer appeared in the colony as His Majesty's duly-appointed stamp distributor. In Williamsburg, he received the kind of acclaim reserved for the bearers of plague...

"[But] violence averted, Mercer beat a meek retreat to England. There, he and others assured Englishmen of the lengths to which Americans would go to resist such taxes." But though the English Parliament made some conciliatory moves, they still insisted on the right "to legislate for the colonies in 'all cases whatsoever.'" Meanwhile, Americans "put their emphasis on the measure that revoked the stamp tax."

"Mason, keenly conscious of the two interpretations, knew that questions of imperial rule had not been settled. When a group of London merchants admonished the colonists for their spirited resistance to a lawful measure, Mason testily denied the implications of treason. His open letter to British businessmen, addressed to the London Public Ledger in the spring of 1766, was signed 'A Virginia Planter,' showing deep concern for strained British-American relations.

"Americans were tired of being treated as a schoolmaster would handle unruly boys, Mason insisted. The repealed Stamp Act dealt with a single grievance and had not wiped out remaining sources of friction, such as the enforcement of the British Navigation Acts. [Many of those statutes, aimed at insuring a healthy trade for the empire, had long gathered dust. Recent tightening of them hampered open smuggling that had gone on for years, proved a boon to informers, and encouraged eager Crown agents to flout trial by jury and due process of law in their search for personal gain.]...

"Mason warned the British that compulsion could not sustain a favorable British-American trade balance. A growing America, nurtured on free principles, would not accept oppression after having once 'tasted the sweets of liberty.' Another Stamp Act, or anything approaching it, 'would produce a general revolt in America.'...

"England was in no mood to heed preaching from America. The Revenue Act of 1767 proved that she was committed to a course of pressure on America, pressure that could be relieved only by compliance. Bold men from Massachusetts southward assumed leadership, announcing bluntly that they would never kiss the rod that flayed their backs. The arrival of British troops in Boston in 1768 revealed the steps London was preparing to take. A grim prospect faced Bostonians: regulations backed with bayonets.

"Clumsily handling the revenue problem as though they were dealing with country bumpkins, the British found too late that their distant cousins were serious, proud, and ready to risk everything."

In March 1773, the House of Burgesses in Williamsburg, Virginia, set up a "Committee of Correspondence and Inquiry" to keep in close touch with events in Virginia's sister colonies, which helped promote a course of unified action among the colonies.

On April 19, 1781, on the anniversary of the commencement of hostilities between Great Britain and America (which began in 1775), Henry Cumings preached a sermon at Lexington to commemorate the event. "To every attentive observer," he said, "it must be obvious that the wrath of Great Britain, so far as it has been permitted to exert itself, has contributed to bring about and establish our independency. It has evidently been the occasion of events, which have raised us to an honorable consideration among the European powers, and induced some of them open to espouse our cause, and aid us by a friendly alliance."

"The pride, avarice, and ambition of Great Britain gave rise to the present hostile contests," said Cumings. "From this source originated those oppressive acts, which first alarmed the freemen of America; and provoked them, after petitioning in vain for redress, to form plans of opposition and resistance." Cumings explained, "This conduct of America exasperated the British administration and roused their entire wrath. Transported with angry resentments, they proceeded from oppression to open war; in order to frighten and compel us into a submission to those arbitrary and despotic schemes which they determined, at all hazards, to carry into execution." "But," Cumings added, "those vindictive and sanguinary councils and measures, which, in the vehemence of their passions, they adopted, for this purpose, have, by the providence of GOD, contrary to their expectations, involved them in the most perplexing difficulties, by uniting thirteen provinces of America in that declaration of independence which they now wish us to rescind."

Conclusion

America's Revolution was over, and the founders of our nation felt God had intervened and allowed our fledging nation to win its freedom. The Constitution was next to protect what every founder felt was liberties granted to every living being from God and would be protected in this nation as long as we had the morals to defend it. Now many will argue that the founders had no religious beliefs, but that is not true. America's creators did not believe one religion stood above any other and that the divine created this nation and helped separate us from the King of England.

George Washington played a major role in both the war and as our first president. Washington often talked of prayer and God. Washington's army was poorly outfitted and trained and outnumbered in New York by about thirty thousand troops to seven thousand. Washington's faith never wavered, and as they waited in New York for the onslaught of British military power, Washington issued orders for his troops to pray for the campaign ahead.

On May 17, 1776, he wrote that that day was "to be observed as a day of fasting humiliation and prayer, humbly to supplicate the mercy of almighty God, that it would please Him to pardon all our manifold sins and transgressions, and to prosper the arms of the united colonies, and finally establish the peace and freedom of America upon a solid and lasting foundation."

Faith guided us through the war, and then we had to form our government, keeping in mind our sacred liberties. The Constitution was as hard fought for as was the war itself, and Benjamin Franklin, being the oldest statesman at eighty-one, and who many today feel did not believe in God in 1731 long before the war, wrote his creed to live by:

> That there is one God, Father of the universe. That He is infinitely good, powerful and wise. That He is omnipresent. That He ought to be worshipped, by adoration prayer and thanksgiving both in public and private.

So in the summer of 1787, as the delegation to create our new government had been arguing for ten weeks, it was Mr. Franklin that gave a stirring request for those gathered to pray.

> I have lived, sir, a long time, and the longer I live, the more convincing proofs I see of this truth, that God governs in the affairs of men. And if a sparrow cannot fall to the ground without His notice, is it probable that an empire can rise without His aid? ...I also believe that without His concurring aid we shall succeed in this political building no better, than the builders of Babel... Therefore, I beg leave to move that henceforth prayers imploring the assistance of heaven, and its blessings on our deliberations be held in this assembly every morning.

But it was not Franklin alone who established that the liberties of our nation were founded by God and meant to be protected by are newly penned constitution. Here are some writings that have always inspired me.

Benjamin Rush

Rush was not only a signer on our Declaration and a member of our Continental Congress. He was a well-known physician. Benjamin wrote in 1806 these amazing words:
"The only foundation for a useful education in a republic is to be laid in religion. Without this there can be no virtue, and without virtue there can be no liberty, and liberty is the object and life of all republican governments."

James Wilson

One of the lesser-known patriots and founding fathers of our nation was Scottish-born James Wilson. The young lawyer's writings on the British Parliament's authority impressed members of the continental congress so much they elected him to the body in 1775. The following year, Wilson signed the Declaration of Independence and later the United States Constitution.

Serving as a United States Supreme Court Justice until his death, James Wilson realized there was a much higher law than man's to consider. When questioning what the ultimate cause of moral obligation is, Wilson determined, "I give it this answer, the will of God. This is the supreme law. His just and full right of imposing laws, and our duty in obeying them, are the sources of our moral obligations."

Quotes by the people who signed the Declaration and wrote our Constitution are endless, and I urge you to follow the path of the enlightenment that this wise men walked in discovering liberty for themselves. Thomas Jefferson has been utilized by the left as an atheist for the purpose to take God from our nation's beginnings. Jefferson's belief in the unquestionable relationship between good government and religious freedom is reflected in article three of the Northwest Ordinance, where he writes:

"Religion, morality and knowledge being necessary to good government and the happiness of mankind, schools and the means of education shall forever be encouraged."

Unfortunately for us, we have stopped paying attention to what was given to us by the generations prior to us. Noah Webster said it best when he penned these words:

> When you become entitled to exercise the right of voting for public officers, let it be impressed on your mind that God commands you to choose for rulers, just men who will rule in the fear of God. The preservation of a republican government depends on the faithful discharge of this duty; if the citizens neglect their duty, and place unprincipled men in office, the government will soon be corrupted. ("Advice to the Young" from Value of the Bible and Excellence of the Christian Religion, 1834)

Today, too many of us vote not on the basis of who will protect our God-given freedoms but on who will promise us something in return for our votes. We have an oath of office for a reason, and it was established by President George Washington who signed the bill into law on June 1, 1789 creating it. The oath is a sacred covenant to God as the creator or liberty and a promise to uphold and defend the Constitution that was created to protect said liberties.

If we as citizens vote for someone once that violates their oath, we are not responsible, but if we continue to elect people who violate the Constitution, we are as responsible to God as they are. At the beginning I gave you two options as to where liberties came from, God or man. This book makes it clear that all that America has all that America is having been a gift from God. Continue to speak out on behalf of our Republic and defend religious liberty or our nation will be lost.

The End

About the Author

TIM AALDERS IS a current small business owner, living in Highland Utah and has held titles, such as CEO, COO, marketing manager, and sales manager. His career has included fields in real estate, construction supplies, retail box stores, and the restaurant industry. And as a business consultant for small businesses, he understands what makes America's economy work. Tim was a well-known voice on conservative talk radio for over ten years, only leaving when his daughter of twenty-five passed from a rare heart disease. He became the voice of Main Street USA with his own radio show, *Buy Back America Radio*. After watching as the assets and resources of this great country were being sold to foreign corporations and powers, he also founded *Buy Back America* to unite the American consumer and small business owners. Tim believed that someone had to shed the light on the corruption of Wall Street and the involvement of our own elected officials in the collapse of the housing market and the dollar. His ability to follow the money helped expose the many backroom dealings politicians with their largest campaign donors and special interests colluded together to put more money in their pockets leaving less in yours.

Even though Tim was a casualty of the economic crash, he refuses to be a victim. Like the multitude of Americans before him, he started over and bounced back to have a small successful building and development company here in Utah. Tim had fought on the radio for conservative Utah values for years and sees this election as an opportunity to go to the front lines of the war Washington, DC. Tim understands that liberty came from God, not man, and has been known as MR Constitution on 100's of radio interviews. Tim understands what is at the heart of the problems with this country and is a key speaker on issues like free trade and globalization, immigration, the Federal Reserve, entitlement programs, special interest, and our broken political system. Tim is an advent supporter of the constitution and the original intent of our Founding Fathers. He is an everyday American that truly believes that everyday Americans can and will make a difference.

Dr. Andrus Summary

Dr. Hyrum L. Andrus (March 12, 1924, to October 23, 2015) was well educated, holding a PhD and was considered an expert in the fields of political science, history, and American citizenship. He was the author of multiple books, articles, and taught many seminars. His research led to the writing of this book because the lessons of liberty, he started needed to be continued in our generation.

My friend Ron Mann, who served as Reagan's special assistant to the president of the United States and without him, this book would never have been finished. In 1987, he was asked by the chief justice of the supreme court to organize and execute the celebration for the bicentennial of the US Constitution. Ron has spent his life defending the Constitution, and I believe if he would have lived during the founding of this nation, he would have been one of the signers.

CPSIA information can be obtained
at www.ICGtesting.com
Printed in the USA
LVHW031056130421
684340LV00008B/202

9 781647 015022